SHERLOCK HOLMES

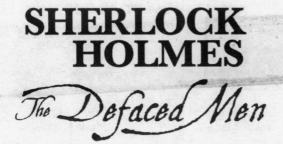

SHERLOCK HOLMES

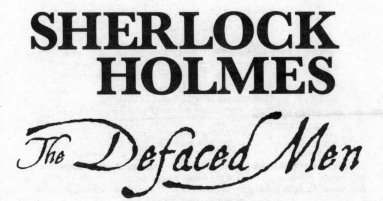

TIM MAJOR

TITAN BOOKS

The Defaced Men
Print edition ISBN: 9781789097009
E-book edition ISBN: 9781789097016

Published by Titan Books
A division of Titan Publishing Group Ltd
144 Southwark Street, London SE1 0UP
www.titanbooks.com

First edition: August 2022
10 9 8 7 6 5 4 3 2 1

Printed and bound by CPI Group (UK) Ltd, Croydon, CR0 4YY.

For Brian and Naomi

CHAPTER ONE

I have known my friend Sherlock Holmes for fifteen years, and consider my understanding of him as full as any single person on this earth. However, I must confess that much of his private life – which is to say, almost the *entirety* of his life, as he is nothing if not private – is yet unknown to me. Consequently, the instances of Holmes greeting a visitor to our rooms as an old friend are few. (A notable example of this phenomenon was in 'The Case of the Haltmere Fetch'; my account of which begins with an encounter with a childhood friend of Holmes's, but which I have no plans to publish due to the great sensitivity of the matter.)

What I mean to say by this preamble is that if Sherlock Holmes greets a visitor warmly I am minded to take particular notice, in the hope of gleaning some speck of detail that might be added to his biography.

In the mid-morning of 16th March 1896 we were working at our own desks: I compiling notes on one of Holmes's previous cases, and Holmes occupied intently on an unknown task, writing furiously in a jotter. We might not have spoken until luncheon had we not been interrupted by the ring of the doorbell. I heard the tread of several pairs of feet up the stairs, then our housekeeper opened the door to our rooms.

"A client for you, Mr. Holmes," Mrs. Hudson said. "A Mr—"

Her words were cut off abruptly as the white-haired man she had escorted upstairs pushed past her and into the room. Our housekeeper folded her arms over her chest in exasperation and stared at the intruder's back, then flinched as a second man eased his way past her, carrying a heavy wooden crate, and moved to stand at one side of the room.

"Thank you, Mrs. Hudson," I said hurriedly. When scorned, our housekeeper's annoyance is liable to manifest in other ways, and she had promised steak pie for lunch.

She grimaced at our visitors again, then left and closed the door with more force than necessary.

I turned in my seat as the white-haired man strode to the centre of the room, looking about him as though the furnishings and hanging pictures were of equal interest as the two human occupants. On closer inspection, I saw that he was not as elderly as he had at first appeared. Though his hair was bushy and wild, and his pointed beard equally as white, and long enough to almost entirely obscure his necktie, his skin was relatively smooth and his eyes alert and intelligent. He wore a good suit and waistcoat, and beneath his arm he carried a large leather portfolio.

His eyes passed over me, then fixed upon Holmes.

"I have come to seek your assistance." His voice was halting, as though this was the first time he had spoken to-day, and his accent was difficult to place.

Holmes watched him for several seconds, then leapt from his seat to shake the newcomer by his hand.

"My word!" he exclaimed. "You're just the person I need!"

I paid close attention immediately, waiting to see what our visitor's response might be. His face was a picture of confusion, but to his credit, he bowed his head politely and said simply, "Oh? How is that?"

Holmes gestured to the jotter on his desk. "I am currently preparing notes on a monograph relating to the uses of collodion – not only the more conventional uses, but also in the cleaning of lenses, in theatrical make-up both as a fixing solution and to simulate wrinkled skin when allowed to harden, in blasting gelatine, and also its potential use in the treatment of warts. It is a wondrous material, is it not? And you would be ideal in advising about one of the historical aspects of my treatise, namely the importance of the differences between wet-plate and dry."

To add to the mystery of how the men knew one another, I understood very little of what my friend had said. I glanced at the second visitor, who seemed content to guard in silence the wooden chest he had placed on the floor beside my desk. He appeared to be in his late thirties, and wore round spectacles.

The white-haired man nodded stiffly. "I would be happy to impart what knowledge I have, in due course."

Holmes had the good grace to let the subject drop. "You have come about another matter, of course. Please, sit and tell us all."

As our guest sat before the fireplace, I rose and took my usual chair and Holmes took his. The white-haired man was unhurried, and did not speak. Instead, he gazed around the room again, then at Sherlock Holmes, a faint frown upon his face. Then he rose nimbly, went behind Holmes's armchair, lifted my friend's prized Stradivarius – I gasped involuntarily – and then he simply placed it down again, several inches to the right from its original position. On his return to his seat he similarly adjusted a lamp upon the dining-table. He sat and his eyes travelled around the room again, but now he appeared content.

Holmes watched all of this strange behaviour placidly.

"Excuse me," I said, "but am I to take it that you know one another already?"

The visitor replied, "No, but it seems that we are both aware of the other's features. Your newspaper caricatures are as ugly yet revealing as my own, Mr. Holmes."

Bemused, I turned to Holmes, who shook his head. "I am not in the habit of reviewing ironic commentaries, and any details to be gleaned from caricatures are decidedly second-hand. No, I recognised you not from your face but from other salient details."

"I have heard much of your gift for observation," our guest said with a nod of satisfaction. "Please, explain."

Holmes tapped a finger against his lips. "I may as well proceed in the order that details presented themselves to me. Your right eye is the first indication of your trade – or rather, the brow above it, which is considerably more lined than above the left, which indicates long hours spent squinting, or looking into a lens of some description. The same applies to many seamen who habitually use telescopes or sextants, but your manner otherwise is entirely unlike a sailor's. I noted next that your eyes moved around the room in constant observation, and at the same time your mouth twitched as though determining some features to be to your satisfaction and others an outright annoyance. Then you spoke, and in your accent I detected English – fundamentally so in the vowel sound 'o' in 'come', indicating that you were brought up in the southern regions of this country – and then, layered upon that, hints of more than one American accent: a harsh 'a' in 'assistance', indicating time spent in the vicinity of New York, and yet at the same time, a softened 't' which suggested exposure to the accents of the west coast."

Although I had seen this sort of trick performed many times over, the fact that Holmes could draw so much from a single uttered statement still seemed a miracle. However, our guest merely nodded and waited for Holmes to continue.

"Then there is the matter of the object you were carrying," Holmes continued, indicating the leather portfolio which our visitor had now leant against the side of his chair. "Its size is notable, of course, but what was more immediately arresting was the pasted paper on its upper corner."

The white-haired man frowned and raised the portfolio, which was evidently heavy, onto his knees. He and I both looked closely at the traces of paper that Holmes described, which had been mostly removed, leaving only faint hints of lines.

"It is clear that it once displayed a circular design," Holmes said, "and within that an image of a tower of some sort. It is a seal related to one institution or another – but which? The only text legible is in the upper-left segment of the circle, and appears to read 'SITAS PEN', which can only lead to one conclusion."

"I am most impressed," our guest said.

I cleared my throat. "Apologies… what is the institution, then?"

Holmes replied before I had even finished speaking; he must have anticipated my question. "The circular text once read 'Universitas Pennsylvaniensis', and the unusual tower is a tower of books. It is, of course, the seal of the University of Pennsylvania. But what is of most interest is that the scuffs and weathering of the leather binder suggests that it has been in regular use for at least fifteen years, yet the particular design of this seal is an iteration which has been in use only during these last… let me see… *eight* years – and the tearing of the pasted paper has been performed imperfectly at a much more recent time." He looked up at the ceiling and sighed. "And then I am bound to confess that my knowledge of public figures played a part in moving from this set of general observations to a conclusion about your precise identity." Hurriedly, as though this confession about possessing some degree of general knowledge might amount to an admission of cheating, he added, "Though subsequently I noticed the attention you paid to the movements of both my companion and I as we moved from our desks to these chairs, and I flatter myself that this may have provided the final clue even if I had not known of your personal history."

With that, our guest pushed himself up from his chair again, and approached Holmes to shake his hand.

"It is a great pleasure to find myself in the company of somebody so attuned to the appearance of things," he said.

Holmes's satisfied expression evaporated. "I am occupied with the *meaning* of things, not simply their appearance."

"As am I, as am I." The man returned to his seat, and when he sat his posture was like that of a schoolboy eager to learn.

For my part, I shifted uncomfortably in my seat. There is always a point during Holmes's parlour tricks when his audience loses its patience.

The white-haired man turned to me. "Mr. Holmes has correctly diagnosed my travels from England to America, with long periods spent on both the east and west coasts. And he has correctly identified that I may be considered both a man of the arts and a man of science – the *mise-en-scène* of any setting is as much of interest to me as the precise, measurable movements of the creatures within it, despite the latter having effectively become my trade." He reached out to offer his hand. "I know that you are Holmes's biographer, Dr. Watson, and my own name is—"

"Muybridge!" I cried out, staring at the man's outstretched hand without shaking it.

He bowed his head and withdrew his hand. "Eadweard Muybridge, at your service."

"I have seen a number of your photographs of human figures in motion," I said. "They are much admired among the medical profession, as they reveal a great deal about the workings of the muscular structure that remains invisible to the naked eye, and which is impossible to determine when the body is at rest. And also… that is to say, I am sure that your pictures have much to offer artists, too, as you have suggested."

I sensed that my cheeks were reddening as I saw in my mind's eye the pictures I had been shown of women going about everyday tasks; those series of sequential pictures revealed ever more about the women's movements due to the models being entirely naked. I now recalled that they had been shown to me not in the company of fellow doctors as I had intimated, but at my club.

"Art was certainly my initial calling," Muybridge said thoughtfully, "though for many years now my specialism has been considered to be the sciences. People have taken to calling me Professor – quite incorrectly, I hasten to add."

Holmes said, "And I maintain that your expertise in photographic techniques will prove invaluable to my study of collodion. But of course you did not come here for that purpose. Now, Mr. Muybridge, tell us of your trouble."

Muybridge's expression darkened. He glanced at the man at the side of the room, who remained as silent and implacable as ever.

"I fear for my life," he said.

"Ah." Our guest's pronouncement had changed Holmes's manner only very slightly: I saw his eyes shine.

Muybridge rose halfway from his seat, at the same time tugging at his white beard. "You appear to care little for my plight, sir!"

I interjected hurriedly. "Sherlock Holmes is simply accustomed to hearing each potential client's circumstances in full before giving a response." I did not add that fearing for one's life was hardly an unusual circumstance for visitors to our rooms.

Muybridge lowered himself into his seat again. "I apologise. I am quick to anger nowadays. I seem to suspect everyone of malice towards me."

My smile seemed to disarm him even further. "Please, continue," I said.

Our guest nodded. "I returned to London in 1894, following a most successful venture at the World's Columbian Exposition in Chicago the previous year—"

Abruptly, he stopped and looked up at Holmes, who merely raised an eyebrow.

Muybridge sighed. "My intuition is that it would be folly to lie to you, Holmes, or even to characterise my actions in a misleading manner. Chicago was no sort of success, and the gate receipts were hardly enough to recoup the cost of the hall constructed to house my galleries and my lectures. Visitors had more hedonistic pursuits in mind; the wax museums and hoochie-coochie dancers did roaring trade."

"Then your return to England is something of a retreat?" I suggested.

"A calculated change of emphasis," Muybridge replied sharply. "I have little interest in vying with cheap entertainments to catch the eye of the masses. I am a serious man, Dr. Watson, and my legacy will be one of advancement of knowledge, not gaudy frivolity."

I nodded and my eyes met Holmes's. We had many times encountered men of a particular age, preoccupied with their lasting legacy. Such self-centred pride had been the downfall of more than one of them.

Muybridge continued, "Since then I have divided my time between two tasks. The first is the selection of images and composition of notes for a popular book dedicated to my studies in animal locomotion."

"Then widespread readership is yet your aim?" I asked mildly.

Our guest bristled. "Anybody with information to divulge wishes to do so to the widest possible audience. What I have to show is of interest to any right-minded person, as evidenced by the fact that very many have already subscribed to the publication in anticipation, more than a year before its advertised publication. I wonder whether either of you gentlemen might be inclined to—" He broke off, and his cheeks flushed, the first appearance of colour on his face. "My apologies. I am not here to act as a salesman. I will continue with my account. The second of my recent occupations is the conducting of a number of lectures on the same subject, in various towns around this country and addressing a variety of audiences. The crowds are not as large as once they were, but their appreciation is sincere. Since October last year, this second activity has occupied more of my time and is due to conclude this very month, March."

"Then this concern for your own well-being is connected to your lecture tour?" Holmes asked. For the first time I saw him look directly at the silent man who must be Muybridge's assistant.

"Yes – and an even greater fear is that the conclusion of the tour may put my pursuer into a new mode, that perhaps all that has happened is only a prelude to something greater."

Holmes nodded. "Perhaps now would be the moment to explain the nature of this 'pursuit.'"

Muybridge turned to his assistant and nodded curtly. At once, the other man became all activity; he hefted the chest closer to the dining-table and began unpacking a collection of bulky objects of wood and brass – the first a box on stilts, the second a device with a small wheel handle on one side that appeared to operate a much larger wheel on its rear, and the third a pedestal upon which was unmistakably a focusing lens. I watched him with interest as he began to make minute adjustments to the relative positions of the items. Though this man was far younger than his employer, his hair was already thinning and the shoulders of his shabby black suit were strewn with flakes of skin.

While this had been going on, Muybridge had lifted his heavy portfolio onto his knees and unfastened the straps that held it closed. Now, with great care, he removed from the binder a large, circular glass plate perhaps fifteen or sixteen inches in diameter. Upon the plate were inscribed a sequence of drawn images of a horse. He stood and moved to the table, holding the glass plate before him as if it were a ceremonial object.

"You are no doubt aware of the zoopraxiscope which has made me famous," Muybridge said, and I detected a change in his tone to a more authoritative address that he presumably deployed during his lectures. "As you see, it comprises a projector connected to a lantern." To demonstrate his words, his assistant opened the side of the box on stilts and revealed the lantern within, which he promptly lit. Muybridge continued, "The projector and lens are just as one might find in a magic lantern used in any phantasmagoria show. However, the unique aspect is this central housing that holds glass plates such as this one, along with a shutter disc, which rotate in opposite directions in order to project one single image at any given moment, producing the effect of animation."

Almost reverently, he placed the circular plate into the similar-shaped housing on the rear of the wooden box with the wheel handle. His mute assistant checked the fit, then darted to the curtains at the windows, drawing them closed. I looked at Holmes, who appeared unaffected by the liberties being taken within our home.

"Of course, it is the photographs themselves that are truly remarkable," Muybridge went on. "They have been captured by a bank of twenty-four cameras positioned in a line, each device triggering moments after its neighbour in order to record the precise motion of the animal subject as it passes. The images are striking when viewed in isolation, but my zoopraxiscope allows me to return that animal subject to motion in a perfect simulacrum of life."

Another nod, and the assistant crouched to work the handle and I saw the disc at the rear begin to spin. Once he had achieved a certain regular speed, he stretched out to remove a cover from the focusing lens. Immediately, an image appeared on the darkened wall of our room. Or rather I should say that it was a *series* of images – yet that was not how I perceived it at all. There upon the wall the silhouette of a horse galloped without moving from its position. Its limbs were a complex, overlapping mesh of activity, its mane and tail rippling like liquid, its rider bracing against the motion, far less supple than the beast he sat astride.

I had heard about the phenomenon of projected moving pictures, of course, but an example of it had not been set before me until now. I found myself quite breathless at its magic.

"I have your recently published brochure titled 'Descriptive Zoopraxography'," Holmes said pleasantly, "but long before that I was highly interested in your photographs of the horse named 'Sallie Gardner', and those later ones of 'Occident'. To have proved that all four legs of a galloping horse leave the ground at once is a capital discovery, and one which I have drawn upon in my own work on occasion. You have provided a great service in proving what the eye cannot see."

I looked again at the miraculous horse in motion. As Holmes had stated, between the flick of the front hooves and the rear hooves there was a moment during which the silhouetted beast and rider appeared suspended above the ground, delineated by a horizontal shadow.

Despite my appreciation of this marvel, I felt bound to say, "But these are drawings, not photographs."

Muybridge's cheeks reddened. "It is a limitation of the technology at hand – silhouettes are required, and fine detail would not be transferable to the plate or visible to the viewer. But each individual image is painstakingly copied from the photographic image, with amendments to ensure greater fidelity rather than corruption of reality." He waved to his assistant, who stopped his turning of the handle and replaced the lens cover. Muybridge took from the device the glass plate and indicated one of the horse drawings inked upon it. "See that each picture is unnaturally elongated, but only in order to appear correctly proportioned to audiences due to the distorting effect of projection."

"I do understand," I said, rather resenting having become the focus of this lecture. "It is not a far cry from the zoetropes that children enjoy so much."

I saw Muybridge's body stiffen, and I realised I had made a gross error.

"My dear fellow," Muybridge began, his eyes filled with sudden fury, "my invention is no more like a zoetrope than a living, breathing beast is like a stuffed toy. The zoetrope is a plaything, whereas the zoopraxiscope is a tool that will promote scientific understanding of the world around us. I suggest that you—"

Holmes interrupted him. "Is there another glass plate that you would like to show to us?"

For several seconds, Muybridge did not respond. Then all of his anger seemed to ebb away in an instant. Our guest was so quick to rage, which then left him with equal speed, that I began to wonder about his state of mind.

Muybridge slid the plate into a paper sleeve, replaced it within the portfolio carefully, then removed another.

"This sequence is one of my many studies of human locomotion, conducted at the University of Pennsylvania," Muybridge said.

The images on this new plate depicted a man striding from left to right. Despite the images being drawn rather than photographed, the artist had succeeded in conveying the figure's bushy beard and lean frame, and the thinness of his silhouetted limbs suggested he was naked.

"I myself was the model for this series," Muybridge said.

Perhaps there was even more of the artist in this man than I had realised. Few scientific men of my acquaintance would offer themselves naked for study, but in the artistic world perhaps this was an everyday occurrence.

"May I?" Holmes said, and took the plate from our guest. Then he turned it slowly before him, crudely animating the sequence. "I take it these scratches are the cause of your anxiety?"

"Yes, they are the principal issue," Muybridge replied.

As I gazed at the glass plate, and my friend's face which was visible through its translucent portions, at first I saw nothing amiss. Then, as Holmes turned slightly, the light from the window glanced at a different angle, and I saw the scratches to which Holmes had referred. I rushed to stand behind Holmes's armchair, and from this new angle the lines became far more visible. Above seven of the fourteen silhouettes were the rough letters 'RIP' carved directly into the glass surface. The letters grew larger on successive appearances. The smallest message hung above the head of the figure, but by the fourth iteration the feet of the letters touched the hair of his head, and by the seventh the letter 'I' bisected the man entirely. Still more alarming, though, was the realisation that the figure itself had not escaped mutilation. A flurry of cross-hatched lacerations made a violent cloud over each and every instance of Muybridge's face in profile.

"And these scratches," I said, addressing Muybridge, "I suppose they are clearly visible when projected?"

Without reply, Muybridge took the plate from Holmes and placed it into his zoopraxiscope device. His assistant turned the handle, then took away the lens cover once again.

Despite having seen the defaced plate, I was unprepared for the effect of the images when projected. The fourteen images took perhaps only three seconds to be shown in their entirety, so the sequence had already repeated several times before I was able to take in the chaotic vision. The letters 'RIP' grew rapidly like a cancer before beginning anew, and the consequence of the letters having been inscribed only on alternate images was a pronounced flickering that was in great contrast to the fluidity of the other parts of the animation. I found it almost impossible to concentrate on the walk of the naked Eadweard Muybridge as opposed to the shifting mass of scored lines that obscured his face, and which suggested the violence of the hand that had made them.

"As you can well imagine, the effect upon my audience was one of mingled horror and excitement," Muybridge said.

"And the effect upon yourself?" Holmes prompted.

Muybridge frowned. "Dismay. Frustration."

"Earlier, you referred to fear," Holmes said.

"A turn of phrase. I fear very little. I have trekked the mountains of Yosemite and dangled above precipices in order to secure the images I require. I have wrangled wild animals. I have—" He stopped.

Now it was my turn to frown. From the newspapers I knew a little of the man's personal history and his past actions, of which some aspects were decidedly unsettling. I pledged to speak to Holmes about the matter at the first opportunity.

Holmes went to open the curtains. Then, when the young assistant had slowed the rotation of the device to a halt, Holmes plucked the glass plate from it, ignoring Muybridge's obvious anxiety at it being handled. Holmes examined the disc for some time before concluding, "The perpetrator worked quickly, but not in a great rush. After each letter is a small letter 'x' – presumably a dot was too difficult or too subtle a character to etch in such a way – but they could simply have been omitted and the effect would have been much the same. Presumably you have interviewed your staff about the matter?"

The young man who had operated the zoopraxiscope did not look up, but instead busied himself dousing the lantern and packing up the device.

Muybridge nodded. "This example is only the first of the defaced slides. After this occasion – which I discovered at an informal lecture at a club near to my home in Kingston upon Thames – I fired my assistant who had been operating the lantern. However, then it occurred at the very next lecture: a crude noose appeared around a motionless portrait of myself seated beneath the 'General Grant' sequoia tree of Mariposa Grove in California. I am unable to show you the evidence of that vandalism, as I smashed the glass plate shortly afterwards."

I found it remarkably easy to imagine this white-haired man bellowing in anger and casting the glass slide to the floor, producing shards that perhaps endangered the front rows of his audience.

"Do you have any suspicions as to the author of these defacements?" Holmes asked.

"None." Muybridge waved a hand at his assistant, whose head was bowed to his work. "You're naturally suspicious of Fellows here, but he has no reason to have committed this vandalism, and as I have already said, he was engaged only after the first occurrence."

"At any rate, do you have any inkling as to the purpose of the threats?"

Muybridge shook his head. "No demand has been made. Whoever did this appears to wish me ill, but wants nothing."

"Might not professional rivalry be the inspiration?" I asked.

"It might. I have had rivals in the past, though none who might have stooped so low. But nowadays there are only disappointments…" Muybridge stared at the glass plate that

Holmes still held before him, and I recalled his account of his disillusionment and failure at the Chicago exposition. "Nowadays it is more difficult to contemplate such a thing."

I was about to question him further on this subject, but Holmes said quickly, "We understand you very well."

"All the same," Muybridge said, appearing grateful to move the conversation along, "these are not hollow gestures. There have been physical attempts on my life on two occasions."

"Indeed?" Holmes said as he passed back the glass plate. His tone was as casual as if Muybridge were describing his holiday plans.

"Twice this year I have been almost run over in the street by horse-and-carriages," Muybridge said. "And before you state that such a thing is not so unusual… both times the carriages were empty, and the driver so wrapped up in scarf and hat as to be unidentifiable to the least degree. I am convinced these were attempts on my life, so you can appreciate why I take these other threats seriously."

"Where did this happen?" I asked.

"In Kingston upon Thames in each case, once close to my home and once directly outside the library where I often go to conduct research."

Holmes clapped his hands together. "Well, you certainly have my attention, and I will do my utmost to help you. You said that your lecture tour is almost at an end – which is the next engagement?"

"In three days – the evening of the nineteenth – in the council chambers of Liverpool City Hall. I will be addressing the members of that city's Amateur Photographic Association."

"And will you utilise your zoopraxiscope machine?"

As though involuntarily, we all looked at Fellows, who had now packed the device into its bulky case and had once again retreated to the shadows.

"Indeed, yes," Muybridge replied. "Though the technology may be old, it is still capable of dazzling and informing in equal measure. Several times I have considered retiring the device and relying solely upon photographs to compare the real motion of animals with those depicted in paintings by the masters… but I have been convinced of the error of such an approach."

"By whom?" Holmes asked.

Muybridge opened his mouth to reply, then hesitated for a moment before saying finally, "By the public."

Holmes nodded. "Then we will accompany you to Liverpool, and let us hope that you will be threatened once again."

Muybridge rose from his chair, watching Holmes warily.

"Yes," he replied, "let us hope for that."

CHAPTER TWO

Three days later, after a long but uneventful train journey and a brief stop to deposit our belongings at the inn where we would be staying that night, Holmes and I walked through the Liverpool streets, passing through St George's Quarter in the direction of the town hall.

In the periphery of my vision I registered my friend's manner of walking, which I determined was more sprightly than usual.

"I perceive that you're looking forward to this experience," I said.

"Of course. It promises an instructive lecture with a diverting visual experience, plus there is the likelihood of directly adding to our understanding of a most interesting case. You, on the other hand, are far more reticent."

"Only because I am conflicted about the type of man who has engaged our services."

Holmes nodded, but did not look at me. "I know that you have been dwelling on Eadweard Muybridge's personal history. You have been doing so since we travelled through Coventry."

I considered this. "Yes, it must have been around that point that I saw a coach and horses through the window, recalling the physical attacks upon Muybridge as well as the publicised events of his past. I believe it made my mind begin turning anew."

"Then let us have it out, Watson. Speak your concerns aloud."

"Is it not obvious? It is no secret that when he lived in California, our friend Muybridge shot dead his wife's lover. That is an undisputed fact which he himself has stated on numerous occasions as the truth."

"And for which he was tried and acquitted. It was deemed justifiable homicide."

"Yes, but—" The heat rose in my cheeks. "After Muybridge's appearance at Baker Street, I could not stop myself from going over the details of that trial, Holmes. The defence team of the accused entered a plea of insanity, and their case was built around his eccentric behaviour, which they ascribed to his serious stagecoach accident some fifteen years previously, in which he suffered a head injury. And yet Muybridge claimed that on the night he killed Major Harry Larkyns he was in his right mind, and the jury agreed with him on that score. Surely, Holmes, no killing in cold blood such as that can be considered 'rightful', even when one's pride and marriage is at stake? I note that all of the jury were themselves married men."

Holmes stopped walking and regarded me. "Our legal system, and its counterpart in America, is constructed around faith in the abilities and good sense of a jury."

I nodded reluctantly. "I am fully aware of that. I know that Muybridge must be considered an innocent man. But that will not prevent me from retaining a healthy degree of scepticism regarding his actions."

Holmes clapped me on the shoulder. "I would go further. You ought to treat *all* people in such a way. Scepticism is the watchword of the consulting detective. Now, we are close to our destination. Use this new-found scepticism of yours to aid observation, but for heaven's sake brighten your countenance, Watson. This lecture is intended to be a pleasant event."

We turned onto Castle Street and then the grand facade of the town hall came into view, and looming behind it a striking dome supported on a tall drum with Corinthian columns. At the foot of a wide, protruding section, the three bays that led to the entrance of the building were obscured by such a scrum of people that they spilled out onto the street.

"It's my recollection that this lecture has been arranged for an association of local amateur photographers," I said. "Does it strike you that there are more people here in attendance than might be expected?"

"Quite so," Holmes replied. "Something is amiss."

We hurried along the remainder of Castle Street and then crossed Dale Street to reach the hall. As we approached, several of the waiting men noticed us, and soon a huddle formed.

"Is one of you Mr. Sherlock Holmes?" one man said, brandishing a notepad and pencil, and others echoed his question, directing their gazes at Holmes and myself in turn. "Care to make a statement about the attempts on Mr Muybridge's life?"

Holmes offered only a thin-lipped smile and tried to force his way through the crowd.

"We're here only to see the lecture," I said. "Please, allow us to pass."

"You Sherlock Holmes, then?" another man asked me, shoving my shoulder roughly, "Or his assistant?"

"I am *not* his assistant," I retorted before I could prevent myself. "I am his biographer and his friend."

My interviewer was unimpressed, and swung away from me immediately. "It's the other one who's Holmes. Hoi, where's he gone?"

The group of journalists became chaotic, each attempting to turn to catch a glimpse of Holmes. Somehow, though, Holmes had contrived to slip away while their attention had been upon me, although that had been only a matter of moments.

I took the opportunity to push my way towards the entrance of the town hall, but the confused mass of bodies prevented my progress. In my desperation I turned fully away from the building and looked over the heads of the newspapermen, craning my neck and staring fixedly as though I had found something I had lost. Once I was confident that I had been noticed, I gestured with a thumb to the right as though suggesting a route.

Immediately, all of the journalists turned in the direction I had been looking, and then in the direction I had indicated. Seizing the opportunity, I barged my way into the entrance hall.

In contrast to the hubbub outside, the lobby of the building was calm, as if some supernatural barrier existed to keep out not only the journalists, but also all sound produced by them.

"Come along, Watson, or we'll be late," came Holmes's voice from above.

I looked up to see my friend halfway up the wide central staircase. My low viewpoint and the backdrop of a blood-red stair carpet made him appear momentarily demonic. The long fingers of one of his hands tapped against the balustrade repeatedly.

"How did you escape that horde outside?" I asked. Then, recognising his impatience, I added hastily, "Never mind. But you are going the wrong way, Holmes. Surely the council chambers are here on the ground floor?"

"It appears that popular demand has necessitated an amendment. The grand ballroom already appears full to bursting. Come *along*, Watson!"

As I ascended the stairs, a distant murmur became the clamour of hundreds of voices in conversation. I hurried in Holmes's wake, through the doors and into the rear of the ballroom. Somewhere between two hundred and three hundred seats had been arranged tightly in rows, occupied by men and a smattering of women, all shifting excitedly in their seats. Latecomers stood at the rear of the room.

Holmes looked at me pointedly, as it had been I who had insisted that we freshen up at our inn upon arrival in Liverpool. He pushed along the row of standing people until he could progress no further, then he stood with arms folded across his chest, giving his full attention to the scene before us.

At the far end of the ballroom a large, white fabric screen had been erected. Before it, facing the screen, I saw the dark wooden blocks of Muybridge's zoopraxiscope projector. It protruded above the heads of the seated audience due to its placement on a pedestal, itself on a raised platform before the screen, from which I presumed Muybridge would provide his commentary. I noted that one of Muybridge's glass discs was already loaded into the machine, a fact that appeared to have been noticed by many of the waiting spectators, who pointed it out to one another.

I leant towards Holmes to be heard over the wash of voices. "From Muybridge's testimony at Baker Street, I understood that his device is now considered less state of the art than once it was. I had no idea his lecture might be so well-attended."

Holmes clucked his tongue. "You were right first time, Watson. His audiences have been dwindling for many years, and his achievements relegated to the status of historical stepping stones. But have you already forgotten the scene outside?"

"You mean the journalists asking for you?"

Holmes nodded. "That can only mean that my involvement is widely known, which in turn has cast a light on the recent experiences of Eadweard Muybridge. The local newspapers must have taken up the story in anticipation of to-night's event."

"So all of these people—"

"—are waiting eagerly for the next instalment of the vendetta against our client," Holmes concluded in a tone of disdain.

I did not have the nerve to point out that we had come here for precisely the same purpose.

The dimming of the gas lamps provided a distraction. A ripple of movement and hushing sounds passed across the room. Then Eadweard Muybridge strode onto the platform and silence fell.

"I welcome you all," he said in a voice far more strident than perhaps his advanced age ought to have allowed. "It is gratifying that so many share my enthusiasm for the point at which art comes into its closest proximity with science."

I wondered if he understood the true reason for the packed hall, and whether the truth would offend him. Quite possibly, he might see this greater audience as an opportunity – both in terms of broadcasting his findings to the widest possible assembly, and also in terms of touting for subscriptions to his forthcoming book.

"As you are all aware," Muybridge continued, "this lecture is titled 'The Motion of the Horse and other Animals in Nature and in Art', in keeping with the theme of my recent publication. I will keep the promise implicit in that title. Together we will examine the true nature of the motion of horses, as proven by my own extensive photographic studies in America, and we will also travel back through the ages to appreciate the understanding – or lack of it – of our forebears. Did the sketches of Leonardo da Vinci capture accurately the horse's gait? Did the famous painter of horses, George Stubbs, do likewise, or was he blinded by what the eye *believes* it can see? Are the more recent studies in paint and bronze by the Frenchman Edgar Degas – which I have been told were inspired in part by my studies – a better reflection of motion in life, and are they therefore better examples of art?"

He paused, looking out over his audience. Despite the continued respectful silence, I had the distinct impression of impatience amid the mass of bodies. From their shuffling and their forward-bending postures, I perceived that few of the audience members were hanging on the details of Muybridge's introduction, but rather they were eager for him to begin his presentation.

Muybridge clasped his hands together. "However, as the title attests, we will not stop at horses, instructive as that noble beast may be. We will look at other animals, including that species at the apex of life on Earth—"

Gasps sounded out from somewhere in the middle of the room. In one region of the ballroom, I saw heads bob.

Muybridge opened his mouth to continue, but then hesitated as the same phenomenon was repeated in another part of the room. To my left I saw Holmes rise to his toes to watch these proceedings with interest.

"What was that?" cried one distinct voice, this time closer to the platform at the front of the ballroom.

"Gentlemen," Muybridge said, "I must insist on quiet. As I was saying, the species at the apex of life on Earth, namely—"

"A bird!" somebody called out.

"No, I was in fact referring to—" Muybridge began.

"There's a bird in here!"

"Turn on the lights!"

As a town hall official fumbled with the gas lamps, I heard the distinct flutter of wings. Then a wave of curses came from my right, further along the row of standing attendees. Within seconds, disturbed air – and perhaps something more physical – brushed against my cheek.

"Don't fuss with the lamps, you fool!" a voice cried. "Somebody open the curtains!"

A flurry of movement prefaced the throwing open of two

pairs of heavy curtains simultaneously. Daylight streamed into the room, blinding white in contrast to the earlier gloom.

All faces turned upwards. Now the source of the disturbance was clear for all to see. A plain grey pigeon with black bands on its wings hung above the lecture audience, flapping madly as if its sole ambition was to remain in place and visible to everybody present. Then it seemed to have a change of heart. It launched itself into a steep descent, hurtling towards the audience members seated in the centre of the ballroom. The effect this action produced was as if a great rock had struck that portion of the crowd: they flung themselves away from the expected point of impact, clawing over one another in their efforts to get away. However, the pigeon rose sharply again, yanking its heavy body aloft, ready to repeat the trick on another group, and leaving its first victims to pat one another down and mutter confused apologies.

I noticed that Holmes paid the bird no attention at all. Following his example, I focused on our white-haired client upon the platform. Eadweard Muybridge stood motionless and his eyes were wide as they watched the swooping creature. He held one hand over his mouth, as if to prevent himself from crying out.

With a great deal of exasperated complaints and shoving, the French windows in two of the four large bays were opened. The sight of many dozens of people attempting to shoo the bird using their hats or their folded programmes might have been comical in other circumstances, and it occurred to me that Muybridge might well find the contortions of their bodies interesting subject matter for one of his motion studies. Then I recalled that his custom was to photograph his subjects naked, and I baulked and put the image forcibly out of my mind.

Finally, the bird seemed to recognise that the world outside presented greater opportunities, and fewer beatings, than its continued presence in the ballroom. It swung drunkenly from side to side, struck a half-open window, then succeeded in navigating to freedom.

In the absence of the fluttering of wings, all sound within the room seemed to have been extinguished; then a collective sigh arose from the crowd; then the sigh became giddy laughter and chatter. Muybridge wavered upon the stage. He staggered forward, and then a man that I had not noticed before now stood up from a chair positioned beside the zoopraxiscope – I recognised him as Fellows, the lantern operator – and offered it to Muybridge, who sat down heavily.

"Either our client is an absolute perfectionist who would have been upset by any interruption," Holmes said quietly, "or the appearance of that bird held particular significance."

In time, the audience settled. The windows were latched, the curtains drawn and the lamps, which the town hall staff had finally succeeded in operating, but to no effect given that they had done so only after the curtains had been opened, were turned down once again. The darkness was more profound than it had been earlier.

All eyes turned to Muybridge as he rose unsteadily from his chair. He patted his assistant on the shoulder, then resumed his central position on the platform.

He cleared his throat. "The species at the apex of life on Earth, namely" – he paused briefly for the inevitable ripple of muted laughter – "ourselves. Humanity provides the greatest variety of bodily movement, both deliberate and unconscious, and study of the human figure in motion will prove instructive to those working in any number of fields, not least artists and photographers such as yourselves."

Now he seemed to regard his audience more critically, perhaps for the first time suspecting that fewer of these men were members of an amateur photographic association than he had been led to believe.

Muybridge looked towards the door of the ballroom. "There is still one light over there. I must have absolute darkness." He waited until somebody hastened to douse the light, then continued, "Now I will introduce to you my invention of the zoopraxiscope. Its workings are complex, but they are less important than the effect it produces, so we will begin with a demonstration. Here, presented faithfully, drawn from life itself, is a horse engaged in a rapid gallop."

I saw a pinprick of orange light at the front of the platform, at the position where I had seen the now-invisible zoopraxiscope. In its glow I made out the huddled form of the lanternist, who bent forward to remove the cap from the lens.

Then my full attention was occupied by the image projected on the screen behind Muybridge, who shifted aside to allow an unobstructed view. At great size and from this distance the moving image was even more convincing than it had been at our demonstration three days earlier. In short, I believed that I was watching a running horse, no matter what my conscious mind understood to be the case. The beast faced to the right, racing continually and yet never moving from its position, but rather than undermining the effect, it seemed as though I were running at equal speed alongside it.

"Now we will slow down the rotation of the glass plate upon which the images are inscribed," Muybridge announced, "in order to answer the age-old question of whether all four hoofs of the horse leave the ground simultaneously."

Again, I saw the silhouetted Fellows bend towards the machine. Then the animated form of the horse on the screen slowed unnaturally to make undeniable the fact that all four feet were above the ground at times. The audience murmured its appreciation.

"Perhaps if some derivation of this machinery were applied more widely," I whispered to Holmes, "there would be no need for anybody to engage your services, as they might simply review events at slow speeds, showing a true recreation of life that might be analysed, in place of deduction after the fact. There might be no mysteries remaining in the world."

Holmes stared at me, his expression inscrutable, then turned away without deigning to reply.

On the stage, Muybridge continued his commentary, directing his lanternist to show first one slide and then another, noting the distinctive arrangements of each limb of the beast pictured, and the consequent knowledge imparted about the function of certain muscles. Following the first horse was another, this time moving at a gentle trot, and then a greyhound, a sheep, and a chicken with jerky, proud movements that aroused amusement within the audience. The interval between slides was brief; I watched the indistinct form of Fellows as he pulled the shutter before the lens, resulting in the animated image disappearing, and only then did he halt the rotation of the glass plate (so that no member of the audience saw any static silhouette, perhaps in order to maintain the illusion of life that Muybridge prized so highly), and then he slid the next glass plate into place, began the rotation and removed the shutter in a motion so fluid as to require only a sentence or two of Muybridge's narration to bridge the gap.

I shall not say that I was uninterested in the slides, though I will confess that after the tenth or so my enthusiasm became somewhat dimmed. Similarly, Muybridge's commentary had become a wash of soothing drone, and I found myself concentrating less and less on his words. As my eyes roved the dark mass of the crowd I fancied that I was not alone in my plight: heads and shoulders bobbed from side to side, indicating impatience, and others

had nodded forward and then failed to rise. When Muybridge's lecture moved on to the study of horses and other animals in the works of the pantheon of great artists – which involved the magic-lantern projection of motionless facsimiles of paintings – I judged by the slumped shoulders of many of the attendees that impatience had turned to despondency.

As the final part of his lecture, Muybridge moved on to the discussion of human figures. The crowd became enlivened at the sight of human subjects in motion, and even more so at the sequence of static photographs depicting naked men and women at work and play.

"As a man of science, I will not be accused of salaciousness or titillation," Muybridge said as the shutters came across the lens and the hall became entirely dark once again. His statement prompted in me a half-memory that he had been accused of precisely those things upon publication of these same images. "The naked person reveals a great deal more about the workings of the body than one that is clothed, of course, and to demonstrate my dedication to the pursuit of knowledge, during my work at the University of Pennsylvania I was frequently required to act as photographic model myself, as you will see."

I squinted in discomfort at a sudden bright light from somewhere above. Then the shutters of the zoopraxiscope were opened and I gasped, as did every other member of the audience.

On the screen was projected a sequence depicting a lean, naked man swinging a heavy pickaxe over his head and striking the ground on his other side. This would not have been arresting in itself; the reason for the crowd's fascination was that the head of the figure was defaced by cross-hatched lines. Their variation in each individual image produced an unsettling effect, as the mass of violently scored lines changed each moment, appearing constantly in motion, and perhaps even more alive than the pickaxe-wielding subject. As if this were not enough, above the head of the miner – who was Muybridge, I reminded myself – flickered other scored lines, which at the end of each sequence of movements resolved themselves into the hovering words 'TO HELL'.

For several seconds we all simply gazed up at this awful vision. Then, as if a dam had been forced open, a swell of muttered voices in the crowd became an uproar.

Muybridge, his face deathly pale, stared mutely around the room, which then became markedly more dim as the bright light I had noticed earlier was extinguished; only now did I recognise that this source of light could not have been the zoopraxiscope, which continued to play its loop of images. Muybridge turned as slow as a sleepwalker to look up at the white fabric screen, and his posture became first slack, then knotted and tense.

When he faced his audience once again, the room hushed. It occurred to me that while the defaced figure had been the expected outcome of the evening, it was Muybridge's response to it that most interested the most opportunistic attendees. I thought of his confession of having smashed one of the previously vandalised slides, and wondered if I might be able to force my way along the aisle to restrain him if he turned to rage.

However, Muybridge only said indistinctly, "That concludes the section on the human figure, and in turn it concludes the lecture." He paused, looking first at his assistant, and then at the expectant faces of his audience. "My intention at this point was to gauge interest in subscriptions for my forthcoming publication about the various gaits of a horse, and a more extensive overview of my animal motion work, with over one thousand half-tone images…" He cleared his throat once, then twice. "But I see that you are all impatient to get on with the supper that our hosts have kindly laid on for us. I thank you for your warm welcome."

With that, he strode to the nearest set of double doors, fumbled with the latch, then finally succeeded in effecting his escape. A stream of attendees followed him onto the first-floor landing.

I made to move in the same direction, but Holmes put a hand on my arm.

"Let him find his own way to the inn," he said. "We have much still to do here."

I nodded and allowed him to lead me in the opposite direction to the tide of bodies. Eventually, we made our way along the central aisle to where the lanternist sat beside the zoopraxiscope, as though he were still waiting for his cue to change one glass disc for another.

He looked up balefully as we approached, and said in a reedy voice, "You'll be wanting to question me, then?"

Holmes nodded.

"You going to clap the cuffs on me?"

"I'm not the police, nor do I have cuffs, nor would I make use of them if I had. Your name is Fellows?"

"George Fellows, sir."

"And how long have you worked with Mr. Muybridge?"

"Just this lecture and one another, though I was engaged two weeks ago in preparation. Mr. Muybridge has fewer public appearances than once he did, as I understand it. I thought it was a real opportunity for me. I'm trained in magic-lantern work, and not so long ago I was part of the revival of Phylidor's Phantasmagoria at the Royal Polytechnic Institution, which was no small business. But there's less call for variety-hall lanternists these days, and these new moving-picture shows you hear so much about… well, they're a closed shop. I'd hoped that dealing with Mr. Muybridge might open those doors, allowing me to show that I'm a dab hand with animated images. But he doesn't know a soul in that world." He sighed. "I'd have lost my job soon in any case, seeing as Mr. Muybridge is talking about giving this all up. My main fear's that when the story of what happened here to-night gets out, I'll be unemployable anywhere."

"I hardly think that the name of the lanternist will feature in tomorrow's newspaper reports," Holmes said.

"But you're asking me questions this very minute," Fellows moaned. "And what'll be next?"

"There will be no 'next', and I assure you that I ask questions of everybody," Holmes said, not unkindly. "Everybody who was present in this room is of equal or greater interest to me than you are."

Fellows's face brightened. "Really, sir? Then you don't suspect me of being responsible for this damage?"

"I have no particular reason to believe so. But you must tell me all you can about any opportunities that another may have had to perpetrate the vandalism."

The lanternist's relieved smile vanished. "I've guarded these discs closely since they were entrusted to me yesterday – and I can tell you I checked them thoroughly more than once."

I looked at the motionless glass plate still fitted into the zoopraxiscope. Even though the cross-hatched lines and lettering were produced by scoring the glass itself, the lines were visible at a glance and as prominent as any other part of the images.

"May I examine it?" Holmes asked.

Fellows nodded and watched as Holmes lifted the plate free. I noticed that Holmes gave the drawn images and scratches only a cursory glance, and his eyes seemed drawn to the centre of the disc, where a square of paper was pasted, bearing the large numbers '4/14'.

He pointed to this legend. "This note represents the sequence of use in the lecture, I presume? Part four, plate number fourteen? And it is your own handwriting?"

Fellows nodded. "Not my normal handwriting, of course. It's written nice and big so I can read it in the dark, but even then it's a challenge to make out those numbers."

As Holmes scraped at the edge of the paper with a thumbnail I noted that it came away easily. He put the disc down carefully.

"When did you last perform a check of the discs?" he asked.

"At around three o'clock, when we were first let into this room to set up. And then I've been sitting right here since a quarter to five, when the first attendees arrived."

"And were the slides left alone for any period of time between your arrival and the start of the lecture?"

"Well, only to allow me to stretch my legs and such like. But I mean only minutes at a time, and I made sure Mr. Muybridge was here in the room on each occasion."

"What was he occupied doing?"

Fellows gestured at the empty chair on the platform. "Sitting, reading, writing his notes. That sort of thing."

It occurred to me that when Muybridge was engrossed in his work, he might well be less observant about the world around him. Like Holmes, his level of concentration was remarkable, but unlike Holmes, it was narrowly focused.

Fellows seemed to have anticipated my thoughts. "But as I say, this was for only minutes at a time. There'd be no chance of somebody stealing in, scratching over every single image on one of the discs, then melting into the background – would there?"

Holmes didn't reply to the question. "Are your responsibilities limited to the changing of slides?"

"It's hardly a trivial business, Mr. Holmes—"

"I mean only that I assume that it is not you who dictates the light levels in the room at large, or who produces any other lighting effects?"

"None," Fellows replied in bemusement.

"Are you referring to that bright light that prefaced the showing of the final slide?" I asked Holmes.

Holmes swung around to look at me. "You saw a light? Describe it to me."

I shrugged my shoulders. "Just that. An exceedingly bright light, from above head height. It made me wince... but then I was distracted by the image of Muybridge on the screen."

Holmes was silent and motionless for some seconds. Then he leapt onto the platform and turned to look out over the ballroom. From this position of authority, he looked down at me and said, "Watson, this evening you must be your most avuncular self."

"I am never less than that," I retorted. "But for what purpose?"

"Speak to staff members, and any attendees that have remained in the building – as I suspect many of them will have done, given the lure of supper and drinks in the dining-room, not to mention the prospect of gossip."

"Are they all to be considered suspects in this matter?"

Holmes raised an eyebrow. "Of course. But as well as that, note their observations related to the defaced slide, and you must also enquire about this bright light that you have mentioned. And be sure that you see their tickets – and record everything."

I noted Fellows flinching beside me, but in my despondency I ignored it.

"Oh, is that all?" I said in a morose tone. "You may recall that there were more than two hundred people in this room. It would be a help if we might share the burden of questioning them."

Holmes shook his head. "I am better deployed here. Hurry now, Watson, before more of them leave the building."

CHAPTER THREE

The remainder of my evening was as frustrating as I had imagined it would be. As if acting as a harbinger of annoyance to come, upon leaving the ballroom I collided with a doughy-faced member of staff, and then rather than apologise, he simply stopped and stared truculently at me, watching on as I picked myself up and dusted off my jacket. Then, no sooner had I sidled into the packed dining-room, than I became mired in repetitive conversations, chiefly centred around the intentions of whoever was threatening Muybridge, and the specific interpretation of the scratched-out face of his image. Worse still, each conversation involved at least three attendees, who all spoke over one another and became louder and more expansive as the evening wore on. Steering each discussion to matters of lighting effects within the ballroom was no easy matter, and my requests to see the ticket stubs of each of my interlocutors were met with outright confusion – until the point when some astute individual identified me as 'Holmes's assistant' and the conversation became derailed all over again. Though on numerous occasions I came within striking distance of the table upon which a buffet supper had been laid out, I had no opportunity to take a plateful of food or even a drink, as each time I attempted to do so I would spy an as-yet-uninterviewed attendee heading towards the door, and I would be compelled to head him off before he exited. After an exhausting hour and a half of conversation my throat was parched and my note-book was full of nonsensical jottings.

At just after nine o'clock I stood in the centre of the dining-room, turning slowly and surveying the remaining people. With no small degree of satisfaction, I saw only people to whom I had already spoken, including the serving staff and another employee of the town hall who had been responsible for the operation of the gas lamps in the ballroom; given Holmes's preoccupation with light, this man's page in my note-book was fuller than any other.

I made for the serving-table, only to discover that it was now empty of food – and as I watched, aghast, two waiters exchanged conspiratorial glances and each took one of the remaining glasses of wine and drank it in a single gulp. Shaking my head, I plodded out of the room and along the corridor to return to the ballroom.

George Fellows sat with his legs dangling from the platform, staring at the floor in dejection. All around him, on tablecloths spread on the surface of the raised platform, were laid all of Muybridge's glass plates. Alongside them were odd-shaped pieces of wood that at first baffled me, but which I finally recognised as the dismantled elements of the zoopraxiscope.

"Good lord!" I exclaimed in horror.

"I may indeed need His intervention," Fellows said in a dismal tone, "when my employer learns what's been done to his machine."

I turned around. "Where the devil is Holmes?"

Fellows gestured with a thumb, upwards. I looked up at the ceiling, half expecting to find Holmes dangling from it, or perhaps hovering like the pigeon that had interrupted Muybridge's introduction. Then I saw what the lanternist was indicating: a bowed balcony protruded slightly from the inner, windowless wall of the room. Beneath its wide arch I saw the silhouette of a crouching figure. Then, much like the painted silhouettes of athletes on Muybridge's glass discs, the kneeling figure burst into motion, standing and waving a hand.

"Come up here, Watson," Holmes called out. "You'll find the stairs through the curtains below the balcony."

I pushed past the heavy crimson curtains and bumped my way up the unlit staircase to emerge beside Holmes. The area was larger than I had anticipated, though most of it was recessed into the wall so that only a small amount of its floor protruded into the ballroom. Behind the arch was a half-dome ceiling lavishly decorated with glinting golden panels that matched the gilt of the ornate two-foot-tall balustrade.

Holmes directed my gaze away from these pleasing details to the carpeted floor, and said, "Well, what do you make of that?"

"I'm sorry, Holmes," I said. "What aspect is of particular interest? The shade of the carpet, or the weave, perhaps?"

Holmes clucked his tongue. "You have my sympathy that you haven't eaten, Watson, but please try to moderate your acerbic tone. I'm referring to the *damage* to the carpet."

I knelt to examine it closer. Sure enough, almost in the centre of the floor of the protruding section was a darker, discoloured patch. I touched it, and found that the carpet was slightly singed.

"Then this indicates the source of that bright light I saw," I said. "But to have produced this burn mark, the lamp must have been placed low to the floor – and yet this balustrade…" I let my words trail away. Shuffling awkwardly, I repositioned myself so that I faced the rear of the ballroom and the wall against which Holmes and I had been standing during the lecture. As I lowered my eyes to a height at which I estimated the lantern placed here might be located, I saw that a large diamond-shaped gap in the design of the gilt balustrade allowed a view of almost the entirety of the room.

"You have followed my train of thought," Holmes said as I rose.

"Only to an early stop, I suspect, and far from the entire journey," I replied. "My mind does tend to work slowly on an empty stomach. Have you completed your investigation here?"

Holmes clapped me on the back. "I have."

With great relief, I led the way down the short staircase and into the main part of the ballroom.

"Well, then," I said, striding towards the doorway, beyond which I saw the same doughy-faced staff member who had knocked me down earlier; however, I refused to be waylaid by demanding an apology from him when I had far more important things to do. "We needn't go as far as our inn just yet; there must be any number of restaurants between here and there."

George Fellows hopped down from the platform. "Surely you aren't going to leave me like this?"

At first I failed to understand his meaning, but then I looked again at the dismembered zoopraxiscope.

Holmes shot me a look that might almost have been interpreted as apologetic.

"It will take me no more than an hour to put the device back together," he said. "Go on without me if you can't bear to wait."

I hesitated. Then, with no small amount of grumbling, I slumped into a seat in the front row, my arms folded tightly to stifle the equally loud muttering emanating from my stomach.

Upon our return to our inn, we discovered Eadweard Muybridge standing alone at the counter in the saloon. His posture said much about his state of mind: his shoulders were hunched and his white beard dipped towards his chest. When he raised his glass it seemed a mechanical motion and his lips barely grazed the surface of the liquid within.

He turned as we approached.

"Where were you?" he barked. "My understanding was that in accepting my contract, you were bound to keep me safe."

"Then we have commenced under a misunderstanding," Holmes replied genially. "I have been labouring under the apprehension that I have been engaged to solve the mystery of the threats scratched upon your zoopraxiscope slides, as opposed to ensuring your welfare at large. In fact, we have made great strides in the case."

"Were you followed far by the journalists?" I asked.

"A better word would be *hounded*," Muybridge replied bitterly, "and no fox ever scurried as far out of his way or performed as many about-turns as I did in my attempts to shake them off."

"I can imagine that reports of those who were within the ballroom only heightened their tenacity," Holmes said, "and of course some of that surprising number of attendees may themselves have been members of the press."

He looked at me for confirmation, and I nodded.

Muybridge stared into his glass. "When I came onto the platform, for the briefest of moments I believed that they had come due to an interest in the subject matter of my lecture."

"Did you indeed?" Holmes said.

I watched my friend warily. It was unlike him to make such a rhetorical remark. However, Holmes appeared to be waiting, as though he yet expected an answer to his question.

"I suppose that tomorrow's papers will be filled with tales of what happened to-night," Muybridge said blankly.

"Certainly," Holmes replied, "and though only the locals appear to have carried the story of the previous threats made against you, over the next day or so I am confident it will be amplified and will appear elsewhere, including in the London papers. You are likely to be the 'talk of the town', as they say."

Again, I looked sidelong at my friend, who rarely deployed such stock phrases. Whatever he was doing must surely be intended to evoke a response from our client.

Muybridge nodded slowly. "They won't stop there. My life will be held under a magnifying lens once again. They'll dredge up…" He stopped and took a gulp of his drink.

I watched our client with great interest, having reached the assumption that he was referring to the killing of his wife's lover. This first hint of talk about this period of his life surprised me; I realised now that I had anticipated a show of defiance in relation to that awful event. Now I recalled a detail from the newspaper reports of his trial: when he had been pronounced an innocent man, Muybridge had convulsed and wept continually, unable to summon the strength to exit the courtroom, and his own lawyer had been forced to plead with him to stifle his emotions enough to leave.

"I take it," Holmes said, "that you refer to your dispute with Governor Stanford?"

Muybridge's face creased. "What?"

"I mean the issue of ownership of your famous photographs of the horse named 'Occident', and the invention of the mechanism of a bank of cameras to capture its sequential motion."

I was too familiar with my friend's methods to correct him. Though his assumption seemed grossly misjudged, I knew that there must be a purpose to his prompt.

Muybridge waved a hand sharply. "That's all in the past."

"Then the ownership of those images is resolved?"

"Well, not entirely, but it is in the hands of lawyers, and—" Abruptly, Muybridge stopped speaking. Then his features transformed into a new expression of wonderment – though it struck me as one suited to the stage, an exaggeration of a natural expression. "Do you think that it may have some bearing on these threats I've received?"

"Who can say?" Holmes said, and once again I stared at my friend, amazed at his callousness. "Do you think that Fellows may have been working in league with such a man?"

Again, Muybridge hesitated. "Ah yes, Fellows. He came highly recommended… but I do not know him at all well."

"It hardly matters now, if you intend to dismiss him. Perhaps we ought to have him followed, in case he mounts some other plot against you."

Muybridge had already drained his glass, and yet now he lifted it again to his lips in an automatic motion. He stared at it, then set it down on the counter. "It's an irrelevance. To-night's lecture was the last of my scheduled engagements of this tour – and now I fancy it will be the last I will ever conduct. I shall dedicate myself to the preparation for publication of *Animals in Motion*, and that will serve as my legacy."

"Very well," Holmes said mildly, waving the publican over and ordering our client another drink.

CHAPTER FOUR

In the days to come, Holmes barely referred to the Muybridge case at all. Upon our return to Baker Street – following a decidedly awkward train journey shared with Muybridge and the hapless Fellows, who sat with the zoopraxiscope crate placed on the seat beside him as though it were a travelling companion, and who said not a word – Holmes had taken my note-book from me, leafed through its pages and then appeared to dismiss the matter entirely from his mind. Several times I broached the subject, hoping to enquire about our next steps, but each time my friend made some excuse or looked about him for a distraction.

The account of Muybridge's lecture appeared in the Saturday newspapers, the speed of which suggested the eagerness of journalists to file copy immediately, in a race to reach the presses that same night. On Friday over breakfast I read the *Times* article with a sinking heart, and I found similar accounts in the *Telegraph* and the *Standard*, the significance of all three papers being upon our table that morning only then dawning upon me. Each of the three articles had a similar bent: 'Professor' Eadweard Muybridge's life was at risk, and the perpetrator of the threats had almost certainly been present at Liverpool town hall (a detail that clearly occupied the mind of each journalist, who appeared to thrill at their proximity to crime). Furthermore, each contained barely disguised insinuations that the affair might relate to Muybridge's past career in California; the *Standard* even carried a miniature sketch of Muybridge's attractive former wife, presumably in lieu of a picture of the murdered Harry Larkyns. But it was none of these details about the case that made me lower my newspaper to peer over it with a distinct sense of trepidation at Holmes, who sat silently in his armchair, his hands clasped under his chin as he stared at the unlit coals in the fireplace.

Cautiously, I began, "I say, Holmes, you must not take this to heart."

Holmes cleared his throat quietly, but said nothing.

I raised the *Telegraph*. "After all, it has been placed only on page seven, which shows the affair is as yet of little importance to its readers." I chose not to add that the *Standard* had placed it on page four, and the *Times* had deemed it a second-page story.

Still the coals seemed to occupy my friend's full attention.

"Moreover," I said, desperation beginning to grip me, "there is a great deal in each article that is *not* connected to you – and nobody could possibly imagine that you have any better insight into Muybridge's past misdeeds than anybody else—"

As Holmes turned slowly to look at me, I realised I had made a grave mistake.

"I mean to say," I stammered, "that you have only very recently been engaged by him. There is nobody in the country who would have expected you to have solved the conundrum by this point."

Holmes's eyes widened very slightly.

"No, I do not mean that as it sounds," I added hastily. "It is only that…" My voice died in my throat; I could not think how to continue, or what I might possibly say to placate Holmes. Despondently, and with the fervent hope that the ground might swallow me up, I looked down at the newspaper lying open on my lap, which began:

Great Detective Baffled by
Threats Against Life

The most puzzling of crimes surely warrants the involvement of the greatest mind of our age. Yet the threats against the life of Professor Eadweard Muybridge, scientist and innovator responsible for the remarkable photographs of the racehorse 'Occident' in full gallop, have bewildered even the remarkable, but evidently fallible, Sherlock Holmes. For he, along with some two hundred and fifty onlookers, was most easily deceived last Thursday evening, when Professor Muybridge was subjected – in plain sight – to another of the mortal threats to which he has received in recent weeks, as reported previously…

On Sunday, Holmes finally broke his silence. We had both eaten at my club and afterwards, accompanied by brandy and cigars, Holmes had proceeded to instruct me about the various myths and religious texts that contained similarities to the tale of the building of the Tower of Babel and the subsequent confusion of tongues. At the point at which he suggested that the Tower may have been inspired by the Etemenanki ziggurat dedicated to the Mesopotamian god Marduk, my eyelids had begun to droop. It was as if from very far away that I heard Holmes say, "Of course, an element of rivalry may well be the key to the threats against Muybridge."

I shook my heavy head.

"You don't agree, Watson?"

"Sorry. I was just clearing my... but I thought we were discussing Babel?"

"Yes, we were – perhaps a quarter of an hour ago."

I rubbed my eyes and set down my cigar, which had burned so low as to present the threat of burning my fingers. "I confess I'm surprised that you bring up Muybridge now. I had assumed you'd grown tired of the case."

"Not in the least. Now, who might be his rivals who might wish him ill?"

I took my time to consider the question. "Well, you have already spoken to him about the horse pictures. That governor in California."

"Governor Leland Stanford, yes. 'Occident' was his racehorse, and the experiment to capture his motion in full gallop was reportedly Stanford's whim. All innovations beyond that point are disputed by each party."

"But Muybridge's attitude suggested that it was unlikely that bad blood might produce so visceral a threat now, fully fifteen years after legal wrangling began."

"I agree. Then who remains?"

"His former wife?" I suggested tentatively. "Or... doesn't he have a son, whose paternity he has denied?"

"Flora Muybridge died in 1875, shortly after their divorce," Holmes said. "The son works as a ranch hand close to Sacramento and there is no indication of him having the least interest in the father who disowned him. But Eadweard Muybridge is one of those men who is defined by his work rather than his friends and family. I urge you to consider *professional* enemies."

"But are there any others working in the same field as Muybridge?"

Holmes's reply came quickly. "There are others that have styled themselves as chronophotographers, dedicating themselves to the study of animals in motion by means of photography. The Parisian Étienne-Jules Marey, for example."

"Then is there bitterness between them?"

"I have heard of no suggestion of it. Muybridge has visited Marey on several occasions, and they speak of one another fondly in public. As much as Muybridge is capable of such a thing, they are friends."

I chewed my cheek in thought. "When Muybridge first visited us, you asked him about professional jealousy, and he alluded to disappointments in his recent professional career."

Holmes nodded. "I believe he was referring to a meeting with Thomas Edison."

"A man with an impressive record in inventions. What was the purpose of the meeting?"

"Some eight years ago, the New York press reported that Muybridge went to Edison's New Jersey laboratory, suggesting they form a partnership. He proposed that Edison's phonograph might be deployed to synchronise a voice with images of a speaking face projected via his zoopraxiscope. An adaptation of *Hamlet* was mentioned."

"But... Edison created a moving-picture machine himself, didn't he?" I asked. "I read about a parlour dedicated to the device, somewhere here in London. Personally, I see no attraction in staring into a box to glimpse only a few seconds of drama."

"Indeed. Edison was evidently impressed by Muybridge's invention, and by October of that same year he had patented his Kinetoscope, which is distinct from that earlier invention in that it deploys celluloid strips rather than glass plates. In fact, he had originally attempted to do precisely as Muybridge had hoped, with a cylinder phonograph playing sounds to match the images, but it is only more recently that the concept has come to fruition."

"I can well imagine Muybridge's frustration. So do you suspect Thomas Edison of making these threats?"

"I think not."

"Then... perhaps some other proponent of these new moving pictures, closer to home? I understand they're quite the draw at variety-hall shows nowadays."

Holmes pursed his lips. "Yes, that certainly warrants investigation."

"Ought we to question Muybridge about the matter?"

"Too blunt. More direct observation would serve us better. I presume that you read in the newspapers that the famous Lumière brothers of Paris demonstrated their cinematograph at the Regent Street Polytechnic only last month?"

I shrugged my shoulders. "I confess I pay little attention to coverage of the arts."

"No matter. While we are too late to confront Muybridge with the Lumières' invention, there is another that might suffice. A canny Briton named Robert Paul is close behind them in the race. Having first produced a workable copy of Edison's Kinetoscope, Paul now has his sights set on the projection of celluloid images. As fortune would have it, he is due to demonstrate his so-named Animatograph this Tuesday evening at the Alhambra Music Hall in Leicester Square."

"And is your intention that we will offer to escort Muybridge there?"

"A capital idea, Watson. I congratulate you."

I frowned and stared down at my brandy, wrestling with the sensation that I had offered no such idea at all, and that Holmes had simply guided me to a conclusion that he had desired from the beginning of our conversation.

CHAPTER FIVE

My suspicions seemed ever more well founded when Tuesday came around. As I was tying my necktie, Holmes's head appeared around the door of my room and he said in an offhand manner, "I won't be coming this evening after all, Watson. I trust you will enjoy yourself all the same."

"What has changed your plans?" I asked in surprise.

In truth, Holmes's callous attitude towards Eadweard Muybridge since our visit to Liverpool rankled a little; I had often known him to dismiss potential clients upon their initial request, but when he accepted a case he was ordinarily bound to see it through.

Holmes waved a hand in the direction of the sitting-room. "I find that my work on this new monograph is at a crucial point. I cannot abandon it and I hope to complete it to-night."

It seemed a hollow excuse, particularly given Holmes's earlier insistence that Muybridge himself would be of great use in advising on the finer points of the monograph. I finished up with my necktie, nodded stiffly to Holmes as I passed him, and made directly for the door.

* * *

Though the Alhambra Theatre of Variety, with its two tall towers
and Moorish dome, dominated one side of Leicester Square
and directly overlooked the statue of William Shakespeare at its
centre, in the past I had scarcely given it a moment's thought
as a potential destination. Now, in early evening, its open doors
represented a narrow, illuminated passage through which a river
of people was determined to flood.

I found Eadweard Muybridge standing to one side of the main
archway, buffeted by this tide of bodies. Rather than surveying the
faces of those who passed him, his eyes were fixed on a garish
yellow poster plastered on the opposite wall alongside an array
of more familiar fare, which boasted of *LIVING PHOTOS BY
ROBT. W. PAUL.* Muybridge's heavy white whiskers did nothing
to disguise his contemptuous sneer.

"It's as well there are numbered seats," Muybridge said by
way of greeting. "You're exceedingly late."

I checked my watch. "But there are fifteen minutes to
spare."

"Yes, and I would like to use those precious minutes to go
backstage before the performance. I trust that Mr Paul knows of
me and will welcome me readily. Simply seeing the projections
from his Animatograph would hardly hold as much interest
without having examined the machine first, would it, now?"

I apologised, at first only vaguely, but in response to
Muybridge's gruffness I continued to do so with more conviction
as we made our way past the auditorium doors and along the
passage that presumably led to the rooms afforded to artistes.
It occurred to me that Muybridge had not questioned Holmes's
absence. Perhaps when Holmes had extended the invitation to
Muybridge, he had not promised that he would be in attendance.

"Halloa!" a voice cried out, and I turned to see a boy dressed
in a theatre attendant's uniform, who hurried after us.

Muybridge continued striding along the corridor until the boy caught up with him and put a hand on his arm, only for it to be shrugged off violently.

"I would thank you not to molest me," Muybridge snapped. "And do not tell me that I may not go this way. I intend to meet with Mr. Robert Paul, and you will see that he will thank me for having done so."

The boy's face creased with confusion. "No, sir, nothing of the sort. Sorry for my excitement, but I only wanted to make certain that it really was you. You are Professor Muybridge, aren't you?"

Muybridge's back straightened and he puffed out his chest noticeably. "I am he. Have you attended any of my lectures, or read my works?"

The boy emitted an involuntary squeaking sound which conveyed his pleasure. "Neither. Ah, Professor... do you suppose that we ought to be on our guard to-night?"

"Whatever do you mean?"

The boy looked around the corridor furtively, though other than we three it was empty. "He could be anywhere, that villain." He shuddered at the thrill of the idea. "You're a braver man than I, venturing out while he's at large. You know what they've been saying, don't you?"

Muybridge's expression hardened. "I confess that I choose not to listen to what 'they' say – if by 'they' you mean the morally deficient men of the press, or worse still, the 'man on the street.'"

The attendant's nose wrinkled. "No need to be short with me, sir." Then he brightened again as he noticed me for the first time. "And is this Sherlock Holmes?"

I stopped myself from rolling my eyes. Being mistaken for my friend was one of the aspects of my career as his biographer that I enjoyed even less than being taken for his 'assistant', especially as my actual contribution to his fame was so rarely acknowledged.

"No," I said simply. "I am not Sherlock Holmes."

The boy nodded sagely. "Then he's given up already. Can't blame him, I suppose; everybody meets their match eventually. All the same, Professor, I can see you're sensible, and you're on your guard. And I promise you now that I will be, too. I'll be watching – like a hawk, as they say, ha! – and the moment that villain strikes, I'll take it all in."

In a scathing tone, Muybridge asked, "For what purpose?"

"To tell the papers, of course. A story like this needs to be told, Professor, and I'm as good as anyone to tell it. How the lads'll seethe when they find out I was here on the spot!" A gleam came into his eyes as he pictured the effects of his imagined notoriety, and he barely seemed to notice when Muybridge extricated himself and hurried away, leaving the boy still wrapped up in his thoughts.

However, after we turned a corner we progressed little further before we were waylaid again. Two women wearing headdresses and gowns with cotton flowers pinned all over approached us, then formed themselves into a wall of sorts, barricading the corridor, whispering to one another and pointing at Muybridge.

"Is it really you?" the taller woman said, her eyes wide.

"Course it's him!" her friend said. "It's only him an' Charles Darwin that have white beards that size. And you're not Charles Darwin, are you, sir?"

"No, I am not the deceased Darwin," Muybridge confirmed laconically, and I found myself stifling a smirk at not being the only one to be wrongly identified to-night. "Now, my good women, will you let us pass?"

The shorter woman frowned. "The show's about to start."

"I'm fully aware of that. I am on my way to see Mr. Robert Paul himself."

She shook her head, making the flowers on her headdress bob. "I won't have you coming back here. We know all about you and the things you've done."

For the first time, a suggestion of real pain crossed Muybridge's features. "I merely wish to—"

The taller woman folded her arms. "Well, you can merely do it in your own time. If we let you past, you might get up to any sort of mischief. Besides, you've just been told the show's about to start. I can't stop you being in the building, but you'll stay at the front like everyone else."

I consulted my watch, then said to Muybridge, "It's true that there is little time to spare."

Muybridge ran his hands through his white hair. "But that's only because these fools have made obstacles of themselves!"

The shorter woman made a harrumphing sound. "These *fools*, sir, will arrange to have you thrown off the premises if you make a nuisance of yourself!"

Muybridge looked at each of his opponents in turn, then evidently concluded that there could be no chance of conquering them. Without a word, he turned and stamped back the way we had come. I flashed an apologetic smile at the flower-women, then hurried away to the auditorium.

CHAPTER SIX

As we edged to our seats in the seventh row, in a good, central location, Muybridge's complaints found a new target: he could not see Robert Paul's projector behind the auditorium seats due to other patrons standing and shuffling to their places. In part to distract myself from his antics, I opened the programme I had been given when I presented my ticket, and began to read. My eyes passed over the advertisements for restaurants, whiskey, hair products and corsets. When they finally settled on the list of entertainments, I froze.

"Is this accurate?" I asked Muybridge, pointing at the programme.

He stopped and looked at it. His eyes, too, widened in surprise.

"I should have expected no more from a place like this," he said. "Now you see why I restrict my own lectures to places of learning, as opposed to shrines to cheap entertainment."

I stared at the list again. Holmes had given me no reason to suspect that R. W. Paul's demonstration of his Animatograph was not the sole attraction this evening, but in fact there were eleven items described on the programme, with the Animatograph placed eighth. No less than two full stage plays were described with a list of actors and their parts, plus singers and dancers and even an act named Emmy's Troupe of Trained Toy Terriers. I groaned and cursed Holmes silently.

As the rest of the theatre patrons began to settle themselves, Muybridge insisted on turning and rising from his seat to look over their heads, shielding his eyes to peer into the darkness. Finally I could take no more, and I promised that we would go backstage immediately after the show to make our introductions to Mr. Paul and to request a personal demonstration of his machine. From this vantage point before the performance had yet begun, the end of the evening seemed so far away as to be unreachable, and therefore I was ready to promise anything in order to navigate a way through the hours without further annoyance.

The screen curtain before the stage, upon which was painted a scene from Ancient Greece with women at leisure amid columns that apparently stretched into the distance, began to rise. The orchestra commenced its overture, and then a male singer who had been revealed upon the stage joined in. I checked my programme and reassured myself that the overture represented one of the eleven items on the list.

Despite my misgivings, the first several acts passed quickly enough. The Musical Korries were perfectly pleasant, and I found myself enthralled by the first play, titled *Donnybrook*, which featured spies and police, and which might even have amused Holmes. Emmy's toy terriers were a delight, and I couldn't help but nudge Muybridge and then turn to see if he was enjoying it as much as I – only to discover that he was asleep. In response to my nudging his head fell back, and this new posture seemed to release pent-up snores which were louder than the barking of the dogs. As gently as possible, I pushed his head forward again so that it lolled heavily, and the snoring ceased.

Next followed lively acrobats upon bars, then Russian dancers and then a selection of pieces inspired by *Romeo and Juliet*. By this point my eyelids were beginning to droop, and it was only the distasteful imagined picture of myself and Muybridge slumped unconscious side by side that forced me into some semblance of wakefulness. When it was announced that Robert Paul's Animatograph would be the next item, I gasped and lurched up in my seat, then shook Muybridge awake.

The auditorium had been dim throughout the earlier acts, but as a white screen lowered and hid the stage lights, for several seconds there was no source of illumination at all. Then a single spotlight lit to reveal a man, who I assumed
himself, striding onto the narrow strip
to introduce his device. I did no
of his speech, as my eyes a
responses. How
been

The spotlight remained upon Paul, though it dimmed noticeably, and then a second beam of light came from the rear of the large room. I expected Muybridge to turn and search for the projection machine, but instead he stared fixedly ahead.

Upon the screen appeared a man dressed in full evening wear. His image flickered somewhat, and though he spoke his words were inaudible. Strangest of all, he seemed a giant, his body aturally large, his face looming above the orchestra pit.

"Ladies and gentlemen, I introduce to you Tom Merry," aul said, now standing beside the flickering image, "the famed lightning cartoonist."

idge had leant any further forward in his seat, he rehead on the back of the one before m Merry turned away and raised r that was fixed on the wall all was within the Merry

I could only smile at the different causes of our appreciation. Whereas Muybridge saw only technical accomplishment, I, like the greater part of the audience, had immediately accepted what we saw projected on the fabric screen as reality, and had reacted to it as entertainment as opposed to acknowledging the miracle of its production.

After a pause of only a minute, during which time Paul detailed more about the creation of his films, Tom Merry appeared once again, his white sheet eerily restored to blankness. Again, he turned to his sheet and began working on a caricature, which soon coalesced into the recognisable form of Otto von Bismarck. I glanced around me and saw that the eyes of my fellow audience members were less alight than they had been. Had we all grown used to this spectacle so very quickly? Muybridge, in contrast, remained entranced.

When Tom Merry's sketch was complete, the applause was decidedly more muted, perhaps this time in recognition of the absence of a real performer to applaud.

"What will be next?" Muybridge murmured. It was clearly a rhetorical question, as he now seemed oblivious to my presence.

Robert Paul cleared his throat and said, "The general manager of this fine establishment, Mr. Moul, is known for his clear-sighted understanding of his audience. The attractions you have already seen so far this evening are testament to that. At the time he made his request to me to demonstrate the Animatograph, he advised me to 'add interest to wonder' – his own words, and wise guidance that I have since taken to heart. So, ladies, gentlemen, I present to you now a film first created by Mr. Birt Acres for the Kinetoscope, which I hope will represent both interest and wonder, and perhaps something more thrilling alongside. It is titled *Arrest of a Pickpocket*."

The screen illuminated again. Now it showed a wall entirely different from the one that we had seen earlier; its scuffed brickwork perhaps belonged to an alley, and playbills were scattered across its surface. Seconds later, a figure appeared from the right, as though he had stepped from the stage itself and onto the screen. He moved furtively, watching around him in all directions, and then he was immediately followed by a uniformed policeman, who seized the first man – the pickpocket – by the neck, only to throw him from the left side of the frame. I registered people around me copying my instinctive motion, heads turning to the left to track the motion of the two men as if they might still exist beyond the confines of the fabric screen. Then they reappeared, scuffling, the policeman's hat knocked from his head to go sliding along the floor, accompanied by gasps from around the auditorium. The policeman lunged for the pickpocket but only succeeded in wresting his jacket free. Then, just as the fugitive seemed bound to escape, another man appeared to block his way. Like others around me, I cried out in unrestrained jubilation. Together, the newcomer and the policeman wrestled the pickpocket to the ground, working hard to overcome his flailing limbs, and finally handcuffs were placed upon him and then he was hauled to his feet. The newly arrived man shoved the criminal roughly, pushing him to the right, leaving the policeman to scoop up the cast-off jacket and scurry after him.

The image disappeared and the auditorium was entirely dark. For a moment, there was no collective response to what we had all witnessed. Then, presaged by a sound like thunder as people rose to their feet, deafening applause filled the hall. I followed suit, clapping until my palms were sore. Then I looked at Muybridge, who was still sitting. His eyes were wet with tears, but there was no sadness in his expression. He nodded again and again, still staring in the direction of the screen even though the bodies of the people in the next row now blocked his view entirely.

I sank into my seat and said, "That was something to be seen, was it not? Do you think it was fact or fiction?"

Muybridge seemed not to have heard my question. His face was as pale as marble.

The applause continued and only died down when Robert Paul raised his hands, a gesture that might have been an appeal for silence or a modest recognition of his triumph.

"Ladies and gentlemen, I must very shortly vacate this stage to allow Mr. Morris Cronin to perform with clubs" – a loud groan echoed around the hall – "but before I do so, would you like me to project *Arrest of a Pickpocket* a second and final time?"

Cheers erupted from all corners.

Paul bowed. "Then I thank you sincerely, and I promise you more of this 'interest added to wonder' in the weeks to come… and here, again, is *Arrest of a Pickpocket*."

People sat so quickly that my own seat shook as though I were at the epicentre of an earthquake. This time, the response to each new event on the screen was both prefigured and followed by whoops and shouts, and I felt sure that if Robert Paul could be persuaded to show his film again, the effect would be amplified to an even more startling degree. When the film finished, after less than a minute, my instinct was to put my hands over my ears to stifle the thunderous applause from all around.

Paul absorbed this congratulatory onslaught for a long while, then bowed deeply and made his way off the stage and into the darkness. The clapping was replaced with a murmur of excited conversation among the crowd.

"Well, the audience certainly enjoyed it," I said to Muybridge.

Muybridge didn't respond. He still faced forward, blinking rapidly. I had the strangest feeling that he was rather like one of his own cameras, or that of Robert Paul and Birt Acres, and that by blinking he was capturing the world around him, one static frame at a time.

"I wonder what Holmes would have made of it," I wondered aloud. "We've found ourselves in enough scrapes similar to the one shown on the screen. No doubt he would have noticed numerous irregularities in the depiction of an arrest, though."

Muybridge looked around him blankly as though noticing his fellow theatregoers for the first time.

"He has done it," he said in a hoarse voice.

"Do you mean Holmes?"

"Robert Paul. He has captured life and now it can be summoned at will."

With a start, I remembered my reason for being here tonight. "And how do you feel about his achievement?"

"He has done it," Muybridge repeated. When he looked at me, I saw tears glistening in his eyes. "It is a wonder, a marvel of ingenuity... and yet these people respond to it as though they were witnessing a true, everyday scuffle between police and criminal in the street. It is as if the screen were simply a window."

"Rather poetic, that," I said, "but I take your meaning. Is it such an undesirable effect?"

Muybridge shook his head. "For so long I have positioned my own work as an aid to study – a tool of science. But this... With this invention, and with this singular work, Paul and this man Acres have created a supreme entertainment. Nobody here in this room desires to know whether a horse lifts all of its feet from the ground when it gallops – or, in this case, how many seconds a policeman's hat remains in the air after being knocked from his head. They want only a spectacle, an illusion which convinces them of its veracity throughout the entirety of its duration."

"I am certain there is room in this new art for both study and spectacle."

Muybridge sighed. "Perhaps. But my time is over. I have long known it, deep down. Now I am reconciled."

I realised only now that this was far from the reaction to another innovator's work that I might have expected. I dwelt on Muybridge's responses during Morris Cronin's act, barely registering the clubs being thrown to and fro. The next attraction was an adaptation of Washington Irving's 'Rip Van Winkle', and perhaps in sympathy for its protagonist, I became drowsy and gradually slipped into sleep.

CHAPTER SEVEN

I awoke after dreaming of tumultuous waves heard from within a cabin at sea, though I soon realised the effect was the result of the sustained applause from all around. When I regained my senses fully, I saw that the painting of Greek columns had been reinstated before the stage, and many theatregoers had already vacated their seats. Muybridge grumbled as he waited impatiently for the stragglers in our row to make way.

I got to my feet and followed him as he succeeded in leaving the row and then marched to the rear of the auditorium. When I caught up with him, he was standing with his hands on his hips, turning on the spot.

"It's gone," he said. "It must have been carted off during that interminable play."

"Perhaps Mr. Paul will still be backstage," I said in a still dazed tone.

Muybridge nodded sharply. With a speed that belied his advanced age, he pushed past meandering theatregoers to walk in the direction of the stage.

"But that is not the way to the backstage area," I said, though it occurred to me that Muybridge may know of another route. I had little idea myself about the layout of any theatre.

Muybridge pointed directly ahead. "There's the stage. The quickest way is clearly best, and those lackeys will be guiding everyone out of the building at this point. Here, I'll need a leg up."

To my amazement, he ascended the steps to the left of the orchestra pit.

"But we must make our introductions and request a meeting with Mr. Paul," I said weakly.

"Do that if you wish."

I watched impotently as Muybridge bent to pull at the lower part of the curtain, then eased his way through the gap as quickly and efficiently as a fox. Feeling distinctly like a schoolchild having been dared to break the rules, I hesitated on the top step.

Consequently, I experienced a great sense of relief as I heard my name called out from somewhere behind me in the auditorium.

"Dr. Watson!" the voice called again.

I shielded my eyes to look around the great room, wondering who might know me here. Then I saw a young man – barely more than a boy – hurrying towards me.

"It is Dr. Watson, isn't it?"

"Yes indeed," I replied, amazed that I was known here, of all places. "What is the matter?"

"My father has taken ill – he is unconscious. Please, won't you attend to him?"

I glanced at the curtain through which Muybridge had passed, but then said with no small amount of relief, "Of course. Lead me to him."

The boy's father, who appeared to be in his late fifties, lay prone before the first row of seats at the other side of the auditorium, in a place where no patrons now passed in order to leave. His left arm was crossed tightly over his body, which immediately suggested to me heart trouble. His head was turned to one side, but when I bent lower I saw that his face was grey and beads of sweat dotted his forehead.

I tended to the fellow and examined him, and it very soon became clear that the attack had passed without causing damage. Soon I had raised him to a sitting position and he looked about him wonderingly, as though not having expected to find himself alive. His son shook my hand again and again, despite the fact that, lacking my bag, I had in no proper sense treated the patient.

Then my head jerked up at a sharp, wordless shout, which came from the direction of the stage.

"Good lord. Muybridge!" I cried. I had almost forgotten my companion, and had certainly had no concern for his safety while in the backstage area.

The sounds of thumping footsteps and grunting came muffled through the sheet curtain.

With a last look down to reassure myself that the heart-attack victim was no longer in danger, I bounded up the steps and wrestled with the curtain to pass it.

The backstage area was dim, and the only shapes I could make out were looming walls of stage scenery, and a web of ropes overhead.

I called Muybridge's name, but there was no response. Then I heard the slam of a door from somewhere ahead and to my right.

The wings seemed crammed with detritus intended to slow my progress. I tripped on cables, snagged my cuff buttons on hanging silks, ducked to avoid being struck by hanging objects that in the pitch darkness defied description.

I heard the sound of a door – surely the same door as I had heard earlier – opening and closing, and I renewed my efforts to navigate the maze.

Finally, I stood before a dark brick wall adorned with illegible chalk marks. A single small door interrupted the black surface.

I pushed through it with some effort to find myself in a narrow alley. Its length was interspersed with barrels and crates stacked with sodden paper and cloth, presumably stage effects no longer required by theatre troupes. Near to the far end of the alley I saw somebody walking purposefully towards the better-lit street that ran perpendicular. At first I took him to be Muybridge, and almost called out, but then I saw that a long cape flowed behind the figure, whereas Muybridge had worn a simple woollen suit, and this man carried a cane. Remembering the shout from behind the stage curtain, I darted off in the direction of this eerie phantom.

Whoever it was reached the main street before me, paused momentarily, then made off to the left. I reached the same position mere seconds later, and yet I saw no sign of a lone man in a cape, nor Eadweard Muybridge.

Cursing, I went left along what I belatedly understood was Charing Cross Road. The crowds became ever more dense, and by the time I had crossed Cranbourn Street and passed the junctions of Little and Great Newport Street, I had no confidence about my ability to track my quarry – or rather, my two quarries. This thought reminded me that I had not actually seen Muybridge leave the Alhambra, and that he might still be there, possibly injured. I could not in good conscience continue racing about the London streets without making sure that it was not a pointless errand. With a sinking heart, I turned to make my way back to the theatre, convinced that this quest, too, would end in disappointment.

My fears were well founded. Fully two hours later, after a thorough search of the theatre backstage and its front of house, and then another fruitless trek around the nearby streets, I set off north-east on foot, having already covered more than half of the distance to Baker Street during my hunt. I tried not to dwell on Holmes's reaction to my news of losing our client in such appalling circumstances, and I constructed a litany of excuses for my actions, most of them based on the fact that Holmes had not warned me that Muybridge might be in danger to-night. However, my attempts to sidestep blame were in vain, and I did not even succeed in convincing myself. I had known as well as Holmes that Muybridge's life was under threat. I should not for a moment have let him out of my sight.

As I turned onto Paddington Street I paused. Directly ahead of me strode a familiar figure. The long cape alone might not have identified him as the man from the alley, but some aspect of his purposeful stride made me certain that it was the same fellow. After a second or two I saw that he held a cane, too – though I noted that he now carried it in both hands like a cudgel, rather than using it to aid his movements. He was making his way along the pavement, never looking to either side.

I moved in his wake in fits and starts, using the doorways and dark awnings of shops as cover and always keeping at least three other pedestrians between myself and my quarry. He turned onto Great Woodstock Street, then Nottingham Street and almost immediately Northumberland Street, a route which afforded me several corners of buildings to hide behind. The journey past the workhouse was more demanding of my skills, but I grew more confident when I realised that the caped man's head never turned. He proceeded left on Marylebone Road, at which point I adopted my former approach of hiding in the doorways of shops.

At the junction my quarry turned right onto Baker Street, his cloak billowing out behind him as he changed direction. Having crept closer to him than ever before, I now caught a brief glimpse of his face in profile. His most notable feature was a beak-like nose.

I froze, replaying in my mind the events of the evening. As the caped man made his way along Baker Street, I abandoned my scurrying and simply followed him openly, watching his motions and trying to add the certainty of evidence to instinct.

I increased my pace to match his long stride, then increased it still further to close the gap.

Finally, I could bear this furtive behaviour no longer. I jogged to catch up with him. I was still unable to make out the face properly, and the head turned not a jot, but all the same I became positive that it was—

"Holmes!" I cried.

"It is a pleasantly still evening, is it not?" he replied, as casually as if we had been strolling side by side for the entire journey. "Like you, I could not countenance taking a cab."

"But—" I began, but then found I had no accusation prepared.

"I have been waiting for you to join me. Perhaps you prefer to walk alone."

I gaped at him in amazement. "If you had only revealed your face, I would have approached rather than skulk around in the shadows."

"Watson, there is nothing wrong with skulking. In fact, I would recommend you practise it more often. To-night you have displayed better skills of concealment than others might, but let us say there is room for improvement."

I stopped walking, but as Holmes continued at the same quick pace I was forced to hurry to catch up with him again.

"If we are speaking of concealment and secrecy," I said indignantly, "then we ought to discuss your activities earlier this evening. I take it that my long search for Eadweard Muybridge to-night has been of no worth, given that you were his pursuer?"

Holmes nodded. "By now he will be in his bed in Kingston upon Thames."

"You followed him there?"

"No. I followed him to the telegraph office."

"Oh," I said. Then, "Should I understand why?"

We were nearing the door to our rooms. Holmes finally slowed his pace and turned to face me. "In your recollection, what occurred this evening? I refer to the part of it *after* the toy terriers, the pickpocket and your nap."

I blinked. I had hoped that my brief episode of sleep had not been noticed by anybody. "You were present the entire time?"

"Naturally."

"I wasn't napping. I was simply less interested in the Irving play, and the…" I trailed off, unable to recall the final item listed in the programme.

"Monsieur Farini."

"Yes." I knew that Holmes was goading me, but I refused to hazard a guess at the sort of entertainment Monsieur Farini had provided. Besides, I was more interested in the other parts of the evening that now came to mind. "The man who required my assistance – that was no true cardiac arrest, was it?"

Holmes gave a barking laugh. "A chemist friend of mine for whom I have performed a service in the past. He was happy to create a distraction as a means of repaying the debt, though I nevertheless paid for his ticket, and that of his son."

I rubbed at my forehead. "That was when I heard Muybridge cry out, behind the curtain. What did you do to him, Holmes?"

Holmes fished for his key as we approached the door. "Nothing that he hasn't experienced before. I simply showed him a projected picture."

CHAPTER EIGHT

Once inside our rooms, Holmes seemed determined to take as long as possible to settle. He went to his room to change into a fresh shirt and dressing-gown, went to his desk where he rearranged the untidy scattering of books into an equally untidy pile, then collected his pipe and shag tobacco, and finally spent almost a minute rearranging the cushions on his chair before sitting primly and finally looking up at me, an expectant expression on his face as if he had been simply occupying his time while waiting for me to speak.

"Have you quite finished?" I asked. I had been sitting in the chair opposite for several minutes, and I was still wearing my coat.

"Quite."

"It is a decidedly unattractive characteristic of yours, this retention of vital information at the most inopportune moments."

"Is it so very vital?"

"That's just it. I won't know until you tell me."

Holmes drew from his pipe thoughtfully, and waved his right hand. "Ask any question you like."

I grunted, but saw no way to proceed other than indulging his childishness. "What image did you project backstage that made Muybridge shout out?"

In a mild tone, Holmes replied, "That is the wrong question."

I rose from my chair in exasperation. "I refuse to play this game."

Holmes gave a curt nod.

I realised immediately that my charade was even less plausible than my friend's. I sank back into my seat, but not before removing my coat. At least I might be comfortable while I was used as a plaything.

"It would be more profitable," Holmes said, "to approach the sequence of events from the beginning."

"The Animatograph?"

"Earlier than that."

"The... toy terriers?" My cheeks flushed. I recalled laughing heartily at that act, but now that I knew that Holmes had been present after all, that undisguised enjoyment seemed a weakness. "No. You mean earlier still. Liverpool. Does this mean that you have not put Muybridge out of your mind since then, as it appeared? Since our excursion to Liverpool you have not deigned to speak to him at all. I might add that I have considered this new coldness towards him only more puzzling due to your initial friendliness when he first appeared in our rooms."

"I do not consider friendliness to be a necessary part of our working relationship. He is our client, is he not?"

"Yes, but hardly one who seems to have commanded your attention."

"There are good reasons for that."

"Which I imagine I will only discover if I ask you the right questions."

Holmes's only response was to draw again on his pipe.

"Very well," I said. I thought back to the lecture at Liverpool town hall. The defaced slide images were an obvious source of mystery, but other aspects of the evening still eluded my understanding. I chewed a fingernail as I summoned the events of that night to mind. Then, finally, I exclaimed with no small amount of triumph, "The bright light!"

Holmes was watching me with interest.

"Here is my question," I said. "What was that bright light I saw at the same moment as the defaced slide was projected?"

"It is almost the right question, and close enough that I will supply the correction. You ought to have asked, 'Who saw the bright light?'

I frowned. "But I already know that. I saw it, and in addition you had me ask everyone in the place whether they saw it. It is all recorded in my note-book."

"Possessing data is hardly the same as understanding its significance. Furthermore, you no longer possess the data."

"Well… that's because I gave my note-book to you."

"I thank you for it, and I am happy to tell you that I make profitable use of your data."

I struck the arm of my chair in annoyance. "Enough, Holmes. Tell me the answer."

Holmes removed his pipe and the corners of his mouth raised, which was as close to an expression of apology as I could expect from him.

"The key to that particular riddle is Muybridge himself. As in his own motion-study work of the last decades, the sequence of events is of as much importance as the events themselves. I will describe to you what I saw, and in what order. The expectant audience finally experienced what it had come to see, and what had in effect been advertised in the local press as the principal attraction of the evening: a defaced picture of Muybridge projected on the screen. Muybridge, too, had a pronounced response at that moment – but the important distinction is that he exhibited it *before* he turned to see the projected image that so enthralled his audience."

A frozen picture of that moment appeared unbidden in my mind's eye, and immediately I knew that what Holmes described was true. Everybody in the ballroom had been similarly alarmed, but it had not occurred to me that Muybridge was standing in front of the projected image, looking out into the ballroom, and therefore could not see it.

"Then what did he see that affected him so?" I asked weakly.

"We will come to that. There were twelve people, including you and I, standing against the back wall of the room. You complained of a bright light at the time that the ruined slide was shown, and it was an easy matter for me to determine that several of the men standing to your left made the same observation. I was aware of the light myself, but not to the degree that I might expect other, less observant, people to see it, and to my left only one man agreed that a bright light had been visible. Later, on my instruction, you made comprehensive work of interviewing the attendees that stayed for supper. While some people left immediately after the lecture, enough remained to paint the picture that we required."

"Paint the picture? That's rather fanciful language, for you."

Holmes smiled. He rose, crossed the room to his desk, and withdrew from its drawer a folded sheet of paper. Then he took from the bookcase a heavy book. When he took his seat again, he placed the folded paper on top of the book upon his lap, hiding the contents of both.

"You will recall my careful study of the orchestra balcony," he continued, "and the burns in the carpet that were produced by a directional lantern. There is no uncertainty about the source of the light. What remains is to determine what image it showed, and therefore what Muybridge saw that night. I myself made certain initial assumptions that proved to be unfounded. Would you care to hazard a guess at what the image might have been?"

I considered the question. "A horse, like the one that made Muybridge famous when he took pictures of it in motion."

"A more-than-reasonable starting point. You will recall my conversation with our client after the lecture, regarding his public spat with Governor Stanford concerning ownership of those same images. There is bad blood there, still, but Muybridge's responses to my questions did not suggest to me that the subject had been uppermost in his mind that evening. How would you describe his reaction to the image that he saw projected from the directional lantern?"

I closed my eyes, trying to conjure the scene in greater detail, but I was not equal to the task. "I had thought it was shock."

"I suspect there is a different sort of projection at work. You were shocked, therefore you expected to see shock reflected in others' expressions."

"Then how would you describe his response?"

Holmes waved a hand. "I would characterise it as intense aggravation – and of course, it was the second time that evening that Muybridge became aggravated by unexpected events."

"You are referring to the pigeon?"

"Very good. It was only upon our return to London that I understood why that might have struck him so conspicuously."

Holmes put the folded paper aside and turned the book to face me – I saw that it was the volume titled *Animal Locomotion* by Eadweard Muybridge himself – then opened it at a bookmarked page. The left side was a block of descriptive text, but on the right was a series of Muybridge's photographs depicting a young, almost-nude athlete in motion. The first twelve images showed him in profile, performing a head-spring, but in the final two of those frames his motion seemed prematurely arrested: rather than continuing the motion of his somersault, his body appeared to stiffen unnaturally, his arms were thrown up and his mouth had opened in surprise.

A series of twelve narrower images were placed beneath the first dozen, which must have been taken by other cameras at precisely the same moments but from a position directly in front of the athlete. These pictures served to explain the unusual reaction, as they contained elements invisible in the initial sequence. In the bottom-left of the first five frames was a pigeon, slightly to one side of the approaching athlete. In the sixth image, it had opened its wings, perhaps having been startled by the man's approach and unusual manner of motion. By the ninth it was in flight, and in the tenth it was finally noticed by the athlete. The eleventh and twelfth frames showed what I had already seen in the sequence above: the flailing limbs of the athlete and his stricken expression – only now, from this angle directly in front, the pigeon was visible, its wings spread and its beak angled directly towards the man's face.

"You believe that the trapped pigeon in the Liverpool ballroom made Muybridge recall this incident?" I asked.

"We have had ample evidence that our client has a long memory for bad fortune," Holmes replied.

"Then perhaps the pigeon's appearance was no accident. It may have been released by whoever is vandalising the glass slides."

Holmes bowed his head in agreement.

In a more excited tone, I said, "So the projected image from the directional lantern was the silhouette of a pigeon!"

Holmes smiled pleasantly. "I think not."

"Why not?"

"Because I know what the image was."

"And do you intend to tell me?"

"I intend to show you, using the data you collected yourself." As Holmes reached for the folded sheet of paper, he continued,

"The pigeon was certainly a deliberate interruption, but an interruption was precisely what it was intended to signify: interference, or what some might call a fly in the ointment. The symbol that was projected upon the audience sitting directly before Muybridge was one that had a more precise meaning."

I watched with unbridled anticipation as Holmes unfolded the paper. At first I did not recognise what I was looking at, but then I recognised the rectangular shape, doors and protruding balcony of the ballroom, depicted from a bird's-eye view (here I could not help but think again of the hovering pigeon). The small squares placed in two parallel grid formations were evidently the seats occupied by the audience on the evening of Muybridge's lecture. Some of these seats were neatly cross-hatched.

Holmes pointed at a location at the rear of the room. "You were standing here, and though I was standing directly beside you, no light from the lantern was projected directly at my position, which is why I perceived its brightness as far lesser than you did. Evidently our unknown lanternist used a crude method of forming a shape, more akin to a magic lantern in a phantasmagoria show than the more advanced zoopraxiscope. That is, some areas were simply masked by thick card, and the light passing through the unobstructed parts created the projected shape. Your diligent investigation revealed that the people in all of these seats I have indicated by cross-hatching registered the light as bright and shining directly in their eyes. It is a compelling demonstration that data is only as powerful as its interpreter, is it not?"

"I suppose so," I said in an offhand tone, "if I only understood what these shaded seats show us."

"I admit that the markings do not amount to a perfect representation, and some use of the imagination is required." Holmes exhaled slowly, suggesting annoyance. "Given the proximity of the seats the margin for error is considerable, plus there is the difficulty of relying upon witness accounts of a brief incident of very little consequence to those people you interviewed. And yet I still maintain that the two letters are clear to see."

"Letters?" I repeated. I peered again at the diagram, squinting to ignore the gaps in what I now saw to be two patterns side by side. Then, slowly, each of the patterns coalesced. "Ah—I see it! They do seem to form a letter I and an F, though only very approximately."

"I insist that had we the full data set, and more observant witnesses, the shapes would be undeniable."

"But as it is, we cannot be certain."

"I say that we can."

I frowned. "Do you have some corroboration? It is unlike you to rely upon such circumstantial evidence."

Somewhat reluctantly, Holmes replied, "As it happens, yes. I paid a call to George Fellows, the lanternist, armed with these new findings. When I revealed to him that I knew about the letters being projected upon the Liverpool audience, and moreover that they were an I and an F, he abandoned all secrecy and agreed that he, too, had seen those same letters that evening."

I nodded, feeling rather a fool for not having realised that Fellows was the only other person in the room who was facing towards the audience, with the same vantage point as Eadweard Muybridge.

"Then do you suspect his involvement in any other capacity?"

"No. Fellows kept the information to himself only as collateral. He feared soon becoming unemployed, and redundant given his limited training, and therefore his instinct was to retain information that might prove to have some value at a later date. His frankness when I challenged him, and his subsequent pleading, convinced me that it is no more than that."

Having absorbed this, I turned my mind to the more immediate mystery. "But tell me, what is the significance of the word 'IF' in this context? A reference to chance, perhaps, like the accident of the pigeon startling the athlete in these photographs. You spoke of a 'precise meaning'. What does it mean to Muybridge?"

"I do not know," Holmes said cheerfully.

I stared at him. "Then why do you appear so pleased with yourself? This message was sent to our client almost a week ago, and you have concerned yourself with the case not at all since then."

"You forget that it meant something to Eadweard Muybridge, and he is our client, as you so regularly remind me. Yet he failed to reveal to us what he saw, and I was foolish enough to allow him to leave the town hall in Liverpool directly after the lecture, so we have no information about his immediate actions."

"Might he not have withheld the information because he was afraid?"

"Would you describe his state of mind as fearful, when we met with him at the inn after the lecture?"

After some consideration, I replied, "No."

Holmes nodded. "Given this reluctance to share information that night, it seemed likely that he would evade a direct question about this message, 'IF', once I had determined it."

"So then instead, you contrived for Muybridge to venture backstage at the Alhambra, and then you—"

"I showed the message to him again. As I had foreseen, his behaviour before and during the programme indicated that he would attempt to approach Robert Paul's projection device at the end of the evening. It took only a little encouragement for Mr Paul to allow me to help him pack up the machine during the final part of the show. This, then, would certainly drive our client backstage in his search. Judicious deployment of Emil Grace, my chemist friend, prevented you from acting as an unwitting 'interfering pigeon', and allowed me to conduct my experiment."

I straightened my spine. "I resent being compared to a dumb beast."

Holmes's eyes flicked up to meet mine, but he did not apologise.

I returned my thoughts to the earlier part of that evening. "I take it that Muybridge responded to your trick with the cry of anguish that I heard?"

"He did cry out. Whether or not it was in anguish is for our client alone to know, at present."

"And then he left by the backstage door."

"After a brief search for the source of the projection, yes – but I had displayed it only briefly and had hidden the directional lantern well. His fumbling was in entirely the wrong part of the backstage area."

"I know the next part of the story. You followed Muybridge, your cape flapping, and proceeded along Charing Cross Road." My face flushed. "Then I lost sight of you. Where did Muybridge lead you?"

"To the telegraph office."

"Ah! And from there he sent a telegram?"

"That is an entirely reasonable inference."

"To whom? And to deliver what message?"

"I do not know."

I examined my friend's placid expression. "Holmes, I have never known you to be so content to state that you do not know what has occurred, and this evening you have said as much on two occasions. What gives you such confidence despite your lack of facts?"

"There is a difference between ignorance of a fact that one does not hope to understand, and not knowing a fact and yet *expecting* to possess that knowledge."

I laughed. "I have full confidence that in the course of time you will know everything there is to know about all things. But when, Holmes?"

"Tomorrow morning."

I nodded, though I was no more the wiser. "By what means? Please, I beg you not to reply, 'I do not know.'"

A smile spread slowly on Holmes's face. "Very well. I *do* know – but I am choosing not to tell you. Good night, Watson."

CHAPTER NINE

I woke with a start, reeling from a vivid dream in which I was upon a theatre stage, haring from side to side to evade pickpockets, terriers and jugglers. The audience comprised only one man, Sherlock Holmes, whose stony expression changed not one iota as I performed my antics, but who laughed uproariously when I stumbled and fell.

I pulled on my dressing-gown and staggered blearily from my room.

Holmes was sitting in his usual seat, smoking peaceably as he stared at the unlit fireplace.

I looked at the clock. It was far later than my usual hour of rising.

"You seem very content," I said gruffly. "Have you already made progress in your ambitions to know the unknown?"

Holmes simply gestured at the table, upon which Mrs. Hudson had laid out the breakfast things. "There is a telegram for you. I have taken the liberty of reading it already, and also replying to it."

I saw that there would be little use in reprimanding him for his impertinence. I picked up the telegram and read:

Dr Watson—

Apologies for leaving abruptly yesterday
due to indisposition.
Hope you had pleasant evening.

E. Muybridge

I brandished the card to attract Holmes's attention. "It seems perfectly polite and rather bland. Surely you can draw no conclusions from it."

"Would you describe our client's usual manner as polite?"

I frowned. "Ah, I see. You're intimating that it is not only the evasion that is suspicious, but Muybridge's broader response to your ploy. That is, he has not drawn our attention to what, from his perspective, can only be considered another threat against him."

"It would appear to support the conclusion that Muybridge is, in some sense, master of his situation. His reaction in Liverpool was one of frustration rather than fear, and his shout when he saw the letters 'IF' backstage at the Alhambra was similarly aggrieved. His sending of a telegram may indicate that he knows perfectly well who is taunting him."

"What did you write in your reply?"

Holmes waved a hand dismissively. "I simply suggested that he arrange another lecture in the future, in order to catch the culprit. He will refuse, of course, but I wanted to maintain the appearance of our straightforward approach to the case. As you have reminded me, there would otherwise be the risk of appearing negligent towards his plight."

We both turned towards the window at a ring of the bell.

"Ah, good," Holmes said without rising. "This no doubt heralds the development I have been waiting for."

I went to the window, but whoever had called had already entered the building. Presently there came a knock on the door to our rooms, and without waiting for a response Mrs Hudson entered, ushering before her a child of no more than twelve. His clothes were not quite ragged, but his over-large jacket and trousers were dusty and dishevelled. His gaze moved around the room before settling on Holmes in his chair.

"I got it, sir," he said. "Least, I saw it over his shoulder, and set it to memory, and then later another boy wrote it down for me on this slip of paper. Then I fought him 'cause he wanted to be the one to bring it you."

Holmes nodded approvingly, as if this series of actions was entirely gallant. "And here is your reward, as promised." I saw that he already held a shilling in his outstretched hand.

The boy leapt to take the coin, as if it might be snatched away at any moment, and he left in its place a grimy strip of paper. Then he said, "Oh, and the gentleman sent a telegram, too."

"We are already aware of that, as it was sent to this address," Holmes said.

I had been watching this exchange with interest. "Then the man you are referring to is no other than Eadweard Muybridge? Has this boy been watching his activities at the telegraph office?"

"Yes, the office closest to his home," Holmes replied. He examined the paper, and I moved behind his seat to see it. It read:

NO FULL ON SUN IF

"This is utter nonsense!" I exclaimed – though the appearance of the mysterious word 'IF' had not escaped my notice. I looked at the boy. "Surely you've misremembered it."

The boy folded his arms over his chest. "That's exactly

what it said. I can read, just not write so well." He turned to Holmes. "If there's nothing else you'll be needing, sir?"

Holmes held up a hand. "I trust your memory, but do you recall whether any punctuation featured in the message?"

"Sir?"

"Dots," I said.

"Oh. Yes, two of them."

"And where were they?" I asked, trying to stifle my impatience.

The boy leant over to see the message. "There and there," he said, stabbing at the paper with a filthy index finger.

Holmes produced a pencil and added the full stops so that the message now read:

NO. FULL ON SUN. IF

"Thank you," he said, and these two simple words were imbued with as much warmth as I had ever heard Holmes express in any utterance. "That will be all."

Immediately, the boy turned and made for the door. His footsteps thundered down the stairs and then the front door slammed, shaking the very walls of the building.

I moved around the chair to stand before Holmes. "Well? You seem satisfied, but this telegram still seems gibberish to me. Do you now understand the import of 'IF'?"

"It is as I anticipated. Clearly, the letters do not spell the word 'if'. They are initials – a signature."

I looked again at the transcribed message. "Then there can be no doubt that the same person who sent this telegram was the architect of the interruptions to the lecture, and the defaced slides!" My breath caught. "But the first word here is a refutation, which suggests that it is a reply to Muybridge's own message – surely that is the message he sent last night after hurrying away from the theatre… so he has known his tormentor all along!"

"It is instructive to observe your deductive process," Holmes said. I fancied I saw a gleam of pride in his eyes, though my conclusion changed abruptly when he continued, "The process is so slow that I am able to witness each new logical step in slow motion, rather like the footfalls of Muybridge's galloping horse."

"Very droll, Holmes," I said. "Now, as for the middle part of this message… Rather than watch me agonise in slow motion, perhaps you might provide the answer. What is the meaning of 'FULL ON SUN'? Some sort of astronomical reference? Is there an upcoming solar eclipse, perhaps?"

"Nothing so oblique. I am confident that 'SUN' refers simply to Sunday, three days from now. The sender, our anonymous IF, knew his meaning would be clear because the schedule was already agreed, or at least it has already been insisted upon."

I clapped my hand onto my forehead. "Then 'FULL' may refer to a payment – this is a case of extortion!"

"I agree."

"Wonderful!" I cried. "Then we must apprehend him before—" I stopped suddenly. "But Holmes, we still have no idea who the sender is, other than his initials."

"Do you really believe that I have been so inert since our trip to Liverpool? I had hoped you might think more highly of my dedication once I have accepted a case."

"You have been investigating the matter since then?"

"Since I uncovered the message delivered by the directional lantern, yes. There were a number of plausible explanations of the meaning of the letters 'IF', but a signature was always pre-eminent."

"Then who—"

"Now that we have supporting evidence that the perpetrator is known to Muybridge, I can say with some confidence that IF is Israel Fay, who was once an assistant to Muybridge during his early career as a conventional photographer. They travelled widely throughout California, and then Fay resumed working for Muybridge during his human-motion studies in Philadelphia. He now lives in Buckinghamshire. Moreover, my research suggests that he has recently invested heavily in companies developing variations on the cinematograph."

"Then the case is a matter of professional rivalry after all!" I said.

Holmes rose from his chair. "Perhaps you would like to breakfast quickly, before we set off to find out."

CHAPTER TEN

I hurried after Holmes as he exited Loudwater railway station, which comprised little more than a signalman's hut and a combined waiting room and booking hall, though 'hall' seemed altogether too grand a descriptor for such a tiny building.

"Slow *down*, Holmes," I hissed, fearing raising my voice despite the lack of other people in the miniature station. "Surely you do not intend to stride directly to the house where Israel Fay lives to accuse him of this crime? It would be utter madness."

Holmes stopped and turned. "Why is that?"

"Because of the infinitely slim nature of the corroborating evidence," I said. Then, in a more placating tone, I continued, "Your deduction about the message of the directional lantern was a true breakthrough. But simply finding a previous acquaintance of Muybridge's who shares the same initials, and who happens to live in the vicinity... surely you cannot be so easily convinced of this man's involvement."

"You are quite right. I am very nearly persuaded by the connections I have found, but not enough to demand entry to his home."

I blinked. "Or to accuse him?"

"Of course not."

I looked around the desolate railway station. "Then why have we come here?"

Holmes took my arm and led me along the road from the station. "Sometimes, Watson, I feel that we begin afresh with every new case."

"Do you mean in the sense that each case demands a return to first principles?" I said hopefully.

Holmes shook his head. "I mean only that you seem to forget everything you have been taught about the art of investigation." Ignoring my hurt expression, he continued, "Our trail appears to have led us to Israel Fay. What would you have us do at this point? Ought we to look for more convenient threads to unravel rather than pursue this one, which has necessitated a short train journey?"

"Two," I said involuntarily, thinking of the change at Paddington, which had required a brisk jog between platforms.

Holmes didn't deign to respond. "We desire to know more about Israel Fay, yet we have no information on him other than his current address. Failing to come to Buckinghamshire would therefore represent a decision not to investigate him at all."

Chastised, I dared not speak again, and we walked in silence along the road that led from the station for several minutes. Then Holmes pointed directly ahead, across the London Road. Within a dense bank of forest I saw wrought-iron gates in a tall stone wall.

"If I am correct, Fay's home is beyond that gate," Holmes said. Then he turned sharply to the left. "But this is our destination."

I turned, too, to look up at the squat building at the roadside, an inn with a hanging sign that identified it as the Dolphin (I determined this only from the writing at the foot of the sign; the garish painting of the beast in question would have been unidentifiable otherwise). Like the railway station, the building seemed more diminutive than its equivalents in the city; its single chimney appeared almost as large as the porch that contained its only entrance.

Holmes pushed open the door and went inside, and I followed.

Whoever had arranged the interior décor of the inn had made no effort to disguise the cramped dimensions of the building. Everywhere I looked there was clutter: stools scattered around even where there were no tables, horse brasses affixed to the walls in between paintings so grimy with smoke that their subjects were indecipherable, a carpet with a design that seemed intended to evoke the labyrinths of myth, ornaments upon every shelf, so numerous and dizzying that my eye could not settle on any one of them.

It was difficult to imagine the room accommodating a great number of patrons. It seemed full already, despite there being only two people present: the white-aproned landlord standing behind the bar, and another man sitting at a table in the corner.

Holmes ordered two glasses of beer and two plates of sandwiches from the landlord, and then we took our places at a table beside the single customer, a man in his sixties with ruddy cheeks and broken capillaries in his nose.

I set to eating my lunch, paying no attention to anything but my plate until Holmes stretched backwards in his seat and said in a long drawl, "Well, all I can say is that if we receive similar treatment next time around, we shan't return to Snakeley Manse, and that's a fact."

I stared at my friend, nonplussed. I had never heard him speak in such a manner, nor stretch and yawn like a housecat.

Holmes's back was to the other customer and the landlord. He fixed me with a hard look.

"Ah… yes," I replied uncertainly. Over Holmes's shoulder, I saw the old man and landlord both raise their heads to watch us.

"I mean, what do they expect us to do in the meantime?" Holmes continued. "Sit here all day, just waiting? Bloody impertinence, that's what it is."

"Well, I…" Having no idea what Holmes required of me as

part of his charade, I spoke slowly to allow him to guide me.

"P'raps this fellow'll be able to put us right." Holmes turned in his seat to face the old man. "Mister, is there anything in Loudwater to occupy people with time to spare?"

The seated man grinned, revealing stained teeth. "You've already found it. Here at the Dolphin you can go on a journey without the need to move a muscle."

Behind him, the landlord clucked his tongue. "You couldn't be less helpful, Harry." Then, addressing Holmes, he said, "Here, you got trouble up at Snakeley?" He gestured in the direction we had been walking minutes ago, in the process confirming that the building beyond the gateway was indeed Israel Fay's home. It occurred to me that there could be no reason for Holmes not divulging the unusual name 'Snakeley Manse' from me, and likewise this absurd plan to acquire information from local people about Fay and his home, other than that he evidently enjoyed keeping me in the dark.

Holmes shuffled his chair around to better see the landlord. "Well, not trouble so much as nothing at all. We were sent away without any sort of apology." He rose and leant over the counter to offer his hand to the landlord. "Frederick Sutherland, of Garridge's solicitors. That there's my partner, Webster."

"Solicitors?" the landlord said. "Is there anything the matter with Mr. Fay?" His tone suggested that it was not concern that motivated his question, but some more wily instinct.

"All I know is we've been sent away and told to come back later," Holmes replied. Then he turned away from the counter, muttering, "Come all this way, documents in hand, only to face this sort of treatment…"

I watched the landlord, whose posture became stiffer and more alert.

"Did you speak to Mr. Fay yourself?" he said. His voice had the rise and fall of a casual question, but the stiffness of his posture betrayed his true interest.

Holmes turned. Though his eyes only lifted for a brief few seconds, I knew that he was assessing the landlord carefully.

"Not as such," he said slowly. Then he seemed about to speak, but paused as though thinking better of it.

The old man sitting at the table put down his glass and cleared his throat noisily. "Then did Fay tell you so in a note?"

Holmes made a show of surprise. "As a matter of fact, yes. How did you know that, Mr…"

"Harry's my name. He's treated others the same, that's how I know."

"See, Webster?" Holmes said, turning to me. "I told you Fay was the inhospitable type. Maybe we shouldn't take it so personal after all."

"What kind of documents are you delivering?" the landlord asked, peering over the counter at our table. I realised neither Holmes nor I carried a bag of any description.

Holmes patted the breast of his jacket. "'Fraid we'd never divulge that, sir. Though I did think Mr. Fay'd be more eager to see them for himself." He went to the grimy window and stared out at the desolate road. "What I can't understand is even if he was busy, why couldn't we wait there in the house? It's a nice big building. We've no objection to waiting in the kitchens, have we, Webster? You'll often get the sympathy of the cook, that way, and the reward of a good feed. Not that this sandwich isn't good, mind you."

Harry gave a rattling laugh. "It's more than you'll get at Snakeley. There's no cook there."

Holmes frowned. "In a building like that?"

"Fay gets his meals delivered. All three meals for the day dropped off at the back door first thing each morning."

"And you're going to tell me he only leaves a note," Holmes said wryly.

Harry nodded.

"The note often dictates errands, too," the landlord added. "Sally, who used to be a maid at Snakeley, she brings the food, and gets her son to run the errands. There's fair payment, but what kind of arrangement is that?"

"Couldn't the housekeeper do it herself?"

"You're not getting the picture here," Harry said. "There's no housekeeper, no cook, no secretary, no coachman, no stable hand. Fallen on hard times, has old Israel Fay – the fact he keeps paying Sally is a miracle in itself. Nobody's seen Fay for more'n a fortnight, and the curtains of Snakeley Manse are always closed. Even in the weeks before that, he was seen less and less in the village, and never here in the Dolphin." He looked around the tiny room, his eyes wide and the corners of his mouth trembling, as if the idea of not frequenting these premises seemed an unacceptable failing of character.

"Fallen on hard times…" Holmes repeated in a wondering tone. It seemed to me that he conveyed a number of things in this utterance, allowing the landlord and Harry to conjure any manner of paperwork that might be in Holmes's jacket pocket. In a sharper tone, Holmes said, "Then the household staff were sent away only recently? That's a shame, as I would have liked to talk with one of them in the absence of their employer."

Harry and the landlord exchanged looks.

"You'd best speak to Joan," the landlord said. "She's working now – she got snapped up by an employer who values her better, though not in monetary terms, if you take my meaning. But no doubt she'll be in here after seven." He paused, thinking. "Tell you what, I'll send word to make sure of it."

* * *

"What I don't understand," I said as we strolled along the path that led through the centre of Fennell's Wood, "is how you knew that Fay was a recluse. That seems a remarkable deduction."

"I didn't know anything of the sort," Holmes replied.

"But you told that old drunk, Harry, that we were sent away with a note."

Holmes shook his head. "Not so. I allowed him to provide that information himself."

I thought back to the conversation, and realised that Holmes was correct. Simply pausing at the correct moment had allowed Harry to supply the key fact himself, without realising that he was doing so.

"Even so," I said, "you were confident that there was something unusual about Fay's conduct, and that your mention of Snakeley Manse would produce a response."

Holmes turned to look at me with an air of quiet amusement.

I groaned. "I know what you are about to say. Your contention is that any large home, situated in a small village, will elicit bad feeling from other residents. In short, you knew nothing."

"There is no shame in knowing nothing," Holmes said, "if one has the wherewithal to ask the correct questions – or in this case, the wherewithal to remain silent to allow others to answer *unasked* questions."

"That's all very well, Holmes, but you must accept that you have had considerable luck on this occasion."

Holmes hesitated, then said, "I will concede that much. I had hoped for some morsel of rumour that might prove profitable. As you say, any mismatch of fortunes in a town will always inspire some degree of contention among those members of the population who have less. But if Israel Fay has sent away his entire household staff, we are confronted with a more interesting mystery than we had anticipated."

"Speaking personally, I anticipated nothing," I said curtly, "because I was told nothing to begin with."

Holmes ignored my complaint. "Well, now. We have three and a half hours to while away until our rendezvous with Fay's former housekeeper. I intend to spend the time profitably."

I gazed along the woodland trail. "Will this path take us to High Wycombe?"

Holmes nodded. "Is that where you will go?"

"Holmes, you're speaking in riddles. I thought we were both going there, given that is where this path leads."

"As far as I am concerned, this path has led us *here*." Holmes indicated the woodland that was all around us.

I stared in incomprehension at the densely packed trees, clumps of bushes and uneven, leaf-strewn ground that appeared boggy in places.

"You intend to spend the next three and a half hours in this woodland?" I asked incredulously.

By way of answer, Holmes reached down to the rough track and picked up a sycamore seed. "Look at the way the wing of this seed has been snapped. It has much to tell us about the foot that pressed upon it, its shoe and its owner's weight, and many more things besides. These are skills that must be honed, Watson. There is no period of time in which one is compelled to be idle, if one is prepared to learn."

I retrieved my handkerchief and mopped my forehead. After having spent only five minutes in Fennell's Wood I fancied I was filthy already.

I made my way with careful steps from the path, to a point where the ground was raised above the damper soil, and I lowered myself to lean against the trunk of an oak.

"All the same, Holmes," I said wearily, "I find that I am prepared to be idle."

CHAPTER ELEVEN

When we returned to the inn shortly after seven o'clock, it was immediately evident which of the half a dozen patrons was Fay's former housekeeper. As we entered, she looked first at us and then at the landlord, who nodded affirmation. A couple of the other customers watched us, too, though it was impossible to know whether that was because news of our errand had spread, or simply due to the novelty of new faces in Loudwater.

"I wonder if you're the former housekeeper of Snakeley Manse," Holmes said, approaching the woman.

"Mrs. Joan Kemplah, at your service," she replied, rising from her seat to allow Holmes to take her hand.

She was a tall woman, but that was not her most imposing characteristic. Her lips were pursed and her eyelids half-closed as she regarded Holmes and I. Combined with the backward tilt of her head, these aspects produced as haughty an impression as ever I had seen. Her fair hair was tied into a bun which was as perfectly circular as the brim of a bowler hat, and it was precisely the same pale shade as the lace of her long, formless gown.

"Indeed I am," she said, indicating that we should take seats at her table.

When we sat, the wash of noise from the other patrons diminished a little, but it was still loud enough that I was forced to lean forward in my seat to have any hope of hearing what she had to say.

"Though I don't mind saying, Mr. Sutherland," Mrs. Kemplah continued, addressing Holmes, "that there are times I wish that I'd never been engaged in that position."

Holmes raised his eyebrows. "We've been told a bit about Mr. Fay's reclusive tendencies. He's been a poor employer in some other respect, has he?"

She emitted a sharp noise that I supposed might have been intended as a display of laughter. "Nothing wrong with reclusive, to a degree. Staying in one place can make the business of household staff a little easier, or at least more predictable. Now, my current employer, he's off and about at all hours of the day, and whether he'll return for dinner or even supper is anybody's guess. And do you think there's ever a word of apology? Ha! I could tell you about this one time, when—"

"How about I buy you another drink?" Holmes said pleasantly. Without waiting for an answer, he gestured to the landlord, making a circular motion with his index finger to indicate the three of us sitting at the table. It was clear that the landlord had been watching us; he lurched up from his position leaning on the counter, nodding rapidly, and set to work pulling pints of beer.

Mrs. Kemplah swallowed the contents of her previous glass, and held out her hand at precisely the right moment to receive a new one from the landlord.

"As I understand it," Holmes said, "Israel Fay has been leaving his house less and less during recent weeks."

Mrs. Kemplah gulped half of the contents of her glass, and nodded. "The last two months at least. Not that he was a gadabout before that time, but he'd be seen around the village, and circumstances took him to London every so often."

"And what do you put this new behaviour down to?" Holmes said, still adopting the informal voice of Frederick Sutherland.

"Two things: his pictures and his book."

Holmes nodded and sipped his drink.

Though I had remained silent up to this point, for fear of undermining Holmes's facade, now I couldn't help but ask, "Forgive me, but those hardly sound like occupations that might take up the majority of a man's time. Were there many pictures for him to sort through, and was it a very long book?"

Mrs. Kemplah looked sharply at me as if noticing me for the first time.

"He was not looking at the pictures, nor was he reading the book," she said, her lips curling in disdain.

I stared at her in confusion, unequal to the task of grappling with this riddle.

To my relief, Holmes said, "I take it that Mr. Fay is an enthusiastic photographer, and that he's been engaged in writing a book."

"Clearly, that's what I meant," Mrs. Kemplah replied stiffly.

"But you said yourself that he has not been leaving the house," I said, but when Mrs. Kemplah swung around to face me again, I immediately wished I had not ventured to speak. I added weakly, "Then what have been his photographic subjects?"

"He seems little interested in *subjects*."

I turned to Holmes, pleading silently for him to interject.

"Then I suppose he's more interested in cameras and mechanical equipment," Holmes said.

"Quite so."

"Then does he have a great deal of that sort of thing?"

"The house has always been crammed with such devices – mementos of Mr. Fay's work. But as long as I've known him, at least until a couple of months ago, all those machines were just that – mementos. An awful lot of clutter, in my opinion, and the very devil to keep free of dust, but he would have them on display. But my word! Once his interests were revived fully, I'd have happily gone back to those early days. The smell of those chemicals he'd have delivered to the house these last months – oh! Like brimstone, it was. I wouldn't handle it myself, even packaged and handed over by the delivery boy. If people knew the horrid stuff it took to produce these moving pictures, they'd think again."

I exchanged a glance with Holmes, then said, "So Mr. Fay has been occupying his time in producing *moving* pictures, rather than conventional photographs?"

"My dear man," Mrs. Kemplah replied haughtily, "if you're not prepared to listen to what I say, then what is the use of me speaking to you at all?"

I bowed my head in apology.

"I'll own that I don't know much about this new industry," Holmes said. "I've heard of moving pictures, and I know they're ever so popular, but I've yet to see them for myself. You say that Mr. Fay's background is in photography, but given that this cinematograph thing is so very new, was his first career in normal pictures? I mean ones that don't move... What's the word? Static."

I could not help staring at my friend. Even though I understood he was playing a part, it was nevertheless remarkable to see him appear to struggle to convey his meaning.

"Of course. Over in America." Mrs. Kemplah gestured over her shoulder, as if directly behind her lay the continent she described. "But now he's mad for this new business – for the most part as an investor, given his age. They say that these days he makes his investments by means of a courier that drops in at Snakeley Manse at least once a week – though the lad's only ever allowed to go as far as the porch. The instructions are conveyed by written note and the payment's hidden under the flowerpot, though don't go telling anybody that. I tell you, I could make a fair penny if I just took that money each day" – she looked around the bar-room furtively – "and there are plenty round here who wouldn't hesitate to do just that, if they knew. It's as well that I'm diligent about keeping secrets."

I opened my mouth to speak, but Holmes silenced me with a look.

"I'm confused about one thing, though," he said. "We've been led to understand that Mr. Fay has financial difficulties."

"He has enough money to fritter, if not to pay his staff." Then Mrs. Kemplah scrutinised Holmes carefully. "What's your business in Loudwater, Mr. Sutherland?"

"I suppose you might say it concerns Mr. Fay's fortunes, but certainly not related to investments." Slowly, Holmes reached into his jacket, and pulled out an envelope far enough that its corner was visible. Then he seemed to think better of revealing it fully, and closed his jacket again, looking around him as he buttoned it.

Mrs. Kemplah nodded solicitously. "Would you say he's in any mood to make amends for... I don't know... any bad decisions in his past?"

"I could not possibly speculate."

She took a long breath and drank the rest of the contents of her glass. "Loudwater's home to several with claims to an apology of some sort. I mean, to dismiss us all just like that... Do you know how difficult it is to make ends meet after being sent away from a position without warning? And to find new employment in a village this size, without time to prepare the way?"

"What were the circumstances around this dismissal, if you don't mind my asking?" Holmes said mildly.

"Your guess is as good as mine!" she replied. "We were all gathered together and told the news by his secretary first thing one Saturday morning – the seventh of this month – and then we were on our merry way that very day."

"His secretary – who's that?"

"Richard Bradwell."

"Does he live in the village?"

"Heavens, no. And he wasn't minded to stay in Loudwater after his own dismissal. He was in a fury, and was preparing to leave for the city immediately. It'd always been clear he was the superstitious type, always going on about portents and signs and suchlike, and if there's a portent clearer than being fired for no good reason and told to pack your bags, I don't know what it is. That morning he went on and on about having been summoned to Loudwater for this position of secretary, which hardly had prospects as it was, and then only being employed for three months. Though he's fairly young, he's always struck me as ambitious, wanting to see as much of the world as possible, and it was clear he felt he'd wasted valuable time indulging Mr. Fay's whims."

I said, "Then it seems that the engagement of this secretary, Bradwell, coincided with Mr. Fay's tendency to stay within his house."

I was rewarded with another scowl. "Well, that's hardly a surprise, is it? Bradwell was engaged specifically to help Mr. Fay write his memoirs, which is what's been occupying him, along with his investments. They'd spend long nights in the study, working and working, and then Mr. Fay would only rise late in the morning each day. Why men can't keep to sensible hours, I don't know, but they will insist that all meaningful thoughts occur to them only after dusk. Not the night before our dismissal, though."

"They didn't spend the evening in each other's company?" Holmes asked.

"They did indeed – I was referring to the idea of 'meaningful thoughts', as they can't have been discussing the memoirs. In a way, it was my good fortune that I heard them arguing on that night, because when Bradwell gathered the staff the next morning, I was prepared for bad news. Judging by his tone of voice, I'd say he'd been protesting Mr. Fay's decision in the strongest terms. But it was all for nothing, as it turned out."

Mrs. Kemplah sighed and raised her glass, then her head tilted to one side as she regarded its emptiness.

"I'll buy you another drink," Holmes said, "and then p'raps you'll tell us more about Mr. Fay's relationship with Mr. Muybridge."

I didn't dare look at Holmes, despite being startled at this new gamble.

However, Mrs. Kemplah only nodded thoughtfully. "Perhaps that was the beginning of it all," she said, still examining her empty glass. Then she looked up. "*Did* I mention Mr. Muybridge?"

"In passing. And of course we already know about their friendship." Holmes patted the breast of his jacket again.

Mrs. Kemplah surveyed Holmes over the tip of her nose. For several seconds she remained in this posture, then she exhaled and said, "Right. And it's certainly possible that Mr. Fay's deterioration – as you might call his adoption of the life of a hermit – was linked to the deterioration of that very friendship."

To Holmes's credit, he didn't respond in any way that suggested that this information was any more interesting than anything else we had been told.

"I had wondered if that might have been what inspired Israel Fay to contact our offices in the first place," he said, and once again I felt to urge to applaud his gall. "Did Mr. Muybridge ever visit Snakeley Manse himself?"

Mrs. Kemplah shook her head. "But they communicated often, and they met in the city. That all stopped a while ago – and it isn't likely to strike up again, in my estimation, ever since this business with the burned picture."

I saw Holmes's eyes gleam, but otherwise his manner was as nonchalant as it had been throughout the conversation.

"The burned picture?" he repeated casually.

Abruptly, Mrs. Kemplah rose from her seat. As she approached the counter, she said, "Benjamin? Do fetch the newspaper article you saved the other week. Oh, and Mr Sutherland would like me to have another drink."

The landlord, Benjamin, bowed his head and disappeared into a back room, and when he reappeared he was holding a cutting from a newspaper. Mrs. Kemplah took it, then waited until he had poured out another drink before returning to her seat.

She patted the surface of the table to determine that it was dry, then produced the newspaper cutting and smoothed it out so that both Holmes and I could see it.

It read:

Tragic Death In Manor Fire

A fire in the east wing of Chaloner House in Bishop's Stortford late last night had devastating results that went beyond the decimation of parts of this historic property, culminating as it did in the death of a guest of the Griffin family, Mr. Martin Chrisafis. Though no destruction of property can match the tragedy of the loss of life, local people who attended the scene and assisted in the eventual dousing of the fire discovered another loss: the partial burning of a valuable framed albumen silver print (pictured) taken by the celebrated photographer of animals in motion, Professor Eadweard Muybridge.

At the foot of the column of text was a sketched facsimile of the photograph in question, though it was so small that at first I could not make out what it depicted. Eventually I determined that the twin lumps at the top and bottom of the picture were actually tall mountains, the upside-down one being reflected in a still lake along with inverted pine trees.

"The link to Mr. Muybridge is clear," I said, "but I fail to see the connection to your former master."

Mrs. Kemplah emitted another short, sharp laugh. "If Mr. Fay was to be believed, he took that picture himself. There were several in the group that trekked around Yosemite, and while Muybridge might have been the so-called artist who produced the pictures, that didn't mean he operated the camera on each and every occasion."

"Is this a matter of contested authorship, then?" I asked.

"Heavens, no. Mr. Fay was pragmatic on that score. He knew his place and was proud of his time as Muybridge's assistant, both in California and in Philadelphia. Some men are destined to be remembered as pioneers, and others are content to work in anonymity. As a housekeeper, I've more sympathy with the latter. People like me, we work diligently for no thanks, but without us everything is bound to fall apart."

Holmes gestured at the newspaper column. "It strikes me that for this article to have caught your attention, and the attention of our landlord over there, the picture itself must have some particular significance."

Mrs. Kemplah's eyebrows raised. "Very good, Mr. Sutherland. I suppose it stands to reason that a solicitor is adept at burrowing for facts, but perhaps you ought to consider an alternative career as a police detective." She followed her statement with another barking laugh.

Unaffected by the irony of her statement, Holmes smiled and allowed her to continue.

"Yes," she said when she had finally composed herself. "This picture's titled 'Mirror Lake, Valley of the Yosemite' and was taken back in 1872, if memory serves. I know this because Mr. Fay examined it often, and would speak of its origins to anybody who cared to listen."

"You mean to say it hung in Snakeley Manse?" Holmes asked.

"For many years, until he presented it to Elias Griffin last year."

Holmes pressed the tips of his fingers together. "The Elias Griffin who owns Chaloner House in Bishop's Stortford."

"The very same."

After a moment's thought, I blurted out, "But why would Fay give away the picture if he was so proud of it?" Then, as both of my companions turned to look at me, I added, "Ah. I suppose that might be further evidence of financial trouble, might it not?"

"That's certainly the conclusion I reached," Mrs. Kemplah said, "but I've no further information on that score. I did love looking at that picture, mind you. Now I have a copy of this newspaper sketch, though it's hardly the same, is it?"

Holmes nodded sympathetically, then patted the arms of his chair twice to indicate that the conversation was reaching a close.

"Thank you for speaking with us," he said. "Men in our position do well to be forewarned about all aspects of a client's circumstances, and in my experience you rarely get the truth from the horse's mouth. But now we ought to go and visit the horse, so to speak."

As he rose to stand, Mrs. Kemplah said, "If he'll permit you to enter the stables, that is."

Now it was Holmes's turn to laugh – a full-throated chuckle the likes of which I have never heard pass his lips before or since. Mrs. Kemplah responded with delight at the results of her wit.

I made to leave, but Holmes paused. "Mrs. Kemplah, I've no desire to interrupt Mr. Fay at the wrong moment, for fear of being sent away again. In your experience, what time of day is he likely to be using his dark-room and therefore wish to be left in peace?"

Mrs. Kemplah stared up at him. "Dark-room? I made it my business to keep the house aired and light. Mr. Fay works in his study, but that's the brightest room in the house, with windows on three sides, and even when the curtains are drawn they let in daylight."

Holmes bowed his head. "Then I'll assume we're safe to call on him. Thank you again for your assistance."

I was about to add my own thanks, but in a single motion Holmes pressed a banknote onto the counter before the landlord, and then swept me in front of him and out of the inn.

CHAPTER TWELVE

"Well, what are we to do now?" I asked when we were safely outside.

Holmes set off in the direction of Snakeley Manse. "To keep our appointment, of course."

I hurried after him. "But Holmes – we have no true appointment... do we? I confess that this lengthy charade has my head in a spin. But you are not Frederick Sutherland of Garridge's, and I am not... whoever you said I was; I've already forgotten. More to the point, Israel Fay still knows nothing about us, as far as I can tell, and will react no more kindly to our appearance at his doorstep than if we had demanded entry to his house when we first arrived in Loudwater."

"I was speaking figuratively," Holmes said. "We have been furnished with a great deal of information about our friend Israel Fay, and now I am determined to gather the last scraps before we return to London."

"Then you see a certain link between the story about the burned picture and the threats against Muybridge? And that it supports your assumption that Israel Fay is the culprit?"

"I see only that each of these cases is interesting, and that both deserve my attention. As yet, the only information to be had about Israel Fay is from this location."

"Unless we might track down the secretary," I said.

"The housekeeper's pronouncement was clear: he is out of our reach, and if anybody were to know of his current location, it would be his former employer – and I maintain we cannot approach Snakeley Manse for fear of revealing our hand."

I nodded, then immediately shook my head to contradict my agreement. "But Holmes, only Eadweard Muybridge is your client. This sudden preoccupation with Loudwater, and unfair dismissals, disgruntled housekeepers and superstitious secretaries… I am sure it is all very interesting to those involved, but I maintain it need not concern us, if all that we desire to know is whether Israel Fay did or did not deface Muybridge's glass slides."

Holmes only glared at me, and it was impossible to know whether it conveyed scorn or guilty acknowledgement that he had strayed from the task at hand. It has long been my suspicion that Holmes's consulting-detective business is merely a means of attracting people bearing puzzles to Baker Street, and that if other, more substantial mysteries were to present themselves by more natural processes, he would have no qualms in shutting our door to those in need of his services.

We passed the gateposts upon which were engraved the words 'Snakeley Manse' and then moved along a sloped driveway with low-hanging trees bowing over us at either side. I noticed that Holmes's pace had slowed, and I matched it.

I saw through the undergrowth a wide, grey stone building with pronounced curves to its walls, giving it the appearance of a very squat lighthouse. Above a central portico was a gable with a large, circular window which put in my mind an image of the eye of the mythical Cyclopes. The many chimneypots atop the conical roof were evidence of a large household, but the walls were in poor repair, with crumbled pointing and ivy that clung to the lower parts in sporadic patches. As Harry at the Dolphin had suggested, the curtains at each window were pulled shut, despite dusk having only just begun to arrive.

"It is a most peculiar building, more like a castle than a home," I said, "and though its name is similarly strange, it hardly suits the place."

"What part of the name strikes you as odd?" Holmes asked.

"In truth, both parts. I assume Snakeley must be a family name, whereas 'Manse'... is that not a name usually applied to some sort of clergy house?"

"Yes, specific to Presbyterian, Methodist and Baptist traditions. Perhaps what you find unusual about the term is its usage as a *part* of a name. Ordinarily, one might encounter a building simply titled 'The Manse', or if it is no longer in use by the church, 'The Old Manse'. Any other appellation is most irregular."

"I'd go further and suggest that the appearance of the house is hardly Presbyterian either. It's far from the austere building I might have expected."

"Quite so. It is most curious."

I made to continue along the driveway, but Holmes held my arm. I noticed he was ducking low, and I copied his stance.

"This will be far enough," he said. "Any further, and we may attract unwanted attention. If we were to leave this driveway, there would be no cover until we reached the portico."

"What do you hope to see from this distance, then?"

"Signs of life."

I peered through the foliage, which seemed to be growing darker by the moment. I saw strips of light at the edges and join of the curtains of the left-hand window on the first floor.

Holmes pointed at the same room. "That must be Fay's study. Recall the housekeeper's comment that it is the brightest room in the house, and spans its depth."

"Yes, but—" I began. Then my eyes went to the eastern part of the house, and I saw that, despite a wide area of loose stones that would make any covert approach impossible, the trees surrounding that part of the building were so leafy at their tops that they shrouded the first-floor rooms and scraped against the roof. Similarly, even from our distant position it was clear that the treeline came close to the back of the building, and within the woodland was a tall wall which enclosed the house, presumably wrapping all the way around to encompass the woodland in which we hid, and joining with the wall that contained the front gate. As Holmes had intimated, the illuminated room was the only one on the first floor that had a window that would be without obstacle during daylight hours.

"Ah. Yes, I believe you are correct, Holmes."

We watched in silence for several minutes, and the leaves around us grew darker still.

"I have seen nothing, Holmes. Have your keener eyes observed what I cannot?"

Holmes shook his head.

"Then what do you conclude? Might it be that Fay is not in the house after all? I mean to say, we have only the word of people in the village that anybody is in there, and only the evidence that the deliveries are accepted, and perhaps that is not directly after they have been left at the door. The notes and payments might be put in place at any time."

"Very good," Holmes said approvingly. "You are right that illuminated lamps are not enough to indicate occupation. It is more difficult to prove a negative than a positive, of course, so all we can do is to wait for confirmation that he is inside the building."

"Confirmation which, at this time of the evening, would likely take the form of the light at that window being doused."

"At *either* of the windows where light appears."

He pointed at the central part of the house, and I saw that the large, circular window above the portico was indeed dimly lit. My impression was that this light came from deeper within the house, or perhaps even from the open door of the study, and that this circular portal was merely a corridor or landing window, grand and eye-like though it appeared.

I looked around me. The trees were now dark wraiths in the gloom, and the slivers of sky that I could see were violet.

"Then you can give me no idea how long we might be compelled to wait?" I asked.

"No, I cannot," Holmes replied calmly.

Abruptly, his head jerked. "Hide!" he hissed.

The sharpness of his tone prevented me from making any argument. I scrambled blindly into the undergrowth at the left side of the driveway, my calves striking protruding logs and thin branches scratching at my face. My impression of Holmes's movements was that they were like those of a rabbit: he bounded over obstacles and then came to a halt in a crouching position.

Seconds later, a two-horse Clarence made its way up the narrow lane. The driver was forced to duck his head to clear the low-hanging branches, and twigs were torn free by the roof of the vehicle and sent skittering in its wake.

The driver made a wide half-circle in the area before the house, producing an amount of noise that made me appreciate Holmes's earlier warning, and eased the horses to a halt. Then he hopped down and opened the door of the carriage – on the side which was obscured from Holmes and I.

As I waited in anticipation of seeing the occupant, I cursed our new position within the woodland, which made visibility of the house even poorer. Presently, the driver returned to his raised seat, and then his passenger appeared, his back to us, and approached the door of the house.

I heard Holmes exhale softly beside me.

"Is that Fay?" I whispered, but Holmes gave no reply.

To my surprise, the man did not unlock and enter the building. Instead, he pressed the doorbell and then waited. Despite the gloom, I saw the gloved fingers of his right hand stretch and curl in a repeated action. He pressed the bell again.

My gaze shifted to the illuminated windows. I saw no sign of motion from within.

The visitor raised his arm and struck the door three times. Then he called out, "Fay! Fay! Let me in, you scoundrel!"

With a start, I realised that I recognised the voice.

"Holmes," I said, forgetting to restrain my voice to a whisper, "surely that is—"

The next moment, my pronouncement became redundant. The man turned away from the door, and his face was revealed in full. There could be no mistaking that head of wild white hair, the pointed beard with its end so low as to be tucked into his overcoat.

All the same, I breathed the name. "Muybridge."

Muybridge stalked to the left of the building, his head thrown back as he looked up at the same curtained first-floor window that we had been watching. Next, he pressed himself up against the ground-floor window beside the entrance, shielding his eyes as if to see through any gap that might present itself, but he soon withdrew. Then he went fully around the west wing of the building, disappearing from view, and once again I heard his muffled shout, "Fay! Let me in this moment!" He reappeared a minute later, shaking his head in dismay.

Beside me, Holmes murmured, "We owe him a debt of gratitude. Now we need not risk being seen in order to check the first-floor windows at the rear of the house."

"If you ask me," I hissed, "this entire situation is absurd. Eadweard Muybridge is our own client, yet we are hiding in the bushes rather than speak to him. I might add, also, that we are hiding in bushes rather than approach a house which is evidently empty."

If Holmes paid any attention to my words, he gave no impression of it. He held up a hand, which now appeared merely a blotch in the murky twilight, as a command for silence.

We watched Muybridge approach the carriage, then heard the click of its door. Responding to an inaudible command, the driver flicked his reins and the horses completed a turn and then eased along the overgrown driveway once again. Only once the sound of hooves came from the London Road did Holmes's posture loosen.

"I'm glad that's over and done," I said, stretching to ease my stiff joints. "Though I suppose I ought to offer my apologies. There can be no denying that Muybridge's case is related to Israel Fay. He defaced the zoopraxiscope slides, then – for whatever foolhardy reason – he revealed his authorship to Muybridge, who is quite rightly incensed and refuses to pay the ransom demand. Even if they were once friends, Fay's housekeeper was clear that Muybridge had never visited Snakeley Manse before, which might have raised our suspicions even if Muybridge had not been so clearly incensed."

"On the contrary," Holmes replied.

I sat up sharply. "Then you have changed your opinion about the link?"

"Of course not, Watson. I meant only that to-night's adventure is not 'over and done', and that we are likely to be compelled to wait here a little longer yet."

"For what earthly reason?"

"The very same that brought us here. To see Israel Fay."

I made a very deliberate sound of exasperation. "More riddles! Shall I make my bed here, then?"

"If you wish, Watson."

I did not do so, but instead spent my time alternating between grumbling and rubbing my arms for warmth – though both were pantomimes with the primary ambition of pricking Holmes's conscience. Yet my friend's conscience is a complex thing, and at times it seems to be entirely absent. He waited placidly, his gaze never straying from the moonlit spectre of Snakeley Manse.

I checked my watch. It was now just after ten o'clock.

"Do you realise that the last train was half an hour ago?" I said in alarm, the prospect of sleeping in the undergrowth seeming ever more likely. "Don't you think that—"

"Hush!" Holmes replied.

I drew myself to my full height. "Holmes, I have had as much as I can bear – and now you are silencing me!"

My words died away as I registered in Holmes's silhouetted profile a greater intent than before. I looked towards the house, and with a start I saw that the light coming from the study window was dimmer than before – a lamp must have been extinguished.

I turned my attention to the central, circular window. There was still a light there, though surely only just bright enough to illuminate the passage from the west to east wing. It occurred to me that if Fay's study spanned the depth of the house, then his bedroom must be within the east wing.

This conclusion was very soon confirmed. At the circular window I saw a figure making his way from left to right, his entire body from head to foot visible in the circular frame for the briefest of moments, before he disappeared into the east wing. I waited expectantly, but no light came from the first-floor window that was visible from our location.

"His bedroom must be the one at the rear of the house," I said. "That is a shame."

"Why is that?" Holmes asked casually.

"Well… were we not hoping to see more than a fleeting glimpse of him?"

Without reply, Holmes rose and then turned to help me to my feet.

"Are we leaving at last?" I asked.

"Of course."

"And you are content with our evening's work?"

"More than content."

"And… are you confident of finding us beds for the night?"

Holmes laughed and turned to stroll along the driveway in the direction of the road. Over his shoulder, he said, "That is a matter for the landlord of the Dolphin."

CHAPTER THIRTEEN

I spent a most uncomfortable night at the Dolphin inn, upon a bed with creaking wooden slats which seemed throughout the night to moan the word 'rickety, rickety'. Upon our return to Baker Street, Holmes went to his desk and set to examining his journals and his library of newspaper cuttings. I watched on for a while, but each time I made a comment he waved me away impatiently, and eventually I retired to my armchair with a book. All afternoon and evening Holmes was occupied in a similar manner, and when I emerged from my room the next morning he appeared not to have moved from his position. Rather than spend my time waiting and being continually dismissed, I ventured to my club, where I might find one or two people who were pleased to see me.

It was with a mixture of surprise and foreboding that, after my early luncheon, I opened *The Times* and discovered another picture of Eadweard Muybridge. Rather, I did not know at first that it was he, but the picture was immediately arresting, and then I read the accompanying article and then understood what had happened. At first glance, in truth, it was not evident that there was any figure at all in the picture, dominated as it was by a mishmash of lush foliage, and its background filled with not sky but a sheer rock face. In the foreground was a jetty that protruded slightly onto a placid river – and on the jetty, stick in hand, stood a man. He wore a rumpled suit and, as far as I could tell, a scarf, but anything above that was impossible to discern. His head was entirely missing, obscured by a swirl of white that appeared rather like foam in a plughole, and which made a stark contrast with the dark trees.

And yet, this mutilation was not what had initially attracted my notice. Above the headless figure were scrawled in white the words 'NO RETURN' in large uppercase letters.

The article read:

Zoopraxographer Fears for His Life – Where is Sherlock Holmes?

Famed man of the sciences and arts, Professor Eadweard Muybridge, has further cause to fear for his life to-day, upon the delivery of an unusual package to the offices of this very newspaper. As readers will recall, Professor Muybridge has recently been threatened by various means, the most publicised of which are attacks in the street by horses and threats made upon slides projected via his celebrated 'Zoopraxiscope' device.

The first of the contents of this mysterious package was a photographic print, which is produced in sketch form above. Once again, the man portrayed is Professor. Eadweard Muybridge himself, and once again, his face has been crudely obliterated – on this occasion by overpainting rather than scratching at the image. At first consideration, the addition of the message 'NO RETURN' may puzzle readers, but working together, the art connoisseur and the classicist may solve the riddle. The portrait is one-half of a pair of stereoscopic images and dates from 1868, taken in the Yosemite Valley. Most significantly, the portrait is titled 'Charon at the Ferry' – a reference to the ferryman of mythology who transported the newly deceased across the river Styx to the world of the dead. If Muybridge is indeed intended to represent Charon, then the inscribed message 'NO RETURN' must surely indicate that the ferry must remain in Hades, and its unfortunate ferryman likewise. If there were any confusion over this message, the second item contained in the delivered package makes the matter clearer still: a single penny coin, evidently intended as substitute of the Athenian obol or danake with which passengers might pay the ferryman. That is, the ferryman has paid his own fare, and now he must retire to Hell.

Professor Muybridge was not available for comment at the time of going to press, but no doubt we will know his response to this dire new threat in the coming days. This gruesome development and the solution of this new puzzle begs another question: where is the famous Sherlock Holmes, who has been engaged to expose whoever is delivering these threats? Has this riddle truly left the great detective of Baker Street dumbfounded?

That afternoon, I climbed the stairs of 221B Baker Street and opened the door of our rooms quietly, fearing disturbing Holmes if he was still occupied with his research – and also, I confess, because I did not relish informing him about the new threat against Muybridge and the insinuations about his own diminished abilities. However, to my surprise Holmes was standing directly before me, empty Gladstone bag in hand.

He handed the bag to me, clapped me on the shoulder and said, "A cab will arrive presently."

I groaned. "Why is it, Holmes, that I am perennially packing my belongings in a hurry?"

Holmes looked askance at me. Perhaps he imagined that I really was asking him to solve this minor mystery, to add to all of the others he had at hand. His eyes flicked to the clock on the mantelpiece.

"I understand your meaning well," I said in a resigned tone. "Perhaps as I gather my things you might tell me where we are going, and for how long."

Holmes followed me to my room. "Overnight, and to Bishop's Stortford, naturally."

"Then we are to visit Elias Griffin, the owner of the house that burned?"

"The very same."

"Holmes, do you not have any impression at all that this case is straying ever further away from its origins? We were engaged to identify who has been threatening Eadweard Muybridge by defacing his glass slides. Then we followed a lead to Loudwater, which culminated in as excruciating a night's sleep as any I endured in Afghanistan. Now we are to leave for Hertfordshire because of a chance mention in a newspaper article. I fear that we may be neglecting our client's situation, which may be dire, even if he is aware of the culprit of the threats against him. Furthermore, even if *you* do not suppose that Muybridge is in immediate danger, the public at large have been led to assume so, and consequently—"

"Then you have been reading *The Times* at your club?"

I exhaled loudly. "I have. I am glad to know that you have read it too, as I did not know how to broach the matter."

"Clumsily, as is your wont," Holmes replied, with no suggestion of admonishment.

I hesitated, but then decided that taking offence would do

me no earthly good. "Do you agree with the assessment of the meaning of the image sent to the newspaper offices?"

"Of course. Charon is a particularly interesting figure in myth – the most pre-eminent psychopomp, one might say. I see from your rapid blinking that you are surprised that my expertise might extend to the classics, Watson—"

I frowned and bade my eyelids to stop revealing my thoughts.

"—but it is as well to understand imagery that the more imaginative criminal mind might draw upon in his striving for significance beyond the mundane."

"And is that what Fay is doing, in your estimation? Striving for significance?"

"Perhaps more for notoriety. We have concluded that Muybridge knows well the identity of his extortioner. He has already received a demand for payment of a sum of money, and he has his deadline. What more is required after that?"

"Reinforcement of that same demand, I suppose, along with a reminder of the consequences of a failure to pay."

Holmes's fingers rapped on the door frame in a complex rhythm. "Those are both reasonable conclusions. Then there is the fact that delivering the threat in full visibility of the English public, and in such a theatrical fashion, will make it far harder to ignore, either by the public or by Muybridge himself."

"You are assessing this matter in a remarkably cold manner, Holmes. What concerns me as much as Muybridge's fate is the sullying of your name. And do not suppose that it is a wholly selfless impulse: don't forget that I myself am reliant upon your good fortune."

Even as I said this, though, I imagined one day telling a very different series of tales about Holmes as an outcast and pariah. Would I stand by my friend if he was no longer considered the 'great detective'? Would I continue to act as his chronicler? I knew instantly that the answer to both questions was 'yes'.

"You have a faraway look in your eye, Watson," Holmes said quietly. "I am not ready to give up on my chosen career just yet. Let us stay in the present, shall we?"

I cleared my throat and shook myself to wake from my daydream. "The point stands," I said gruffly. "Are you really not concerned about the damage to your reputation?"

"I am not."

"But if you lose the trust of the public—"

"The public are fickle, and I hardly desire more callers at present. We have much to which we may apply ourselves, Watson."

"You refer to these trips, to Loudwater and now Bishop's Stortford. Are they really so closely related to our starting point of the threats made against Eadweard Muybridge?"

"It is fascinating how far the current might take us, is it not?" Holmes replied, apparently unconscious of the criticism in my tone. "I am convinced that Elias Griffin is a piece of the puzzle. Even if it were not for the Muybridge link – and I remind you that Muybridge himself was in Loudwater, making clear the relationship between extorted and extortioner – then Griffin would be a man of interest to us. Alongside the connection of the Yosemite photograph, Israel Fay has invested in companies that are engaged in developments that match precisely Griffin's own work."

"And what nature of work is that?"

"A new type of celluloid that is to be used as a means to project moving pictures."

"Like Mr. Paul's films, which I saw at the Alhambra?"

"Quite so. In Paris, Louis Lumière has overseen the creation of photographic plate emulsion which may be used on rolls of celluloid, but the issue of orthochromasia continues to bedevil most of the men who have their sights set on the projection of moving images."

"Ortho…" I began, then trailed off.

"The failure of a dye to change colour upon binding to a surface. Aniline-based dyes are one remedy, and more recently there have been some who endorse erythrosine."

I turned to the bag upon my bed, with the dual purpose of continuing my packing and also hiding my confusion.

"Indeed," I muttered.

"Griffin has produced numerous academic papers on the subject," Holmes continued. "I will allow you to read them during the journey to Hertfordshire."

Before I could conceive of a sardonic response, Holmes turned and said, "There is our cab."

I paused in my packing and said, "I hear nothing," but then seconds later I heard the clip of hooves and then the slowing of wheels outside the window.

"It was the hurried footsteps as pedestrians moved aside from the oncoming carriage that I identified at first," Holmes said, gathering his coat. "Now do hurry, Watson. Next time we are to adventure I will pack your bag myself."

CHAPTER FOURTEEN

Chaloner House was everything that Snakeley Manse was not. It was larger and a good deal more conventional in appearance, it was freshly painted, and though ivy climbed its walls it was not in sparse, messy arrangements but relegated to one end, coating the brickwork entirely with a pleasant deep green. The house was unobstructed by trees save for a grand oak that served as a useful means of determining the scale of the grand building, given that it reached only to the sills of the second-floor windows.

As our cab slowed to a halt, I bent to peer out of the window, frowning. "The recovery from the effects of the fire appears to be remarkable," I said.

A side door, which was almost hidden amid the lush ivy, opened and a woman wearing an apron over her dark dress emerged. Her face was open and pleasant, and though her hair was worn loose, I felt no sense of impropriety about it. She wiped her hands on her apron as she hurried to our cab.

Holmes greeted her warmly. "You are Miss Edith Griffin?" he asked.

She nodded. "I am pleased to meet you in person, Mr. Holmes. I've read several of your tales."

Holmes smiled. "This is Dr. Watson, the author of those same accounts."

Miss Griffin allowed me to take her hand, but her acknowledgement of me was far less effusive. "Shall I take you to your rooms? And then perhaps some tea?"

"Yes, that would be—" I began, but at the same moment Holmes said, "There is no need. We are content to set to work immediately."

Perhaps it was Miss Griffin's snubbing of me that made me bold, or perhaps it was simply ill temper produced by my two brandies after luncheon at the club, and their having been swilled in my stomach over the course of a cab ride, a rail journey and then another short but violent cab ride from the station. Whatever the reason, I said sternly, "Holmes, I insist. I would very much like some tea."

"Very well," Miss Griffin said. If she was critical of my weakness, she hid it well. "We will have cake and tea in the drawing-room."

The maid seemed to have anticipated our arrival, and the tea arrived almost the moment we took our seats. The sustenance was very much appreciated; the cake was excellent. Once I had had my fill, I looked up at Miss Griffin, who was watching me with an expression that hovered somewhere between expectancy and revulsion.

She inhaled sharply, then addressed Holmes. "I am sorry to say that my father will not see you to-day."

"Why is that?" Holmes asked bluntly.

"He is in a nervous state, and has been ever since the accident. He has not once referred to his work, and of course he could not conduct any even if he wished to do so."

I wiped crumbs from my mouth with a napkin. "About this fire," I said. "We saw no sign of it from the front of the house. Was it really only a matter of a fortnight ago?"

The flicking of Holmes's eyes in my direction told me that I had

stumbled again. To Miss Griffin, he said, "We have learnt little from the newspaper reports, but I take it that the fire broke out in your father's workshop. Might I ask where that workshop is located?"

Miss Griffin gestured vaguely. "It is an annexe to the north-west, which is hidden from the gates. We call it the annexe, but in fact it is entirely separate – a distinction for which I am now grateful, as you can imagine."

"Then the fire affected the annexe alone, and did not touch the house itself?" I said.

Both Holmes and Miss Griffin turned to look at me. Neither answered, and I realised just how inane my question had been. I resolved to pay better attention, now that my stomach had settled.

"I would appreciate it if you would take us there," Holmes said.

"But Mr. Holmes," Miss Griffin said, and for the first time she sounded exasperated, "it is hardly our primary concern, and I do not particularly like to revisit that place. It would be better to begin upstairs." She nodded to the waiting maid, who left the room.

I wondered at this pronouncement. Why might it *not* be our 'primary concern' to understand what had caused the fire, and the conditions in which the house guest, Martin Chrisafis, lost his life? But a warning glance from Holmes cautioned me to remain silent.

"It may be," Holmes said, "that some scrap of evidence there might help our cause."

After a hesitation, Miss Griffin relented. She led us from the drawing-room, along a dark hallway, through a scullery in which a balding footman was engaged in examining silverware, and then we passed through a door at the west side of the house, and presently I found myself blinking in the late-afternoon sunlight dappled by the swaying branches of the oak.

Our hostess's description of the 'annexe' building was accurate. It was a bungalow, though its roof rivalled that of the main building with regards to its vertiginous slope. It was separated from the house by a distance of around twenty-five feet. At one time I presumed it must have been a stable or a groundsman's workshop of some sort, but over time it seemed to have been reconceived as a miniature version of its neighbour, with identical window sashes and door.

Its main characteristic, though, was its poor state of repair. The frames of those windows on the longest side of the building, which had no door, were black and, in one case, missing entirely, the panes shattered on the trampled soil outside. Near to the rear of the building a black smear like an enormous inked fingerprint marred the stucco. Wordlessly, the three of us walked around to the rear, and I drew in a sharp breath. Here, the wall was similarly black, and worse still, the greater part of the triangular section of roof was entirely missing – this absence had been until now hidden by the tall front part. Similarly, the door that had once been in the centre of this wall was little more than a vertical strip of charred timber hanging in the frame, the remainder now ashes at its foot. Through this cavity I glimpsed the interior of the building, though the contents were difficult to make out despite the bright sunlight. Everything within the building appeared black, and upon the surfaces were ghostly, unidentifiable objects that glinted as though the fire had only minutes ago been extinguished.

"I suppose you wish to go inside?" Miss Griffin asked with a shudder.

"I am convinced that it will be profitable," Holmes replied.

Miss Griffin considered this, then said, "It would be as well to enter by the less damaged part. Wait here, and I will return to the main house to fetch my set of keys."

However, before she had time to leave, Holmes had returned to the undamaged front of the annexe and had tried the handle of the door beside a partially open window; the door opened outwards without obstruction.

Miss Griffin stood motionless, looking at the open door. Then she shrugged her shoulders and gestured for Holmes and I to enter the building before her.

It was with a certain amount of surprise that I saw that the room we entered, which comprised roughly half of the space within the building, was a bedroom. There was a desk and washstand alongside the narrow, unmade bed, and a tall coat-stand stood beside the window. All of these items were speckled with soot, and the floor rug had evidently caught alight: it was stiff to walk upon and it crackled dully with each of our footsteps. Even so, the greatest damage from the fire was relegated to the wall against which the head of the bed was pressed, and while the pillows upon it had been partially burned, the lower part of the bed was intact and relatively clean. The black streaks on the rug and floorboards – some of which appeared on the cusp of falling away into the foundations – were most pronounced around the frame of an internal door, through which I made out the same blackened workshop that I had seen from outside the rear external door. This inner door hung loosely from its warped hinges, and was made skeletal by the absence of a large glass pane which now lay in shards on the floorboards.

However, it was the framed picture that hung above the bed that most attracted my immediate notice: it could be none other than the Muybridge photograph that had been described in the newspaper article. The sketch in the clipping did no justice to the image at all, and what struck me was that the reflections of the blunt cliffs of the mountain range and the spindly pine trees were more defined and pronounced in the inverted reflection within the still lake than their actual forms above. It seemed ill fortune indeed that the symmetry of the picture was now ruined irrevocably, as its bottom-right quarter was missing entirely. It was an easy matter to track where the flames had leapt from the bed-head to the picture frame, and then licked along the corner of the picture.

Holmes stood beside me with his arms folded, as though we were two visitors to an art gallery. Then, without warning, he sprang onto the bed and reached up to remove the picture frame from its hook. Resting on the plain wooden bedstead, he brought the burned part of the picture close to his face. Now I saw what he was looking at: the letters 'Mu' were written there in a looping hand, but the rest of the writing was truncated by the missing section of the photographic print.

"Would being signed by the author of the picture make it more valuable?" I asked.

"Yes," Miss Griffin and Holmes replied at once.

Addressing Miss Griffin, I asked, "By what means did your father come by the picture?"

"I do not know," she replied. "All I can say is that he has had it a year, and he is very proud of it. Or perhaps I ought to say he *was* proud of it. But Mr. Holmes, none of this is pertinent to the task you agreed to undertake. When you contacted me I told you of my reluctance to go over what happened that night. It was a dreadful accident, one that is better relegated to history. What occupies my mind now is the unfortunate Martin Chrisafis, and his remaining family, who may not even be in this country. Given that nobody has contacted my father or I about the matter, it remains possible that they are as yet ignorant of his fate."

Now I understood the awkwardness over tea. Holmes had contrived for us to visit Chaloner House under false pretences. If Edith Griffin had been puzzled at his offer of tracing Martin Chrisafis's family, her desire to make amends must have overwhelmed her caution.

For his part, Holmes seemed not to be listening to our hostess. He had put the picture down to rest on the pillows, and now his fingers played lightly on the wall to the left of the position where it had hung, which was free of soot. I now saw that a long scratch had been made in the wall, descending vertically from the bottom-left corner of the frame. Holmes examined the scratch for a long while before he replaced the picture. Then, without reference to his findings, he hopped down from the bed.

Next, he approached the burned internal door. He bent onto one knee and sifted carefully through the shards of glass that had fallen from its central pane, then lifted several of them in turn and held them to the light. The glass appeared very thick and uneven, like that of an old church window, and the daylight produced strange, mottled patterns which made the pieces look alternately like emeralds or sapphires. My friend then picked up and examined a section of the door through which were still threaded the doorknobs on either side. He turned it several times, peering at each smooth knob in turn. I saw that the brass was badly discoloured on one side, no doubt due to the intense heat of the fire.

As Holmes rose he picked up a cream-coloured water-jug which lay on its side beside the doorway, and he replaced it on the washstand, beside a basin which contained another, smaller jug. Then, cautiously, he entered the next room. I hesitated, but then followed, wincing as the floorboards beneath my feet creaked violently.

Instantly, I was obliged to cover my mouth with my handkerchief against the reek of smoke. The room appeared more a laboratory than a mere workshop. The surfaces were crammed with soot-streaked equipment, including oil burners and trays for holding chemicals, and though they were all shattered, I identified a number of glass flasks. The ceiling had almost entirely been demolished, and ragged strips of celluloid hung from the remaining rafters, the sight of which made me shudder as I could not help but liken them to cuts of meat hanging in a butcher's shop.

Holmes moved from item to item, his magnifying glass always held before him, examining all with equal scrutiny. Every so often, he turned and warned me to move more cautiously for fear of upsetting anything, which was made far more difficult by the slickness of the floorboards, some of which still held small puddles of water. Eventually I grew tired of the challenge and passed through the room to emerge into the sunshine at the rear of the building. I found I was surprised by the bright light, which seemed to have been leached out of that dismal studio despite the hole in the roof.

"Your friend's dedication to observation is admirable," Miss Griffin said. "However, it seems unnecessary. No information about Martin Chrisafis or his family is to be found in the workshop."

I gave what I hoped was a reassuring smile. "You say you have read some of my accounts of Holmes's work, so you will understand that he is reluctant to ignore any potential means of learning the truth. You cannot deny that this location is significant in the life of Martin Chrisafis. You must have faith, Miss Griffin."

She sighed, and wrapped her thin arms around herself. For almost a minute she was silent, and then she said quietly, "No doubt it was the celluloid that caught fire initially. It is hard to accept, though – my father has always been well aware of its flammable nature, and he is scrupulous about its storage and treatment."

As Holmes stepped from the burned room, he said, "There are clear indications of a great quantity of celluloid strips having been left on the counter beside that internal door. Has anything been disturbed?"

"Nothing. Nobody has entered these rooms since the fire was put out," Miss Griffin said. "I know my father too well to act without his permission, even though it is clear that he is in no state to contemplate what to do next."

Holmes nodded. "It is a pity that the recent bouts of rain have made the circumstances even more difficult to visualise than did the water used when fighting the fire."

Miss Griffin crossed her arms. "Letting the fire run where it liked would hardly have been an improvement."

Embarrassed, I interjected, "Furthermore, Miss Griffin can hardly be held to account for the weather, Holmes."

Holmes nodded, appearing unconscious that he had caused offence. He turned to Miss Griffin. "Tell me about your house guest. Was it the case that he was found directly in the centre of the workshop room, halfway to the internal door?"

Miss Griffin turned to look in the direction Holmes indicated, as though she expected to find her guest still lying there. "Indeed, yes," she said. "I did not see the body myself, but my father did, and I rather regret that he described it to me in detail, including the awful burns all over – I understand why the vision might haunt him as much as it does." She paused. "But how did you determine that position so accurately?"

"It is only a faint indication," Holmes replied, "but there is slightly less damage there, and less soot has settled, suggesting that a large object prevented the burning of those floorboards."

I grimaced at the picture my friend was painting. To her credit, Miss Griffin seemed unaffected by Holmes's words.

"I suppose he might well have fallen to his hands and knees to avoid inhaling smoke," I said thoughtfully. "But what I don't understand is why this man Chrisafis would pass from the bedroom of this annexe, which it seems was relatively unaffected by the fire, and then enter the workshop, if he understood that within it was a blaze that was out of control. Do you think he was trying to save any item in particular? Miss Griffin, did he understand your father's work well? Did he assist in it to any degree?"

Miss Griffin shook her head. "My father never allowed anybody to work alongside him – I suppose it was the same impulse that made him refuse all offers of investment from various quarters. He was determined that his accomplishments would be his alone, and that he alone would stand to profit if he succeeded. But as for your other questions, you have made a wrong assumption. It was not Martin but my father who was sleeping in the annexe bedroom, as was his custom. Though his working hours were rarely out of the ordinary, he preferred to sleep close to his workshop, as inspiration would often strike him immediately upon waking, and then he would simply rush to the room next door without breakfasting. The desk in the bedroom was frequently where he would take his meals, which I or the maid would bring him – sometimes all three meals in a day."

"Then why was your guest here at all?" I wondered aloud. "The newspaper article claimed the fire broke out at night."

Miss Griffin pointed to the upper rooms of the main house. "That room at the end was the one assigned to Martin. As you can see, the part of the annexe most affected by the fire would have been visible from there. I cannot say why he was awake at three o'clock in the morning, of course, but it seems possible that some sound might have woken him. A number of bottles were smashed, for example, not to mention the noise of the conflagration itself. And then, presumably, he dashed outside wearing barely anything at all – my father told me that when Martin's body was found, he was wearing nothing more than his purple pyjamas. The door to my father's bedroom would have been locked, so Martin must have staved in the outer door of the workshop, to gain access in the hope of saving him… but all for nothing, as by that point my father had already been woken by the blaze, and left his room, rushing to the house to fetch help to put out the fire." Her voice grew distant. "Martin died in pursuit of a noble cause, but it was needless."

"Were you very close?" I asked, uncomfortably aware that we had not yet offered our commiserations.

She looked up. "What? No. I barely knew him."

"But we were told he was a family friend."

"He was the son of my father's childhood friend, who himself passed on some years ago. Now you can see why my father has taken Martin's death so much to heart. Inadvertently, he has snuffed out the last remaining memory of someone who was once his most beloved friend. I wonder if this awful association will mean that he refuses to continue his work. Celluloid is a dangerous material, and it is certainly not worth the loss of a life. You see now what inspires my quest to contact any member of Martin's family, to make amends. I do not wish to be needlessly dramatic, but there is another life at stake: my father's. If things are left as they are, I believe he will deteriorate rapidly."

"In your estimation, was your father complacent about the dangers of the materials he used?" Holmes asked.

Miss Griffin shook her head firmly. "I have already said as much to Dr. Watson, and I do not like the insinuation you are making, Mr. Holmes. My father was well aware of the need for precautions, which is why I am so surprised that the fire was able to spread so quickly. For example, he was diligent about locking both outer doors of the annexe, either when he left the building or when he was within it, asleep. In addition, he kept his supply of chemicals well away from both the annexe and the house. Perhaps you do not believe me, and you wish to lay blame at my father's feet? Here, I will show you."

As she strode away in a direction beyond the annexe, I held back to speak to Holmes.

"You might have told me that we were here on a false pretext," I said in a low voice. "You are pushing your luck, Holmes, and I tell you that she will not take kindly to your insistence on unearthing new information about her father's mistake. You ought to place more emphasis on the aspect of this situation that Miss Griffin has engaged you to examine: the means of contacting the house guest's family."

Holmes put a hand on my shoulder. "I thank you for putting me right. Navigating the emotions of a woman is hardly my suit, particularly when there is tantalising information to be had. Please, watch out for my conduct."

Ahead of us, our hostess approached a small brick building which was little more than a potting-shed, though more substantial in construction than most I had seen. She produced from her apron a key, and unlocked the door to reveal an interior that would barely allow access to a single person. Upon opposing walls were several rows of shelves, and each of these contained a great number of bottles, tins and buckets, all neatly labelled with the same handwriting, and alongside these were various garden implements: watering-cans, forks and spades, which I supposed explained the fact that Miss Griffin kept a key to the shed upon her person. This prompted another thought: might there be others in possession of a key? I looked around me and was startled to see a groundskeeper watching on from the lee of the trees at the periphery of the grounds to the west, where until now he had evidently been engaged in raking leaves.

With a sigh of something rather like contentment, Holmes edged into the small space and, without hurry, began examining each of the containers. Soon he produced his pen-knife and eased open the lids of some of the tins, lifting some to his face to smell them. Miss Griffin and I watched this behaviour for some minutes, then turned away. Standing side by side, we watched the sun set over the perimeter wall of the grounds. I noticed that the groundskeeper had returned to his work with the rake.

"I am sorry for your loss," I said awkwardly, aware of her

increasing dismay as Holmes continued to investigate aspects that seemed of no importance to her. "Though you say you did not know your guest well, I can only imagine how awful your experience has been."

Miss Griffin's smile appeared genuinely grateful. "Thank you. He was kind to my father, and indulged stories of his own father's exploits. At dinner-times – of course, Martin and I sometimes dined together alone, with my father busy in his workshop – he often spoke of his plans to travel. I have no doubt that an interesting life would have lain ahead of him. We were hardly close, but I confess that at times I hoped…" She broke off and stared above the trees with renewed intensity.

I registered that the sounds from behind me had ceased. Holmes backed out of the shed and closed the door.

"For how long had Chrisafis been staying with you?" he asked.

"Three days, on this occasion, and one overnight stay some two months ago, soon after he had first made himself known to my father. Had it not been for the fire, he would have left the very next day, which makes his fate all the worse." She took a deep breath and then exhaled slowly, her cheeks puffed out in a fashion that was decidedly not ladylike – but of course I forgave her.

"By what means did he intend to travel?" Holmes asked.

"I do not know. I suspect he preferred not to know himself, and to develop his plans as he went along. He arrived here on foot carrying only his light case, and he seemed sprightly and accustomed to making his own way. Though…" She trailed off.

I put my hand on her arm. "Please, do continue."

"It has only now come to me that at the beginning of his most recent visit – I mean, his *final* visit – I had come out of the house to greet Martin only because my maid had heard a cab slowing to turn into the gates. But then when I left the house, there was Martin walking up the path on foot."

I glanced at Holmes, who seemed lost in thought. Addressing Miss Griffin, I said, "It is easily explained. Chrisafis must have paid the cab at the gates, and walked the rest of the way. Some people do prefer to get the measure of an unfamiliar building without the frustration of a rocking carriage."

Miss Griffin hesitated, then nodded. "Soon it will be time for dinner. Will you accompany me back to the house? You have not yet seen his personal effects."

We returned the way we had come, but as we passed the burned annexe Holmes slowed to a halt. He was standing at the corner of the front end containing the bedroom, gazing at the ground, which had evidently been churned up when the locals had assisted in fighting the fire. I saw footprints in the exposed soil, and assumed these were what attracted my friend – but then I saw him raise his head so that he was looking at the sand-covered track that led around the building to the outer entrance to the workshop.

"Go inside without me," Holmes said absently. "I will join you, in…"

Then he bent to his work, oblivious to our presence and not seeming to realise that he had not finished his sentence.

CHAPTER FIFTEEN

At dinner, my eyes kept straying to the empty chair at the head of the table.

Edith Griffin noticed my distraction. She dabbed at her mouth with a napkin, then said, "I can only apologise for my father's absence. I suppose that after what happened, and now that he is no longer at his work, I might at least have hoped that I would see more of him. But that has proved not to be the case."

"Will he eat in his room, then?" I asked.

"Yes," Miss Griffin replied. She looked down at the still half-full tureen of soup in the centre of the large dining-table, then, with a glance at the maid standing to her right, added, "He tends to eat only simple foods, which are easily transported. No doubt he will have only a bread roll, cheese and some cold meats."

This correction struck me as odd, but I said nothing.

"Mr. Holmes," she said, turning to my friend, "do you feel that you have learned much from examining the scene of the fire?"

"Naturally," Holmes replied. "It is a fascinating case."

I winced involuntarily. After Miss Griffin and I had returned to the house, Holmes had been absent for so long that I was compelled to return to the annexe to look for him. He was not there, or at the chemical store-room, and my search took me entirely around the periphery of the grounds until I located him as he emerged from a thicket halfway along the track that led to the entrance gates, holding before him like a relic a single thread, which, upon inspection, we both agreed was purple. ("Were not Chrisafis's pyjamas purple?" I asked, and Holmes nodded happily. But he would not speculate about what Chrisafis had been doing skulking in dense bushes at some point before he perished.) When we had both finally dressed and made our appearance downstairs to be greeted by Miss Griffin, dinner had already been laid out upon the dining-table.

"You say it is fascinating, rather than tragic – an interesting choice of word," Miss Griffin said reproachfully. "I do wonder about your priorities, Mr. Holmes, or at least whether your priorities align with my own. In what sense is the 'case', as you call it, fascinating?"

"I mean that it is immensely complex, and yet the simplest situation imaginable."

Miss Griffin's shoulders stiffened. "A guest staying in this house saw that an awful accident was occurring, and he rushed to help, then he perished in the most unimaginable manner. Where is the complexity in that?"

Holmes put down his spoon, leaving his bowl of soup untouched. "For one thing, there is the question about why Martin Chrisafis broke down the external door to the workshop."

"Why, to gain access in the only manner he knew how!" I exclaimed before Miss Griffin had opportunity to reply.

Holmes arched an eyebrow. "I beg you, continue with that line of thought, Watson."

"Well… this man Chrisafis saw the fire from his bedroom window, then he dashed downstairs, in his haste neglecting to rouse anybody else in the house as he passed. Seeing the extent of the conflagration, he naturally feared for Mr. Griffin's safety. Therefore, having tried and failed to open the locked bedroom door, he ran around to the only other door – that of the workshop – which is where he had seen flames emerge. With no other course of action, he struck with his full weight against this door, which was no doubt already weakened by fire damage, to gain access to the workshop. Then" – I glanced at our hostess and blanched at the prospect of summoning the awful image of the burned body once again – "he never made it as far as the internal door leading to Griffin's bedroom."

Miss Griffin folded her arms and looked to Holmes. "Do you dispute the sense of what your colleague has said?"

"I do," Holmes replied simply.

"Mr. Holmes, may I remind you that I invited you here on the understanding that you would help me to locate any persons connected with Martin Chrisafis, in the absence of his father who was once known to my family, as the police have been singularly unhelpful in that regard. My concern is to assuage the guilt suffered by my father every day. I am entirely uninterested in your desire to introduce additional complexity to these dreadful circumstances. Nevertheless, if you have some complaint to make about our understanding of what happened—"

"The bedroom door was not locked," Holmes said calmly.

Miss Griffin blinked rapidly. "I beg your pardon?"

"What was your father's experience that night?" Holmes said. His eyes rose, and mine followed suit, as though we might look through the ceiling to Elias Griffin hidden away in his room.

"He will not speak of it," Miss Griffin replied tersely. "I believe he *cannot* speak of it."

"Might we attempt to coax the information from him?" Holmes asked.

"Certainly not. I will not have him disturbed. The fact that you would suggest doing so is further evidence that you have misunderstood your invitation to our home."

Holmes nodded, clearly having expected this response. Still aloof to the intensity of our hostess's glare, he continued, "Then I would ask you to visualise the events as if from your father's own eyes. You are sleeping soundly. Then you are roused, either by an unexpected sound, or perhaps smoke, or a perception of heat. What occurs next?"

Miss Griffin only frowned, so I ventured, "I open the internal door to my workshop."

Holmes shrugged his shoulders. "Very well. Having done so, you perceive a fire which you determine is already beyond your capability to fight."

"There was a water-jug discarded beside the internal door," I muttered. "A meagre weapon against a blazing fire."

Holmes nodded. "Then what is your next recourse?"

"It is just as Miss Griffin described to us earlier. I rush from the annexe and hare to the house, where I begin to rouse members of the household staff who might help extinguish the fire."

"You are going too fast," Holmes said placidly.

"Too fast?" I exclaimed. "There is a fire blazing, Holmes!" I stopped, realising that I had entered too wholly into the part of Elias Griffin. "Ah, I see what you mean. Very well. I leave the annexe in a hurry—"

"Stop there," Holmes said. "What are your *precise* actions at this moment?"

"Simply that," I replied. "I am intent on getting outside as quickly as possible. This is no moment for the adage 'more haste, less speed.'"

Holmes patted the table twice, one of his tell-tale signs of self-satisfaction. "Then you have said it yourself. Almost certainly, Elias Griffin did not lock the door behind him."

Miss Griffin had been watching our exchange with horror. Now she said firmly, "This is conjecture. Furthermore, it proves nothing. When he hurried from the house, Martin naturally assumed that my father was still in his bed. Equally, upon his arrival at the annexe, he may quite reasonably have assumed that the outer door to my father's bedroom would be locked. I have already told you that my father is diligent about locking the annexe at all times, whether he is within it or without."

"It was not locked to-day," Holmes said. "You expected it to be so, but the outer door to the bedroom was unlocked."

Nonplussed, Miss Griffin retorted, "That is hardly the same, Mr. Holmes. The annexe is now but a shell, and it has been trampled by those people who bravely fought the fire, and my father has not yet so much as returned to it."

"I am simply pressing the point that in unusual circumstances, people may behave in uncharacteristic ways. Earlier, you announced that you would fetch a key from the house. Were you referring to your father's own set?"

"No. I have always kept a spare set, in case of emergency. They are locked in the drawing-room safe."

"Are you certain of that?"

"What are you suggesting now, Mr. Holmes? Would you like me to march in there and prove to you that they are in their proper place?"

"I would be grateful if you would check that they are – but there is no need for either Watson or I to accompany you. We will trust your word."

Astonished, Miss Griffin rose from her seat and crossed the room. The maid waited for a few seconds, then scurried after her. A minute later, both of them returned to their places.

"You will be glad to know that the keys are untouched," Miss Griffin said.

"An unusual choice of word," Holmes said softly.

Miss Griffin's eyes glinted. "Is this another accusation? I tell you that the keys are in the safe."

Holmes nodded thoughtfully. "Very well."

I understood his meaning well: just because the keys were in the safe, that did not prove that they had been untouched since Miss Griffin last had cause to use them. Still, I was grateful that Holmes seemed content not to pursue this line of argument.

My heart sank, then, when he said instead, "And what of your father's set of keys?"

Miss Griffin stared at him without answer. Then she shuffled in her seat. "There is no set, to speak of. He keeps his keys loose, making the claim that if he were to mislay one, the others would not also be lost. They tend to be kept in his jacket pockets. But why are you fixated on this aspect, Mr. Holmes? First you say that the door to his room was not locked, and now you are occupied with the locations of the keys that would lock them. None of these parlour games are of any interest to me, and none will put me in contact with Martin Chrisafis's loved ones."

Holmes gave a wan smile. "It is as I described: complex, but simple. What was the weather on the night of the fire?"

Miss Griffin flashed me a desperate look, and I returned one which conveyed that I could no better predict the workings of my friend's mind than she.

"Very warm," she replied. "As had been all the evenings leading up to it. No doubt that was a contributor to the rapid spread of the fire."

Holmes responded with a long, slow nod, as though this detail explained much.

For the rest of dinner-time Holmes was reluctant to divulge anything more, though I found myself thanking him silently for no longer torturing our hostess. The meal was excellent, but the food stuck in my throat due to the hard glares directed from Edith Griffin to Sherlock Holmes. When we had finished, I made a show of fatigue and announced that I was for bed, and would forgo an after-dinner drink.

"Before we retire," Holmes said, "I beg you, might we see the room in which Martin Chrisafis stayed?"

Miss Griffin hesitated, as if she suspected trickery. Then she said, "Of course. All afternoon I have been attempting to have you do precisely that."

She led us up the main stairwell, then past the rooms allocated to Holmes and I, where we had dressed quickly for dinner, and past doors with grander architraves which belonged to the bedrooms at the front of the house. At first it seemed to me odd that Martin Chrisafis had been allocated the room furthest from the stairs, but when we entered it I revised my opinion: this bedroom was almost double the size of the one in which I would sleep that night, and as it was at the corner of the house it had windows on two adjoining walls, which would no doubt let in a good amount of light during the daytime.

Almost involuntarily, I went to the west-facing window and looked out. The moon had risen, and though it was only half-full, the annexe building was clearly defined by its pale light. I could only imagine how stark the vision must have been of flames bursting from Griffin's studio that disastrous night. I had not appreciated just how close this bedroom window was to the smaller building, and therefore the blaze; now my mind filled with images of Martin Chrisafis sprinting along the corridors, away from the fire in order to reach the stairwell only to then dash back along the ground-floor corridors, towards the danger. It was no wonder that by the time he reached the annexe building his mind was addled, inspiring him to make a calamitous error.

I shook my head to clear this nightmarish vision, then looked at Holmes, who was preoccupied in examining the carpet to the left side of the bed. Then he rose and joined me at the window, but instead of looking out at the annexe, his neck craned as he stared up at the curtain-rail.

"Has anything been disturbed?" he asked without turning.

"Nothing in the room at large," Miss Griffin replied, "save for the suitcase. I assure you that I was merely attempting to glean a home address, after tragedy had struck, as that might have been a first step towards contacting Martin's family."

"And yet you found no address?"

"I did not. Mr. Holmes, I do not think you have been listening to me at all. The lack of an address is the very matter that you have pledged to resolve."

Ignoring her scolding, Holmes said, "Chrisafis spoke of nobody in his family, nor any other person?"

"As I have said, he spoke only of his father, which was the only subject that mine was interested in discussing. My own conversations with Martin seemed to involve concepts and ambitions rather than people."

Holmes spun around. "What ambitions?"

"Well, travel, as I mentioned already. Martin denigrated the failure of most people to see much of the world beyond their own cities, towns or villages. And then..." Miss Griffin's face clouded. "Now that I think about it, perhaps we talked more of *my* ambitions than his."

Holmes nodded, but appeared entirely uninterested in learning what Miss Griffin's ambitions might have been. I was tempted to ask her myself, if only to indulge and placate her, but then I realised that I really was tired and had no desire to prolong the conversation.

More surprising still was Holmes's lack of curiosity about the contents of Martin Chrisafis's suitcase, which remained open on the sideboard. Evidently, Chrisafis had packed it in readiness for his departure the next day, and despite Miss Griffin's subsequent investigation the clothes were folded neatly – I supposed that she had rearranged them after her examination. Holmes gave each item only a cursory glance, then moved away from the sideboard to perform a lap of the room. Finally, he came to a halt to gaze for almost a minute – and as far as I was concerned, entirely inexplicably – at an empty wash-basin.

CHAPTER SIXTEEN

Sleep did not come easily, and when it did I might have wished it away. Images of fires and blackened bodies flickered through my mind, frequently interrupted yet always distinct, like sequences from a moving-picture programme.

However, the sound that woke me finally was most definitely of this world.

I sat sharply upright in my bed, my attention fixated on the door. The sound had come from the hallway beyond. I checked my watch to discover that it was a little before three o'clock.

Despite the certainty that I was awake, an impulse took me to the window and I pulled back the curtain. The view from my room was directly to the north of the grounds, and I was forced to throw up the sash and then contort my neck to allow me to see the corner of the annexe building. It was dark.

This was not that night, and I was not Martin Chrisafis, and the sound had come from within Chaloner House, not without.

I crept to the door, pulling my dressing-gown tight around me. Quietly, I turned the handle and exited into the corridor.

My first thought had been that Holmes was prowling around the house, but the door to his room was closed and yet another on the opposite side was open. I peered through the open doorway to see a large, plainly furnished bedroom in which the bed was placed discreetly against one wall and the greater part of the space was filled with shelving, chests and two desks arranged lengthwise and cluttered with books, mugs and dishes. This could only be Elias Griffin's room.

As the occupant himself was missing, I continued along the hallway to the stairwell. I trod carefully as I descended the stairs, then froze and winced at a sound, before realising that it had been produced not by my own weight upon the steps, but by somebody below, passing directly beneath me where the staircase bent around. I leant on the balustrade and strained my eyes to look in that direction, but the gloom prevented me from making out anything more than a vague shape of a slow-moving figure. I waited several seconds, then resumed my descent.

By now I might have expected my eyes to have adjusted to the darkness, but glimmers of moonlight snaking between the gaps in the curtains confounded this ability, making me wince and then begin squinting afresh. All that I could determine was that I was now tracking my quarry westwards, below our bedrooms – which meant we were moving in the direction of the annexe.

Sure enough, I passed into a room which was a ghostly shadow of the scullery I had entered earlier in the day, and I saw that the door at the opposite side was open. Cold night air came from it, easily penetrating my gown. I hurried to the wall, then eased myself along it to look outside.

Somebody was walking heavily along the sand track that led to the nearest door of the annexe, at the front part which was relatively unaffected by the fire. The wide shoulders clearly identified the figure as a man, and a large one at that. I had seen photographs of Elias Griffin in the house, along with a great portrait that hung in the dining-room, which depicted a broad-shouldered man consistent with this figure before me. From his square silhouette I deduced that he wore something more substantial than night-clothes.

When he reached the door of the annexe he let himself in without pause.

I considered hurrying upstairs to wake Holmes, but then concluded that if I did so Griffin might soon complete whatever activity he was about, and then return to bed without us having learnt a single thing about our mysterious, evasive host. So, ignoring the prickling of my skin in the chill air, I left the safety of the house to approach the annexe.

Instead of going to the door, I continued past it to the first of the two front windows, which was partially open. Immediately, I saw Griffin. His back was to me, and he had halted in the centre of the room, beside the bed. In what seemed an unconscious, automatic motion, he shrugged off his dark jacket to reveal pyjamas, and then held the jacket at arm's length; I ducked down as I realised that the coat-stand was beside the very window through which I was peeping. However, when I dared rise from my haunches I saw that he was once again wearing the jacket; he must have become suddenly conscious of the night air.

He stood for some moments, his hands visible even from behind, so tightly was he hugging himself. The meagre amount of moonlight that reached this part of the building did not allow me to determine what he was staring at; it might have been the destroyed photograph by Muybridge, or the view through the internal doorway to his workshop, or, indeed, the unmade bed. Presently, his shoulders began to heave with sobs and his hands fell away to clasp at one another. I wondered if he was praying.

It did not take long for me to feel that I was intruding unforgivably upon another man's grief, yet I found myself fixed to the spot. It was only when Griffin turned, perhaps five or ten minutes later, that I was shaken from my paralysis. I saw a flash of a broad, whiskered face – it was grey rather than florid, but certainly it was the same face I had seen in the dining-room portrait.

I fled. At first I made for the house, but only moments later I recalculated how far I might be able to travel before Griffin emerged from the annexe, and then I veered sharply away. Soon I had sequestered myself behind the trunk of the giant oak.

The annexe door clicked open and Griffin appeared. He closed the door behind him absently, without locking it, then he set off towards the open door leading to the scullery of the main house. My hiding place afforded me an excellent vantage point to watch him. His pace was slow and regular, and he only gazed ahead of him, without seeming to observe his surroundings to any degree. I registered the peculiar positions of his hands; again, at first I took it to be a posture of prayer, but then I saw that the fingers of his right hand were continually rubbing in wide circles on the palm of the left.

I watched as he re-entered the house, then became suddenly frantic as he pulled shut the door, fearing that I would be locked outside for the rest of the night. However, he had left the door unlocked. It was with a sense of profound gratefulness that I padded along the corridors of the house and returned to my bed.

CHAPTER SEVENTEEN

"May I speak to you alone?" I asked Holmes as we finished our breakfast, watched on by the ever more judgemental Edith Griffin, whose attitude towards us appeared to have hardened still further overnight.

Holmes nodded and presently we retreated to the drawing-room. I closed the door and sat in closer proximity to my friend than was our custom, to ensure that our voices would not be heard from outside the room.

I related my night-time adventure to Holmes, who listened impassively throughout my explanation. When I had finished, he asked, "What colour were his pyjamas?"

I frowned. "It is difficult to say, given the moonlight. Certainly pale, perhaps grey."

"Good. And was the jacket dark blue, and rather shapeless, like that of a navy engineer?"

"Why, yes," I said. "I had taken it to be more in the line of a gardener's jacket, but now that you supply that description, it seems to describe it exactly. How on earth could you know that? Did you find some other thread of that particular colour and coarseness?"

Holmes laughed. "Nothing so impressive. I broke into Griffin's bedroom around midnight last night, and found the jacket hanging on the back of a chair. I was determined to know whether he was in possession of all three of his keys: those of the two outer doors of the annexe, and the shed in which his chemicals are stored."

I stared at him. I knew well that Holmes was prepared to ignore orthodoxy in pursuit of his investigations, but entering a room while its owner slept in its bed seemed not only foolhardy but downright uncivilised.

"And were the keys there?" I asked, despite myself.

"They were."

"And yet Griffin continues to break his custom of locking the annexe," I murmured.

"His workshop is burned beyond repair," Holmes said. "There is little to safeguard now – even Muybridge's prized photograph is of no worth. Besides, it is my suspicion that Griffin's behaviour regarding the locking of doors was motivated more by fears for safety of his family and staff than security. You may recall, for example, that the window beside the front door of the annexe remains open since that warm night on which the fire broke out. However, your tale is instructive in several ways. Here, let us return to the annexe, and I will show you."

Despite my fears that she had been listening at the keyhole, Miss Griffin was nowhere to be seen as we exited the room. We passed out of the house and into the dawn sunlight.

Holmes strode to the annexe, his face downturned like a bloodhound sniffing a scent. He pointed at the sand track directly before the door to Griffin's room in the annexe.

"See, there are multiple instances of the same footprint, evidently made recently since rain has softened the ground," he said. "I noted them yesterday, but my late-night intrusion into Elias Griffin's bedroom in the main house, and your observation of his nocturnal activities, have supplied the answer."

"The answer?" I retorted. "All that I saw was him arriving here and weeping. Surely that is not a full and complete answer."

Holmes beamed. "Very good, Watson. But for the moment, let us concern ourselves simply with *movements* rather than chasing the phantoms of full and complete answers. I note your appreciation of the niceties of the deductive process, all the same."

He moved away on the path that led alongside the building to the outer door of the workshop.

"Having cleared up the peculiarity of the recent footprints, we are immediately presented with another puzzle," he said, indicating the path.

I bent to look at the track, which here was a mixture of sand and darker grains which I identified as ash. As before, I made out multiple scuffed footprints, some of which must have been our own and Miss Griffin's, made the previous day during our assessment of the ruination caused by the fire. Alongside these recent marks, though, I saw a strange linear trail that continued along most of the length of the path.

"Is it a track made by the wheels of a bicycle?" I asked, but then I added hurriedly, "No, it is too wide, and there is only one trail, not two overlapping ones. A wheelbarrow, perhaps?"

"A reasonable guess, but there are no regular footprints in the wake of the trail."

"They might easily have been obscured by other people passing this way. That is, if this trail relates to the night of the fire, as I presume you are intimating."

"Certainly I am, and I have good reason for doing so. See that there is ash embedded in the track at various points – that shows that the track predates the fire, or at the very least it predates the settling of the ash after the fire was put out. Another piece of evidence supports this: the reason that this odd mark remains visible to us, more than a fortnight after the night in question, is that the heat of the fire has baked and hardened the sand."

I rose from my crouched position. "This is all very impressive, Holmes, but you will get nothing more from me. If you know what made this track then say so, because beyond the possibilities of a snake or a circus unicycle, I have exhausted my well of ideas."

"I do not know, as yet," Holmes replied. "As I have said, for the time being I am content to understand movements. All we may conclude is that this trail was made by no vehicle, as it is too irregular to have been formed by a wheel – see that it veers often to the left, almost to the grassed area, then back again. Another aspect of note is that the trail deepens markedly at these same diversions. You do not appear to be looking closely, Watson."

With a sigh, I lowered myself to my hands and knees to gaze at the path. Just as Holmes had suggested, the trail was dug deep into the sand at the very places where it wavered to the left. At these points, the edges of the trail, which from close proximity resembled walls of sorts, were perhaps a quarter of an inch in height. In places, the apex of these raised banks had crumbled so that the light sand lay on top of the dark ash which filled the gulley throughout its length.

I rose and brushed the dirt from my knees. "I presume you have followed it to its end?" I asked, though I knew the answer already. "Where does it lead?"

"See for yourself," Holmes replied.

I followed the trail fully along the path, careful to keep to its opposite side to avoid making any disturbance. Where the path made a right angle the trail was still visible, but beyond that point the soot and debris that had belched from the demolished doorway made further sightings of it impossible.

"I can only say that whatever made this trail may have gone into the workshop," I said, "or else that it continued over the grass, towards…" I shielded my eyes to look across the grounds.

"Towards the shed that is filled with chemicals, or the outer wall, beyond which I believe are simply fields, the village of Bishop's Stortford being located on the opposite side of Chaloner House."

Holmes rubbed his hands together. "An excellent summation. We have learnt a great deal from our visit, but it will not have escaped your notice that Edith Griffin would rather we took an early train to-day than a late one. We will be on our way as soon as I have had the opportunity to ask her whether her father is right- or left-handed. Oh, but before we go, perhaps I might interest you in one further observation about this already compelling scenario."

I watched on as Holmes knelt in the ashes. Carefully, he sifted through the debris to retrieve a bulky metal object the size of two packs of cards: upon scrutiny I identified it as the handle and lock mechanism of the destroyed door. He passed it to me and I took it gingerly, turning it over. Both handles were filthy with soot, and sharp splinters of black wood still clung to the main plate.

"Do you see anything of interest?" Holmes asked quietly.

"Other than its dire state, you mean? I'm afraid I don't, Holmes."

Wordlessly, Holmes reached out to place his index finger on the narrow end of the plate which contained the lock mechanism.

I stared at it in confusion for several seconds before I realised what he was showing to me. The latch protruded from the upper part of the mechanism, as might be expected. However, below it the square lock bolt was withdrawn, sitting flush with the plate. The door had not been locked.

CHAPTER EIGHTEEN

Our journey from Bishop's Stortford did not take us directly to Baker Street; rather, after alighting from the train at Liverpool Street, we hailed a cab which took us in the direction of the Victoria Embankment. Presently, we arrived at the tall yet oddly bulbous exterior of Scotland Yard.

We traipsed along corridor after corridor, and I was still none the wiser about the purpose of our visit. Eventually we reached Lestrade's office and Holmes knocked and pushed open the door in almost a single movement.

Lestrade himself was standing at the window, his hands in his pockets as he gazed out. As he turned to acknowledge us, he clasped his hands before him instead, his thumbs drumming together.

"Thank you for waiting for our arrival," Holmes said. "I'm sorry the delay to our train has made it later than I anticipated, but I am sure that there will be at least one remaining portion of cold beef when you go to luncheon."

Lestrade shrugged his shoulders and nodded wearily. Then he said sharply, "How did you guess that I was thinking about cold beef?"

Holmes chuckled quietly.

"Apologies, Holmes," Lestrade went on. "I am sure it was not a guess, but the result of a series of fine observations. Much as it pains me to ask, do tell me how you reached that conclusion in – what, a matter of no more than a second or two."

Holmes gestured to the view from the window. "Your favoured restaurant is in that direction, is it not? It is past two o'clock, and you expected us to arrive before one, so it is reasonable to suppose that our delay has produced yet another in your own plans, with your empty stomach the innocent victim. Nobody could blame you for wishing yourself at a table in that restaurant at this moment, with food before you. The drumming of your thumbs adds to this unconscious sense of impatience, or simply low blood sugar."

"And the beef, specifically?"

I could not help but interject. "You *always* eat cold beef for lunch, Lestrade – or, at least, whenever I have had cause to meet you in the early afternoon, near to Scotland Yard, it is clear that you have eaten cold beef some little time beforehand."

Lestrade turned upon me with an incredulous expression. "Have you been studying Holmes's methods so very closely, Dr. Watson? How on earth can you say that? Next you will be telling me that I customarily go about with the aroma of beef surrounding me like a miasma." His proud posture faltered. "That is not the case, is it?"

I looked at Holmes, but he nodded for me to continue.

"It is not so much the scent as the physical evidence," I began. "And it is not so much the beef as the mustard which, no doubt, you habitually add to it. The fact is that, ah, it tends to remain evident for a time afterwards. Upon your whiskers, that is."

Lestrade cleared his throat and, involuntarily, his fingers went to stroke his moustache. "Is that so? I always take great pains to cover my shirt with a cloth, but I... Well, well." His eyes moved around the room. "Perhaps I ought to install a mirror somewhere in this room. Yes, that would do it."

Then he laughed. "So, Holmes, your conclusion was reached by means of an observation of a stain which I do *not* have to-day. That is rich, and I'm not so much a stick-in-the-mud that I fail to see the humour in it."

He was interrupted by a groaning sound, and then all three of us looked at his stomach, which had produced the noise.

"Let us dispatch this small matter quickly, then," Holmes said.

Lestrade first went to the door of his office and made certain that it was securely shut. Then he moved to his desk and opened a drawer. Before he retrieved anything from it, though, he looked up at Holmes and I uncertainly.

"You understand that this is most irregular?" he said.

"And I thank you for it," Holmes replied. "I would ordinarily have approached the constabulary in Chelmsford, but as the fire at Chaloner House is no longer an active case, we both know that I would have made no progress there."

I searched my friend's face for any clue as to what evidence he sought, but learnt nothing.

Lestrade glanced into the drawer, at whatever item was yet kept out of sight from us. "That's just it. It's not an active case, which leaves me in a most awkward position. It's one thing to provide you with evidence and details pertaining to a case that I myself have asked you to contribute your skills – though even that is frowned upon by many here at Scotland Yard. However, now you are asking me to act as go-between, fetching documents rather like those street-boys you employ. Which clients you take on yourself are your own business, but they are not police matters."

"Oh, this matter is not on behalf of a client," Holmes said. "Neither Edith nor Elias Griffin would support my continued involvement, of that I am certain."

Lestrade blanched. "Then what on earth is your interest in this fire? You understand that the Griffins are important people in the Hertfordshire area, and even beyond? That by their influence they could cause great difficulties if provoked?"

When Holmes barely reacted, Lestrade's eyes darted uneasily. "And, I must add, Holmes... I have read a little about your current case involving the moving-picture chap, Professor Muybridge. The newspapers are, well, rather scathing about your conduct. I would suggest that you ought to avoid adding more difficulties to those that are already approaching you at speed. And... it may be that I will no longer be indulged in my tendency to involve you in police affairs, if this keeps up. There will be no support in consulting a failure."

He winced and swallowed, as if he now regretted his choice of the word 'failure'. I saw that, despite his gruff manner, it pained him to criticise Sherlock Holmes, who had been of such vital importance in solving so many crimes in place of Scotland Yard and yet permitted many of the solutions to be attributed to Lestrade himself. Not only that, I felt sure that beneath his hard exterior and his world-weariness, Lestrade considered Holmes a friend.

Holmes smiled. Acknowledging only the first part of Lestrade's statement, he said, "You spoke of my 'interest' in the fire at Chaloner House, and that is perhaps the right word. I am interested, even fascinated by the situation. In addition, though I cannot yet prove it, there is a link to the case brought to me by Eadweard Muybridge, though he himself is ignorant of it."

"Riddles. When I ask you questions, all I am given in return are riddles." Lestrade took a long breath, his face raised to the ceiling as though he were consulting with a higher power. "I will only say again that none of this sits comfortably with me, Holmes."

"I understand," Holmes replied. "But your beef is waiting. Will you show the photograph to me, or not?"

I fancied I heard Lestrade's stomach complain again, though I could not swear to it. He puffed out his cheeks, then bent to retrieve the item in question from the drawer. He placed upon his desk a single photographic print, and shook his head slowly as he looked at it, then turned it around to allow us to see.

At first I could make no sense of it. The contrast between light and dark areas was stark, but made the image seem more a pattern than a depiction of anything of the real world. The darkest areas were in the centre of the picture, forming a long, thin shape across the diagonal. I presumed that the patches of brightness across the length of the strange object were simply the reflections from a magnesium flash.

Then the details coalesced into a recognisable form – and I wished that they had not.

The picture showed a body, which could only be that of the unfortunate Martin Chrisafis. Perhaps the camera had failed to capture all of the detail of reality, but even allowing for imprecision, what was immediately clear was how badly burned the body had been. The limbs were bare, and though the legs stuck out straight, the arms were bent inwards as though defensively, the hands little more than curled claws, like those of a bird. When I looked closer I saw wisps of ragged pyjamas that were stuck to the skin of the torso and legs as though fixed with adhesive, and then upon the face…

I gagged twice, then in desperation ran to the window, threw open the sash and gulped in air.

"It's almost enough to put me off my cold beef, too," Lestrade said, coming to my side and offering me a handkerchief.

I dabbed at my mouth gratefully. I turned, but remained close to the window in order to continue breathing the air from outside, which was admittedly not fresh, but its scent was certainly an improvement on the taste in my mouth.

"Holmes, you might have—" I began, but then was forced to gulp down rising nausea once again. "You might have warned me what I was to see."

"Next time I will," Holmes replied absently, which I supposed was as close to an apology as I might expect. He continued scrutinising the photograph, humming to himself as though he were an art aficionado presented with a hitherto-unseen work by a favoured painter.

"I don't know how he can bear to look at it for any length of time," Lestrade said to me. "I consider myself hardened to such things, but Holmes seems to be positively enjoying himself."

I nodded heavily, then regretted the motion and the spinning sensation it caused. "In all my time in service I've never seen a face so badly burned. As a doctor I ought not to use such emotive language, I suppose, but it's *grotesque*." Then, addressing Holmes, "I suppose that this is a property of a celluloid fire, to burn so badly. This is an aspect of this new moving-picture industry that has not been made public, it seems. We must assume that Chrisafis attempted to directly approach the pile of celluloid strips in the hope of quenching the source of the blaze, and that he suffered the consequences."

Holmes did not respond to my hypothesis directly, but said, "I only wish that I might examine the body myself, rather than relying upon a photograph."

"Absolutely not," Lestrade interjected. "There is no question of it, Holmes. Do not ask me."

Holmes raised his head, blinking as though awoken from sleep. "I did not ask, Lestrade. But I did make one other request of you." He pointed at the picture. "Were you able to ask your contact at Chelmsford about the pyjamas?"

Lestrade frowned. "I was, and I felt a damned fool doing it. I'm told they were purple."

Holmes resumed his humming, and again began to examine the photograph.

Lestrade jammed his hands in his pockets. "Now, have you had your fill of looking at that atrocious picture?"

Holmes stared at it for a few seconds more, then pushed the print across the desk, whereupon Lestrade took it up and placed it back into the drawer.

"Thank you, Lestrade," Holmes said.

All three of us turned at a knock on the door. The moment Lestrade called out "Come in" a young-looking officer scurried into the room. He blanched as he recognised Holmes, then hurried to Lestrade and murmured something in his ear. Lestrade's eyes widened immediately.

Lestrade, Holmes and I remained motionless in an awkward tableau as the junior officer made his retreat, once again glancing at Holmes as he passed. Then Lestrade slumped back in his chair.

"It seems that you were not exaggerating in your assessment of the Griffins' attitude to your behaviour," he said in a tone as weary as Sisyphus.

"Then I assume that was a message from Edith Griffin?" Holmes asked politely.

"From Elias Griffin, in fact, plus an additional word of commentary by that young chap, Preston, who was on the receiving end of the telephone call. 'Incandescent' was the word he used to describe Griffin's tone, which I suppose shows Preston's mastery of vocabulary, if nothing else. So, Holmes, it seems that you not only tricked your way into the Griffins' home, you then insulted the man's daughter continually, and finally you left without so much as a by your leave. What the devil has got into you?"

I shot a look at Holmes. As the butler of Chaloner House had escorted me rather forcibly to the waiting cab that morning, Holmes had assured me that he would make our farewells to

Edith Griffin, along with supplying the apology that I maintained was necessary due to his conduct.

Holmes clasped his hands together in a gesture that seemed to say, *Well, it's all in the past now.*

"I had intended to make clear to you that locating the morgue photograph would be the limit of my assistance in the near future," Lestrade said. "But now I will go further. I will not have you haring all over the country, involving yourself in whatever circumstances take your fancy. You are not a police officer, nor a man of the courts, and besides, the law has already determined that this fire was a dreadful accident and nothing more. You said yourself that the Griffin family have no interest in pursuing any suggestion of wrongdoing, and since his diatribe which was directed at me personally, Elias Griffin's view on the matter could not be clearer. I am tired of being known as your lapdog, Holmes, not least when your methods are so far beyond the pale. In recent days you appear to have lost the patience of the English public, and I am afraid to say that you have now lost mine in addition."

"Very well. Are you finished?" Holmes asked pleasantly.

"I must know that you accept what I am saying. There will be no further information passed to you from police files, and the only circumstances in which I would approve any requests for police officers to support your endeavours would involve your reporting an actual crime in the usual way, rather than your customary smoke-and-mirrors approach in which you hold all of the answers and we poor fellows are simply told to—"

He stopped abruptly at a loud creaking sound like the groan of a ship's mast in high winds. With a shamefaced expression, he hung his head so that he was looking at his own stomach, which continued to gurgle.

"Right, then," he said brusquely. "Off you go, both of you. I have more important matters to attend to."

CHAPTER NINETEEN

"I fear I will not rid my mind of that image for some time," I said morosely as we returned to the waiting cab.

Holmes nodded. "The level of devastation was certainly surprising."

"Surprising?" I retorted. "Is that all you have to say about the matter? Utter, bloodcurdling shock might be a better characterisation, at least as far as I am concerned, and I am sure any person possessing human emotions might agree with me."

Holmes gestured for me to enter the cab first. "You are upset, Watson. Like Lestrade, you have not yet eaten your luncheon. Shall we go to your club?"

I stared at him, ready to make another accusation, but then I said, "I confess that I would very much like a drink."

Holmes directed the driver, then settled back into his seat. I tried to rest, but every time the carriage jostled, my efforts to empty my mind were confounded, and the spectre of the faceless Martin Chrisafis loomed before me, blackened and diabolic.

After several abortive attempts to find solace in drowsiness, I groaned and rubbed at my face to wake myself fully.

When I took my hands away I discovered that Holmes was staring at me intently.

"It is perplexing, is it not?"

"You assume, Holmes, that when I am not actively engaged in conversation or some other action, then I must be ruminating on the details of the case upon which we are currently engaged. I have told you before that I am not like you. Sometimes I am just relaxing."

"I am confident in saying that you were not relaxed."

I sighed. "It's not only Martin Chrisafis who haunts me. Increasingly, I find myself unnerved by the memory of Muybridge's projected slides, despite the fact that those attacks are only representations of real ones. All of these mutilated faces, Holmes! A procession of defaced men. Is it any wonder that I am struggling to sleep at night?"

I did not expect my friend to provide solace in relation to my fallibility, and my assumption was proved correct.

"As to how the vision of that awful cadaver might shed light upon any aspect of the fire at Chaloner House, I have no earthly idea," I continued. "Moreover, Holmes, I still fail to see why we are concerning ourselves with that dreadful accident at all. First Edith Griffin, then Elias Griffin, and now Lestrade have all made it abundantly clear that we are not welcome to pursue that particular mystery – if there ever was one in the first place. I only wish that we had been commanded to leave it alone *before* we had been shown the photograph from the morgue."

"I can only insist," Holmes replied, "that there are not two separate cases, but one."

"You say that because of the photo of the Yosemite Valley, I presume."

"That is only the most visible connector, but yes. It is certainly key to our full understanding."

I fell silent, in deep thought. After some time I said, "No – I still do not see the significance of it. We have been told that the picture once hung in Israel Fay's house, and then that it was moved to Elias Griffin's bedroom in his annexe. There is no mystery there. The two were friends, and the picture was Fay's to pass on as a gift."

Holmes nodded. "I suspect it was more in the vein of a payment of a debt, but you are right – there is nothing untoward in the scenario you have described. Of course, one cannot help but wonder when Muybridge's signature was added to it."

"Why, at the point when Muybridge himself presented it to his colleague, Israel Fay!"

Holmes laughed. "For a time I entertained that idea myself. Eadweard Muybridge is a complex man, and the head injury he suffered some decades ago may well have had lasting consequences. It is not inconceivable that his posture might change gradually over the years, or the workings of his mind likewise, either of which might affect the precise movements of his hand."

"Holmes – once again, you have lost me," I said wearily.

"I am speaking of Muybridge's unfortunate stagecoach accident, which was in the summer of 1860. There are accounts of people with injuries affecting the brain whose accent changes, or their preferences, or their behaviour towards their families, for example. It does not seem unreasonable to suggest that such a person's handwriting might be noticeably distinct before and after that event. However, there is little evidence to support the idea of handwriting changing continually, and to such a dramatic degree, during a long period *after* the head injury. We have now had ample opportunity to study our client. Adopting your role as doctor, would you say that he is unstable?"

"Unstable? No. A cantankerous old fool, at times, and I suppose he is prone to sudden rage. But his behaviour is consistent enough, and I have seen no indications of lasting damage as a result of his accident – which, I will remind you, was the very

same assessment reached by the jury in his trial. But Holmes –
you spoke of handwriting… Then you mean to suggest that the
signature upon the photographic print—"

"It is a forgery, of course."

"You could tell as much from the small amount of it that
remained intact after the rest was burned?"

"Naturally. Even the smallest fragment would have allowed
a comparison. We were fortunate that two entire letters were
visible in the burned corner of the paper, and it was evident to
me immediately that they were formed in a way that is distinct
from Muybridge's own hand. His signature is readily available
for study, as it appears in his printed works."

"Yet you did not have an example of it before you in the
annexe, to aid comparison."

"True enough," Holmes said, looking at me curiously, "but
that is what the memory is for."

I nodded without further remark, as if the idea was perfectly
reasonable that the memory might hold faithful copies of
everything one sees.

"What has occupied my mind," Holmes said, his gaze drifting
out of the window, "is *when* the forgery was perpetrated. My brief
examination of the picture was enough to allow me to conclude
that the name was added relatively recently – that is, it was not
signed when it was in Israel Fay's possession. What concerns me
is whether it was appended before or after the picture was taken
down from the wall."

I cast my mind back, imagining that I was once again standing in
Griffin's bedroom in the annexe in the grounds of Chaloner House.

"Are you referring to the long scratch you discovered?" I asked.

Holmes nodded absently. "It was certainly recent, but it was
made before the fire, as evidenced by the specks of soot within.
What does that tell us?"

I considered this. "Only that somebody inspected the picture closely, just as you did, some little time before the terrible events of the night Chrisafis was killed."

"You saw me take the frame from the wall myself," Holmes retorted. "It was not fixed any more securely than one might expect. Therefore, the scratch could only have been made due to notable carelessness, or great hurry."

"That is curious," I admitted after a time. "Even so, you seem to be doggedly seeking mysteries in relation to Chaloner House, as if you are determined that your eye should remain turned away from our actual client, Eadweard Muybridge."

Holmes scoffed. "If the plight of Eadweard Muybridge was our sole concern, I would at this moment be making enormous strides in my collodion monograph."

"What do you mean?"

"I mean that the case as far as Muybridge perceives it is simple, and that our services were engaged based upon a fallacy."

I blinked, feeling distinctly foolish. "Then the threats against him – did he confect them himself? Has he lied outright to us?"

"I did not say that, Watson. Eadweard Muybridge may be many things, but he is not a liar, at least not by choice."

"Holmes, I beg you, speak more plainly."

"That I will certainly do, Watson. When we have finished at your club, we will go to Muybridge and have it out with him."

I sensed that this was as much as Holmes would say about the matter for the time being. He continued gazing out of the window, his eyes darting but not seeming to take in the buildings that we passed, and his lips forming shapes as though he were engaged in a long monologue, or even both sides of a discussion. It was at moments like these that I wished that I could see inside his mind, to understand the routes taken by his thoughts. However, no sooner had this idea occurred to me, it was followed by another, more awful image inspired by recent events: Holmes with his face removed, exposing instead of the pathways of his brain merely a blackened mass.

I shook my head violently to dispel the vision, and in doing so I attracted Holmes's attention. He examined me placidly, both eyebrows raised.

I cleared my throat. In an attempt to suggest that my thoughts had been far less phantasmagorical than they had been, I said, "It appears that you are already satisfied as to your stance towards our client – whatever that stance may be. I suppose, then, that your thoughts are at this moment centred upon the Chaloner House fire?"

"Quite so."

"And is the unlocked door to the workshop the uppermost detail?"

Holmes drew a thumb along his lips thoughtfully. "Certainly that, but also the water-jug."

It was with a certain amount of pride that I realised that I understood what he meant. "The jug that was lying on its side in the internal doorway of the annexe."

"The very same, though I suppose the additional jug in Griffin's basin is of equal importance – or, depending how you choose to frame the problem, the absence of a water-jug in Martin Chrisafis's bedroom in the main house."

At the time of our investigation I had noted that there had already been a jug in the basin in the annexe bedroom, and indeed I had seen Holmes dwelling upon the empty basin in Chrisafis's room. To my shame, though, neither of these details had seemed of importance. Even now, I failed to comprehend why they might occupy Holmes's mind to such a degree.

"Is the presence of a second jug such a curiosity?" I asked. "I find that I can visualise the situation very well. I see in my mind

Chrisafis woken abruptly by the sound of demolished timbers, then his rushing to the window, and his consequent shock at the sight of flames leaping from the door or the roof of the annexe. He rushes downstairs, but has the foresight to bring with him the water-jug from the basin in his room – it was a vain hope that he might douse the fire with its contents, but an understandable impulse, surely."

"There are certainly merits to your explanation," Holmes said, though I knew better than to congratulate myself at this half-compliment. "There is no water supply to the annexe itself, so it would be necessary to transport water from the scullery of the main house, at the very least."

"And Chrisafis could not have been certain that the water-jug in Griffin's bedroom would be full, or even that he might access it," I added.

"Then the puzzle becomes one of character and mentality," Holmes said.

"How so?"

"We know very little of Martin Chrisafis, therefore we can only speculate as to his outlook. It is reasonable to suppose that he was the sort of fellow who would not rush into a dangerous situation unprepared – that is, he might indeed take with him the water-jug in the hope of making use of it to fight the fire. Of course, without the detail of the additional jug, one might reach an entirely opposite supposition: that Martin Chrisafis was foolhardy and headstrong. That is closer to the narrative that we have been encouraged to accept."

"You mean because he rushed into the workshop despite the fact that it was ablaze."

"Yes, but what is more significant is that he did so alone. The remainder of the household were awoken not by Chrisafis, but by Elias Griffin when he came in from the annexe in a wild panic."

"Good lord," I said. "You're absolutely correct."

"Whichever version of Chrisafis's character one chooses to believe in," Holmes said, "I maintain that it requires great contortions of the imagination to explain why he might have had the foresight to take from his room the water-jug, and yet he might fail to rouse anybody in the household as he left the building."

I stared at my friend. "He would have passed the door to every bedroom in the building on his way out."

"You see now why my mind is occupied with the puzzle," Holmes said.

He returned to gazing out of the window, his lips pursed again. I marvelled that there was no more trace of annoyance in his manner than if he were working over a challenging clue in the *Times* crossword.

CHAPTER TWENTY

We had been waiting in the parlour of Eadweard Muybridge's home for more than five minutes when I said, "Holmes, why are we here? First you appear dismissive of our client's case, then you take us across the country in either direction to pursue another one entirely. Furthermore, you said to Lestrade that Muybridge has no direct connection to what happened at Bishop's Stortford, and yet you maintain that that is the true puzzle with which we are faced. So, with what information do you hope he might provide us?"

"I believe I said that Muybridge was ignorant of the events at Chaloner House, which is entirely different to your characterisation," Holmes said. "Though that may be the case, Muybridge has much to tell us that will illuminate the truth – something that he has singularly failed to do thus far. But wait, Watson—"

This urgent command was made in response to a sound from the hallway. Like my friend, I listened intently. Two voices came from the other side of the door, both female. I could make out none of their words, but their tone was hushed and serious.

Holmes strode across the room and flung open the door.

The two women – the maid who had led us into the parlour to wait, and a smartly dressed woman I had not seen before – stood with their heads almost pressed together in close discussion, and they retained this posture even as they turned abruptly to look at us. The maid staggered back, looked at her mistress with wide eyes, then scurried away.

The remaining woman performed a slight bow, and said to Holmes, "I am Miss Catherine Smith, Eadweard's cousin. I came downstairs to tell you that he is not home at present."

"Is that so?" Holmes asked politely. "Your maid seemed under the impression that he had been at home all day."

"Indeed, but then he left." Miss Smith smoothed her hair, which was already immaculate. "Some time ago, actually."

"For what destination, may I ask?"

"He did not say. I should add that he is liable to be away for some time."

"For *some* time, you say? I would be grateful if you might quantify that amount, even if it is an estimate."

Miss Smith's eyes strayed to the mantelpiece clock. "Oh, a very long while, I should think. He customarily goes away for many hours, when he goes. I suppose he may even stay away to-night."

Holmes nodded. "Then it would be folly for us to continue waiting. Thank you for informing us, Miss Smith. Perhaps we will meet with your cousin on his return."

As Miss Smith led us to the front door, she made repeated assurances that she would inform her cousin that we wished to speak with him. Presently, we found ourselves on the street once again.

"Well, Holmes," I said, "that was a rum business."

Holmes smiled. "I had anticipated that Muybridge might not wish to be apprehended. But I suspect we will find him easily enough."

With that, he set off in the direction of the centre of Kingston upon Thames. After a mile's walk, we stood outside the imposing, red-bricked town library.

"How can it be that you are certain he is here?" I asked.

"Muybridge is occupying himself ever more with the preparation for his book concerned with the motion of animals. Certainly, much of his work involves sorting through the photographs he himself created in California and Philadelphia, which no doubt requires being within his own home. But recall how eagerly he spoke of his upcoming publication, when he first visited our rooms. Therefore, even though he left his house in a marked hurry to avoid meeting us – and I am confident that he *did* leave, as his cousin's eyes continually strayed to the front door when she delivered her statement, as opposed to the ceiling as an unconscious indication that he was hiding upstairs – his first impulse will be to work. Moreover, his tendency to advertise his work and his own person is an unconscious thing, after many years of self-promotion. If he cannot access his own study, he will have chosen somewhere public where he will be noticed and remarked upon."

Though I accepted Holmes's logical processes, I nevertheless saw other possibilities, such as Muybridge ignoring his work for the sake of putting more distance between him and us. I supposed that this fear of encountering us was due to his evident knowledge that Israel Fay was responsible for extorting him, which must relate to a matter far more personal to our client than he had suggested when he first described the threats against him.

Within minutes, I was proved wrong. The moment we entered the upstairs study room, I saw Muybridge at its far end, his case upon a large table and documents spread over its surface, and two members of library staff at his side, one of whom was bringing him an enormously thick reference volume.

Muybridge looked up, and his face paled as he recognised us. He snapped instructions at the two members of staff, who immediately fled like startled deer.

"How lucky that you found me here," he said weakly as we approached.

I could not prevent myself from saying, "But surely you did not know that we were looking for you."

I had not realised that his face could yet turn a shade paler. "Quite so. Quite so."

"Let us dispense with this charade," Holmes said. "It is time for you to answer questions frankly and, this time, I would ask you to cleave to the truth."

Muybridge's eyes scanned the study room. There were only two other men in sight, and both appeared almost asleep over their dusty books; they were much older than Muybridge, whose long, white beard I took to be an affectation with the presumed purpose of making him appear wiser, or perhaps more like a wizard as befitted his magic lantern show. Holmes's remark about his tendency towards self-promotion rang truer than ever.

"We cannot speak here," Muybridge said. "This is a library, after all."

"I think you will find that the staff will indulge you, should you wish to entertain visitors," Holmes replied.

Muybridge regarded my friend curiously, and then his posture slackened. "Very well. The staff do seem to be in good spirits to-day. What is it that you want to know?"

Holmes took a seat at the table and motioned for me to do the same. "We have a great number of questions. Watson, would you like to begin? What question do you care to ask?"

I stared at him in horror, still unsure which cards must remain close to our chests and which we were permitted to reveal. The pieces of the puzzles we had uncovered seemed to multiply daily.

"I'm content for you to lead the conversation," I said finally.

Holmes bowed his head. "Very well. Mr. Muybridge, I would be grateful if you might provide information about 'Mirror

Lake, Valley of the Yosemite', and in particular, a print of that photograph signed by your own hand, which was found partially burned in the fire at Chaloner House in Bishop's Stortford?"

I noted that my friend was watching Muybridge even more closely than was his custom when questioning clients. I concluded that some part of his question was a test, and that Muybridge's response – both the conscious and unconscious elements – was of importance.

Muybridge wet his lips before speaking. "It is from one of a series of fifty-one mammoth plates that I produced in the Yosemite Valley, in 1872. That series was a marked success, winning a prize medal at the International Exhibition in Vienna the following year. The print of which you speak was produced by the albumen silver process, which is—"

Holmes stopped him with a raised hand. "Then you are aware of its destruction in the fire at Chaloner House?"

After a momentary pause, Muybridge replied, "I was told as much."

"And, in your estimation, who was it who forged your signature upon it?"

Muybridge's mouth opened, but no words came forth.

"Come, Mr. Muybridge," Holmes continued. "You must have your suspicions."

"I do not know Elias Griffin," Muybridge said in a hoarse voice. "I could not possibly guess."

"Of course, but you did not give the print to Elias Griffin. You gave it to Israel Fay."

Now Holmes's posture had become entirely more casual, whereas I continued to stare at Muybridge, intent on understanding what he knew about the extortioner's activities, given that this was the first time Holmes had uttered Fay's name in our client's presence.

The gift of speech still seemed to elude our client.

"I trust that you are aware of the previous partnership of Fay and Griffin?" Holmes asked. His eyes flicked to Muybridge briefly. "Yes, I see that is the case."

"I know only a little of it," Muybridge said in a guarded tone. "It was a business venture to produce stereoscopic portraits, some two or three years ago. A folly, by all accounts – stereoscopic pictures are relics of the past, and even if one were to produce them to-day, one will find no suitable subjects in a studio, as opposed to outdoor vistas."

"I hope that you cautioned your friend at the time," Holmes remarked.

"It is hardly my place to pour cold water upon—" Muybridge stopped abruptly. "I told you I do not know Elias Griffin."

"But the business did not belong to Elias Griffin, at least at the time of its financial trouble. He only supplied the funds that allowed Fay to avoid bankruptcy. Therefore, might it not be the case that Israel Fay's gift of the Yosemite photograph might have been a recognition of this kindness, or even the repayment of a debt?"

"It might," Muybridge conceded.

"And might he not also have forged your signature to increase its perceived value?"

Muybridge inhaled deeply, then nodded.

"It would be a great service to me if you might describe Israel Fay's character," Holmes said.

Watching my friend suspiciously, Muybridge replied, "Then you know that he accompanied me on my Yosemite excursion."

"I do."

"He was always the wiliest member of the group." Muybridge's eyes became glassy in recollection. "If I complained that a certain tree interrupted an otherwise perfect landscape view, he would immediately begin sawing away at its trunk to remove it. Though we parted ways for years, when I proceeded in my work commissioned by the University of Pennsylvania, which was more demanding a project than any I had attempted before, I thought immediately of Fay, whose ability to solve problems was second to none."

"And did your relationship remain amiable?"

"It was... strained at times. One night, under the influence of drink, Fay revealed to me that he resented the fact that he had not been part of my team when I had made the breakthrough in California – I am referring to the motion photographs of Leland Stanford's racehorse. God help me, if Fay had been present I might have reached the solution sooner, and I would have trusted him better than others to operate the cameras that produced those images. But it was not to be, and yet it seemed that Fay had always carried that regret."

"Is regret the correct word," Holmes asked, "or might it be more in the vein of rancour?"

Muybridge sighed and clasped his hands together. "I confess that I do not know."

"And yet this stereoscopic-image business you describe would also represent being a step behind you, would it not? It is easy to imagine its failure exacerbating Fay's strong feelings towards you."

"One might conclude as much, but failure is often the impetus to strive for success, as I myself have proved," Muybridge said proudly. "Fay's investments have more recently grown shrewder... In fact, his anticipation of the public interest in moving pictures has been far in advance of my own. Perhaps that has been the influence of Elias Griffin, who may yet prove one of its formative architects, if his celluloid experiments bear fruit."

I noted that Muybridge's understanding of both Fay's and Griffin's fortunes and recent occupations was in stark contrast to his original claim of ignorance. Once again, I wondered whether a simple matter of professional rivalry was at the heart of the strange events we had uncovered.

"I think it is time that we stopped skirting around the principal question," Holmes said. "Let us go directly to the source of the matter. Watson, what is the single question now uppermost in your mind? Feel free to ask anything without fear of saying the wrong thing."

Despite his reassurance, this seemed a test of my comprehension, and I did not enjoy the sense of expectation from both men. I kept my thoughts to myself for almost a minute, before finally blurting out, "For how long has Israel Fay been attempting to extort you?"

After I had spoken, my eyes went to my friend rather than Muybridge. To my great relief, Holmes's mouth curled upwards at either side in the merest hint of a smile.

For his part, Muybridge responded like a pricked balloon: his body seemed to slump more and more until I feared that he might topple onto the tabletop, unable to hold himself upright.

"Then you know all," he said quietly.

I did not, of course, and yet I gave a stiff nod.

Muybridge tugged at his long beard. "Our relationship has had as many highs and lows as his personal fortune. At times I have considered him the closest of friends, and at others..." His voice trailed off, and he looked around the room, blinking as though he had forgotten that we were in a library. Then he opened his lapel and produced a pocket-book, from which he drew two telegram slips. I recognised one, which read:

NO. FULL ON SUN. IF

The second – or rather, I perceived it must be the first, in chronological terms – was equally brief, but more immediately decipherable:

100 POUNDS TO KEEP SECRET.
PAY MIDDAY NEXT SUN. BOX AT REAR OF HOUSE. IF

"So it has all been a sham!" I exclaimed. Then I put my hand over my mouth and looked over Holmes's shoulder at the other occupants of the study room, who, thankfully, slumbered on. In a hiss I said to Muybridge, "Why did you engage Holmes's services if you knew all along what was occurring?"

Muybridge shook his head vigorously. "I did not, I swear. And it was not my idea."

Holmes interjected, "Then it was Israel Fay himself who recommended that you consult me?"

The absurdity of this suggestion made me laugh out loud. The body of one of the elderly scholars jerked in an unconscious response to the abrupt sound.

"Yes," Muybridge said. Then, in response to my obvious surprise, he pointed to the dates in the corner of each slip of paper. "I received the first of these telegrams after my lecture at the town hall in Liverpool. Before that event, I had no idea who was the culprit. But Fay himself had at the start of this month suggested that I speak to the famous Sherlock Holmes after I told him of the attacks upon my person by horse-and-carriage drivers and the first of the threats made via a vandalised glass slide – though I only did so almost a fortnight later, after the second such threat was made against me."

"Though during the Liverpool lecture you determined Fay himself was responsible for those same threats," Holmes said.

"Of course. I suspected it when the pigeon was released – the frustration of the interfering pigeon was a private joke between myself and Fay, harking back to our work in Philadelphia. Then, at the moment of the appearance of the defaced slide, there was an additional projection—"

"The letters 'IF', representing Israel Fay's initials," I said, eager to prove that I was keeping up.

Muybridge's eyebrows rose. "Very good, Dr. Watson."

I allowed myself a flush of pride, despite the information being second-hand. Then I frowned. "But still, what would be the purpose of revealing to you the identity of your extortioner… and what earthly reason could Fay have had for desiring Sherlock Holmes to investigate the crime at the very moment it was being perpetrated?"

"There is a very simple explanation," Holmes remarked.

"Then I'd be delighted to know of it," I retorted. "And furthermore, what is this secret to which Fay alludes in his messages?"

Muybridge's body sagged. "The answers to each of those three questions are ultimately one and the same. The word 'secret' in Fay's message simply refers to the very knowledge that he himself supplied to me at Liverpool: the fact that he was my torturer. He knew that I would not expose him, because ultimately his tampering would benefit me."

I stared at him without comprehension. "Benefit you? He has been destroying your glass slides, ruining your livelihood and making a mockery of you!"

Muybridge gave a long, slow nod.

"But people have begun to notice," he said quietly.

My eyes darted as I took in this statement. I looked around the room, recalling once again Holmes's comments about our client's tendency to self-promote. "Are you saying that the defaced slides are intended as a means of advertisement?"

"Indeed. Just as, I now understand, were the near-miss encounters with horses in the street. Fay hoped that the public would find accounts of those events particularly memorable, given my own association with horses in the past. I suppose there is a delicious irony in the idea of my being struck down by the very beast that made my name and fortune, and indeed the event might also have recalled the stagecoach accident that befell me so long ago. If Fay had only dared to allow me to be truly injured, the newspapers might have taken up the story there and then, so that Fay might not have decided to amplify his threats."

I glanced at Holmes, whose expression was impassive. "Then," I began slowly, "the engagement of Sherlock Holmes… that, too, was a part of the ruse?"

"It was," Muybridge said, and his ordinarily pale cheeks flushed. "Mr Holmes, I can only apologise – though I think you have suspected the truth for some time."

Holmes nodded. "By what means did Fay make his suggestion that you come to visit me?"

"By letter. At that point I had become afraid, and angry. None of the account I gave you upon my visit was a lie – or, at least, I did not know then that it was not true. The threats against my life appeared to me entirely real."

I groaned as realisation dawned upon me. "But then, after the lecture in Liverpool, you hurried away, and you have been avoiding Holmes and I ever since, due to your shame about having engaged us under false pretences."

"Yes – and due to my great shame that Fay's ugly plan has worked," Muybridge replied sorrowfully. "The newspapermen have indeed paid attention to me after ignoring my work for a number of years, and my public profile has been restored, or perhaps it is greater than ever it was. Even this very hour, the staff here at the library received me with such delight and attention… I am ashamed to confess that I enjoyed it very much."

Holmes surprised me by laughing. "You may find there is more than one ruse at work, in that respect."

Muybridge scrutinised my friend, but before he could ask a question, Holmes said, "Let us get to the heart of the matter.

The book that Israel Fay has occupied his time writing – is it an account of your life and work?"

Muybridge's eyes became wild. "How did you—" Then he sighed, and settled back into dejection. "Yes. He pleaded with me to be allowed to write my biography."

Holmes held up a hand. "Forgive my interruption. Was that by letter, too?"

"Certainly not. He made his request over dinner, at Christmastime. It has been our custom to meet every month, though it is a great irony that his dedication to his work on the book has since prevented him from doing so. I found that I could not refuse his request, in part due to my guilt that where I have profited, he has singularly failed to make his mark, and partly... well..."

"Partly because you relished the idea of his creating a legacy for you," I said.

Muybridge's pale eyes met mine. "I am growing older every day, but I am secure in the knowledge of my great contribution to both the sciences and the arts, and I am proud of my work. My life has been a string of successes."

I was tempted to remind him of his killing of his wife's lover in California. His omission of this aspect of his biography said much about his ability to mythologise his own history, so it was no wonder that Fay's proposal had appealed to him.

Muybridge continued, "However, my career is reaching its end. This task which occupies me, the collation of images that will comprise my book *Animals in Motion*, is a matter of curation alone. I have no original work ahead of me. Others have already taken my mantle and are progressing far beyond what I envisaged."

"You are referring to the new industry of moving pictures, I take it?" I asked.

Muybridge nodded. "I had hopes of striding ahead with them. But Edison saw through me immediately – he recognised my desperation. Fourteen static images upon a glass slide, presented in quick succession, may trick the eye into perceiving motion – but it is a child's illusion. The ambition of Edison, or, better still, of Mr. Robert Paul, or of those Parisian Lumières, and of many other men, is not simply to show repeating series of actions, but *stories*. I have given the public the thrill of introducing motion to pictures, but I can testify from my dwindling audiences that motion alone is no longer spectacle enough. We have resolved the matter of whether a horse's hoofs all leave the ground during its gallop; we have determined how the spine flexes when a man catches a ball, or swings an axe, or the precise motion of a woman's limbs when she descends a staircase, or pets a dog. These actions are simply constituent elements of something far grander and more absorbing: life itself. And life is comprised of tales, and an understanding of those tales lies in the understanding not of motion but of human minds. We all crave to know one another, and the cinematograph will allow us to watch and learn."

He reached into his pocket for a handkerchief and dabbed at his eyes.

"But, of course, Fay reversed all of that decline, if only for a time," he continued. "The town hall at Liverpool was filled to capacity. No doubt, audiences would now flow into other venues to see me, if only I responded to the requests to conduct additional lectures." He looked at each of us in turn, his eyes pleading silently. "I have refused all of those requests. I am not so callous as to accept the gift that Fay has given me, unbidden. At least, not entirely."

"But neither have you been prepared to reveal Fay's plot," I said, unable to disguise my accusatory tone.

Muybridge shook his head. "I considered that what had happened was in the past. It could not be reversed, therefore I must accept it and move along."

Once again, the name of Major Harry Larkyns came to mind. That other crime had also been relegated to Muybridge's past, and the notoriety it gave Muybridge himself had been used, arguably, for profit.

"I only wish," Muybridge said sombrely, "that I had not agreed to request your services, Mr. Holmes. It has been a torment, knowing that you have been on my heels, rightly seeking the truth. I wonder… now that you have acquired it, might we part ways without recrimination, and as friends?"

Holmes rose from his seat to loom above our client, and an image flashed into my mind of Holmes as presiding court judge, and Muybridge as the accused awaiting a sentence.

"I accepted your case in good faith," he said sternly, "and now I am bound to see it through."

"But I… I release you!" Muybridge protested. "There is no further obligation. I only ask that you do not advertise the, ah, confusion that has marred your investigation. I will pay you an additional amount as recognition of the lengths to which you have gone."

"Those lengths have taken Watson and I further than you realise."

Muybridge blinked as though stunned. "Are you threatening me, Mr. Holmes?"

Holmes gave a barking laugh. "Not in the least. I am inviting you to give your assistance to solve a *true* case of criminal wrongdoing."

Muybridge turned to me with a questioning look. Though I understood what my friend was alluding to, I could not think how to begin to explain it to Muybridge.

It transpired that Holmes's answer to that conundrum was to speak plainly.

"The newspapers reported that a man named Martin Chrisafis burned to death in the fire at the home of Elias Griffin," he said. "I should remind you that the body was discovered within a few feet of a hanging print of your own photograph of Mirror Lake in the Yosemite Valley, upon which was a forged version of your signature. I ask you to lend assistance to reveal the crime that has been perpetrated."

Now Muybridge stood, too, and ran his hands through his hair. "The crime of the forgery of my signature?"

"Certainly not."

Muybridge stared at him. "But you must believe that I know nothing of the rest of that business! The name of the man who died carries no meaning to me, other than having read it in the report of the fire. And I have already told you that I did not condone or know of the forgery of my name before that point, either, though it was certainly made by..." He stared at Holmes for several seconds. "Do you suggest that Israel Fay had some part to play in that awful accident?"

"I am suggesting that it was no accident at all," Holmes replied.

For a time, Muybridge appeared to have lost the power of speech. Finally, he managed to say, "He is no murderer, Mr. Holmes!" Then Muybridge clapped a hand over his mouth and swung wildly to look around the room. One of the elderly scholars had left before we had discussed anything of importance, and the other had now slumped fully over his books. In a much lower tone, Muybridge insisted, "I will say it again: Israel Fay is not a murderer."

"No man begins life as a murderer," Holmes noted calmly. "It is only after the crime has been committed that he becomes one."

Muybridge shook his head, but conviction seemed to be abandoning him rapidly. As if speaking to himself, he said, "His actions have been extreme, I grant you. And each of those horses really did almost strike me down..." Looking up again, he asked, "Might it have been the case that I have underestimated my old friend? That I have been sending him accusing telegrams, when all along my own life has truly been in the balance?"

"These are some of the questions I hope that, together, we will answer," Holmes replied.

A sharp tug of his beard seemed to indicate that Muybridge had come to a decision. "Then I will help you. But by what means?"

"By luring the extortioner out of his house."

Muybridge gaped at my friend. "You have just told me, or at least intimated, that I am personally at risk."

Holmes made a gesture to me, and I rose to stand above Muybridge.

"We are not armchair detectives," Holmes said, "and frequently we are required to put ourselves in danger in pursuit of our goals. You have agreed, now that you can hardly be considered our client in the ordinary way, that you will assist us. Naturally, that assistance harbours some small risk. However, all that you are required to do is the very thing you have done regularly these last years. You will give another lecture."

"I refuse!" Muybridge said instantly. "You have no interest in a lecture, only in allowing me to offer myself as bait!"

Holmes tapped his lips twice with a long index finger. "Yes. I suppose that is a fair summary of the situation."

"But—" Again, Muybridge appealed to me. "This is monstrous! You have told me that Fay is a desperate man, capable of killing in cold blood. The very idea of bringing him out of his den to threaten me openly is—"

"Surely, though," I said thoughtfully, "he can present no *true* threat to your life, until the deadline of Sunday that he has given."

Muybridge froze. I imagined that I could chart the thoughts passing through his mind: first relief that what I said afforded him effective invulnerability, then the recollection that he was as yet liable to pay one hundred pounds to the extortioner within two days, and then the awful understanding that he would, after all, be compelled to act as 'bait'.

"Where?" he said in barely more than a whisper.

"Here, at Kingston library," Holmes replied immediately.

Muybridge looked around the room blankly. "Why?"

"A lecture anywhere else, arranged at short notice – it will be tomorrow evening – would not be plausible," Holmes said. "Here, the circumstances are entirely understandable. You will let it be known that you had not intended to give a lecture, but that the staff here requested it with such humility, and that it seemed only fitting to agree, coinciding as it does with your gift of your papers to the library—"

"What?" Muybridge exclaimed, slamming his palms upon the table and then rising to his feet. "Why the devil would I do that?"

Holmes seemed entirely unperturbed by the explosion of anger. "To ensure your posterity, I suppose. And because you have already promised to do so."

"I tell you I've done no such thing."

Holmes raised an eyebrow. "The library received a letter only yesterday afternoon, in which your offer was made abundantly clear."

Once again, Muybridge's body seemed to deflate. "So that explains my warm welcome here," he said distantly. Then his expression hardened. "Then you, too, have stolen my identity. Just like Fay, you have forged my signature."

Holmes pursed his lips, affecting concern. "I was under the impression that I was simply enacting your wishes. Was I wrong to do so?"

For a time, Muybridge continued staring at my friend as he considered his options. Presently, his shoulders slumped and he said in a dejected tone, "No. Those are my wishes. I look forward to my papers being held here for all to see, despite their very personal nature, and I look forward to this blasted lecture I'm to give."

He sat down heavily. "Might I be allowed to get on with my work now? Though I suspect my mind will be rather distracted after all of these revelations."

Holmes began to gather documents from the table and place them into Muybridge's case. "I think you would be more comfortable working in your own study. We will accompany you back to your house. Besides, I have another favour to ask of you, which will require the generous loan of some items from your paraphernalia."

CHAPTER TWENTY-ONE

Despite my repeated requests, Holmes preferred to keep his immediate plans to himself, though he insisted I make the next two days free of all other engagements. For the greater part of the following morning, he spent his time consulting maps, some of which appeared ancient and were ragged at the edges and at their folds. In the late morning he announced that we would leave by train at four, but then waved away further questions and rushed back to his desk. By midday he relented and revealed that our destination was to be Loudwater once again. By one he finally responded to my query about the nature of our activities, but would only agree that I ought to dress in warm clothes. At two o'clock we climbed into the waiting cab and Holmes sat silently, holding bestride his knees the plain black, bulky travelling case with which he had been presented at Muybridge's home, the contents of which I had not been shown. At three o'clock we boarded the train, an act that I found most awkward due to the bulkiness of my dual layers of clothes beneath my overcoat, and by half past four we arrived at Loudwater, and walked past the Dolphin and then through the gates of Snakeley Manse, and I finally settled myself in the undergrowth of its driveway in preparation for a long wait.

For several minutes, Holmes observed the house in silence. As on our previous visit, all of the windows were curtained, and there were hints of illumination only in Fay's study, and at the circular window of the landing.

I watched with interest as my friend placed the carrying case onto the ground, and then withdrew from it a variety of objects. The two identical ones I found bewildering: each was a black drum around six inches in diameter, and upon one side numerals were written in tiny script around the perimeter. The third item was more immediately recognisable, and the sight of it made me gasp in astonishment.

"Good lord, a rifle!" I exclaimed.

Such it was, evidently: there could be no mistaking the large wooden stock and the oval-shaped grip within which housed the trigger. The only oddity was that its barrel was wider and at the same time more snub than any hunting rifle I had seen, so that the overall dimensions were more akin to those of a shotgun with the barrel sawn away.

"Holmes, what on earth has possessed you?" I hissed, as Holmes set to examining the contraption. "I see no call to have brought a weapon, and even if we had cause, my revolver would surely have sufficed!"

Holmes peered down the length of the barrel, pointing it uncomfortably close to where I was standing. I edged away instinctively. Ignoring my distress, he set to work attaching one of the drums to the top of the device. Then he cast about around him, alighting upon a number of stones which he then fashioned into a rudimentary rest, upon which he placed the barrel. Finally, he lowered himself to the ground to lie behind the weapon, closed one eye and adjusted the angle until it was directed at the circular window in the centre of the house.

"Are you stark mad, Holmes?" I demanded. "Can you truly

be the same man I have known all these years? I tell you, I have never known you to be so cowardly as to fire upon a man without warning, and from a position hidden in the bushes, no less! This is the behaviour of the very types of people that you and I seek to bring to justice. Put the thing away, man, I beg you!"

Holmes turned his head only a very little, still keeping the house in view. "Might you lower the volume of your voice a touch, Watson? And do be a good fellow and avoid jostling my arm. There's a distinct possibility that you'll upset the image."

The meaning of his words took some time to sink in. I backed away on my haunches.

"Then this is not a true rifle, but a… camera?" I asked in amazement.

"Of course," Holmes replied, his voice now slightly muffled, as he had turned to look along the barrel again. "It is an invention of the Frenchman Étienne-Jules Marey, and it is dubbed the 'chronophotographic gun'. In this new era of variety-hall moving pictures, one may characterise this device as old-fashioned, but it suits my purposes to-night most admirably. It is lucky for us that Muybridge was presented with one of his own, in recognition of the inspiration that his own work on motion studies has provided to Marey. I have told you before, the two are firm friends."

I shuffled over to the case and lifted from it the remaining cylinder. "Then within this drum are photographic plates?"

"A dozen of them. Muybridge was kind enough to load both drums for our use, but I suspect that there will be opportunity to deploy only one of them. That is, if the chance is missed, there will not be another to be had to-night."

I turned to look at the house. "A chance to… photograph Israel Fay? But why?"

Holmes only made a muted grunting sound in response to my question. As quietly and unobtrusively as possible, I lowered myself to lie beside him, still staring in the direction of the circular window.

"Muybridge's lecture will commence in a little over three hours," I said. "I assume that you expect Fay to be present in Kingston, even if it is in secrecy, and that he will tamper with another of Muybridge's glass slides?"

"My hope is that the means to provide additional motivation to pay the ransom on Sunday will prove too great a temptation to ignore."

"So then you hope to catch a glimpse of him as he emerges from the house." My gaze travelled around the wide, open area before the building. "I suppose a cab will call for him in due course. Do you expect it to park before the doorway, blocking our line of sight? Otherwise, why are you targeting that round window rather than the front door itself?"

Again, Holmes muttered something I could not make out. Chastened by his obvious concentration upon his task, I fell silent.

Minutes passed, then what seemed like hours, though when I checked my watch I saw that it was still not yet six o'clock.

I was about to make a pithy remark when a suggestion of movement within Fay's study attracted my notice. I had seen nothing directly, but I supposed that somebody had passed before one of the lamps within the room, momentarily changing the quality of light that was visible at the edges of the curtains.

"There—" I said, but stopped as it became clear that Holmes was fully aware of what I had seen. His face was pressed tight to the drum atop the rifle, and one eye was squeezed tight shut, the other squinting so narrowly that one might have taken him to be asleep. Then, a fraction of a second before I registered another movement, this time within the circular frame of the central window of the house, Holmes had depressed the trigger, and a brief fizzing sound came from the cylindrical drum. I saw for a moment the silhouette of Israel Fay pass by the circular window, but he was gone again before I could take stock of it.

One or two hushed seconds passed, and then Holmes rose from his prone position and began disassembling the mysterious rifle.

"I believe that ought to have done it," he said, with no small amount of triumph.

"Capital!" I said. Then I added, "But what is it that you have done?"

"I have captured our quarry, though admittedly not in the usual sense."

"Very good," I said laconically, "although I think I am owed a little more than puns. I still don't see why you mightn't have waited. Fay is surely on his way downstairs, and will appear at the door, perhaps as soon as the cab arrives."

Even so, I could not help but notice that my friend paid no further attention to Snakeley Manse. When he had put away Marey's gun, he stretched out full length amid the undergrowth, hands behind his head and facing directly upwards with his eyes closed, as though he were sunbathing on a bright summer's day.

CHAPTER TWENTY-TWO

I was far from reassured by my friend's distracting nonchalance, so I continued watching the front door of the house – but it remained firmly shut. After a long while I checked my watch to see that it was twenty minutes to seven, and remarked, "If Fay is to reach Kingston library in time for the lecture – or indeed, with time to spare to allow him to deface another glass slide – he will certainly have to hurry. I am not sure that he can make it there in time, given that his transport has not yet arrived. Perhaps the lure was not as great as you supposed."

Holmes responded by easing himself to a sitting position. He, too, checked his watch, and then said, "You are right, Watson."

"I am?"

"By any means of travel, one would have to have set off from here by now in order to reach the library before half past eight."

"Then he had no intention of going, after all."

"On the contrary, Watson." Holmes stood and brushed the leaves from his suit. "The only conclusion must be that our extortioner has already left."

I stared at him. "But nobody has left the house. Even if Fay had exited through a door at the rear, he would have to walk the

length of the driveway, walking directly past our position. There is no other means of travel. Are you suggesting that he swung through the trees like an ape, perhaps from a first-floor window?"

Holmes paused and regarded me levelly. "That is an elegant solution, though I understand that your suggestion is made in jest. But no, Watson, we are not pursuing an ape. Stand up, now. It is time for us to break into Snakeley Manse."

I struggled to my feet, intent only on better seeing my friend's expression to determine whether he, too, was joking. However, Holmes's eyes glimmered with fervour.

"Holmes… we cannot break into this house," I said in a halting voice.

"Oh? There is no longer any need for caution, and I think that the locks of the rear door will not cause undue trouble. I have brought my tools." With a flourish, Holmes produced a leather-wrapped package from his jacket pocket.

"That is not what I meant. We cannot in good conscience allow ourselves to do such a thing – and even if we were minded to do so, I still maintain that Israel Fay is within his home at this very moment. The lights of his study are still lit, and evidently he has not left, no matter what you had hoped would be the case."

Unperturbed, Holmes set off directly across the open space before the house, making no attempt to move quietly on the loose stones. I winced, waiting for a twitch of the curtains, but thankfully none came. I hurried in Holmes's wake, raising each of my feet high and treading carefully.

Holmes had already laid his leather bundle on the stone shelf that comprised part of the rear porch, and beside it I saw a tin box which must have been the means of Fay making payments and exchanges with his delivery boys, which we had been told about by the landlord of the Dolphin and Fay's former housekeeper.

I watched Holmes at work for only brief periods, as I was

continually distracted by the impulse to check the front of the house, and indeed all around me, for fear that Fay might approach from any angle. My friend worked with unwavering concentration, often gripping between his pursed lips whichever pick he was not currently using. Not for the first time, it occurred to me to wonder whether Holmes might have been even more profitably deployed in a life of crime rather than this most antithetical career he had chosen for himself. I was hardly surprised when, less than five minutes after he had begun, Holmes stood back with an air of quiet triumph to allow the door to swing open.

He looked at me expectantly, then gestured to the open doorway.

"I am *not* going first," I hissed.

Holmes shrugged his shoulders, then produced from the carrying case a pocket-lantern, which he lit with a match. He secured the case in the lee of the porch wall, then walked into the house as easily as if it were his own. I half expected him to call out Fay's name, and perhaps ask him to bring drinks to the drawing-room for his guests. For my part, I entered the building with an inexorable sense of being watched.

We passed through a dark kitchen, then made our way along a passageway with an uneven floor that seemed designed to wrongfoot and therefore keep one in a wary, panicked state. Evidently, Holmes shared none of these qualms: he strolled to the main staircase and bounded up the steps two at a time.

I found little solace in the thought that, if Fay truly was still in the building, Holmes would be waylaid by him first. My legs were heavy as I ascended the stairs, passing shelves laden with bulky cameras that appeared to be considered decorative objects. Upon the landing at the head of the staircase I stopped before the circular window, staring at it blankly and fighting the odd sensation that I was in a dream, and that it had been I, and not Israel Fay, whom

Holmes had photographed from the bushes outside.

I started as a figure appeared from the gloom to my left –
but it was only Holmes emerging from the direction of the unlit
bedrooms. He crossed the landing and made for the door of the
study, from the edges of which lamplight still leaked.

"Careful, Holmes!" I whispered, but my fear made my voice
so quiet that I felt sure my friend had not heard me. And what
good would it have done, anyway? Holmes was intent on acting
in the most foolhardy manner imaginable.

He opened the door and immediately cried out, "Halloa!"

At first I was convinced that he had encountered Israel
Fay, despite his assurances. But no – his remark was simply an
exclamation of delight. I made my way to the doorway, then
squinted due to the light from two lamps within the study, one
beside a trio of armchairs and the other in the centre of the room,
standing beside and above a pair of mahogany desks which had
been pushed together to form a single large surface.

The items that had evoked Holmes's excitement lay upon the
twin desks. I counted a dozen circular glass plates, identical in
size to those that Eadweard Muybridge had shown us at Baker
Street and then used during his Liverpool lecture. As I moved
closer I saw that their subjects were primarily human, mostly
naked forms, and the leaner male bodies, with knotted muscles
and white hair, may well have been Muybridge himself. None
of the slides appeared to have been damaged, but I reminded
myself that if Fay had indeed vandalised any slide in such a way,
it would now be upon his person, en route for Kingston library.
Alongside the glass slides were books and printed pamphlets,
some of which I recognised as Muybridge's published works,
whereas others appeared to be private journals. It was only
now that I recalled the more reputable of Fay's occupations
of recent months: not the writing of his own memoirs as his

former housekeeper had attested, but rather the preparation of Muybridge's biography.

I pointed at the few glass slides that did not feature images of Muybridge. "Unless we suppose that the threats against Muybridge might take the form of defaced animal pictures or people other than Muybridge himself, perhaps the presence of these slides indicates a conflict in Fay's attitude. That is, he really has been studying Muybridge's life and work, even at the same moment he has been making these threats."

Holmes nodded. "Or it indicates sentimentality."

"Because these were shared triumphs, these sequences of pictures?"

"I suppose one might suggest so. But rather I was referring to this slide." Carefully, Holmes raised one of the large discs to the light, and we looked at it from either side so that, from my perspective, Holmes's own face was eerily superimposed upon the miniature images.

In this sequence, a figure, who I presumed was a younger Eadweard Muybridge, was clothed in a light suit and walked directly towards the camera – that is, he appeared to move closer towards me in each image.

"Why do you speak of sentimentality in relation to it?" I asked.

"Because this is not Muybridge in these pictures. It is Israel Fay."

Startled, I looked closer. Now I saw that it was true that it was not the same man as in the other sequences. I had been used to seeing a Muybridge a decade more youthful than he was now, but I realised that this man was younger still. However, his face did not have the innocence of youth. His blonde beard was neatly trimmed, his hairline was high, and his nose was off-centre, perhaps indicating an old sports injury or a violent episode in his life.

"I confess I am surprised that Fay ever acted as model for

Muybridge's studies," I said. "Though we must remind ourselves that their relationship was close for many years."

Holmes hummed absently. He brought the glass plate to his face and peered at it for a long while. Then he put it on the surface of the desk again, and used his thumbnail to scrape at a point near to its centre. I saw something come away.

"What is that?" I asked.

Holmes held up his thumb. "There are traces of paraffin wax."

"You seem surprised, Holmes, but surely it can be easily explained. Candle wax has simply been transferred to the disc during projection."

"Certainly not," Holmes retorted.

Rather hurt, I said, "It is only a suggestion."

"And it is one based on nonsense. Firstly, I see no zoopraxiscope here, which indicates that the slides have been studied but not projected. Secondly, the lantern used in the device is a variation of the Drummond light, operating by limelight rather than candlelight, which would provide too little illumination to produce the required effect. Thirdly—"

"I rather think a third refutation is hardly required," I said wearily.

Holmes ignored me. "Thirdly, during projection the lantern is kept well apart from the housing of the slides. Even if a candle were used as a rudimentary light source, it would require great contortions to have it come into contact with any of the slides."

I bowed my head. "Very good. You have certainly put me in my place, Holmes. I hope you are well satisfied."

However, Holmes appeared satisfied to no degree. He continued staring at the slide, moving around the desk to view it from different angles, and then he once again bent close to examine the wax, which I now saw formed a conspicuous crater-like shape near to the centre of the disc.

Then he rose, gazed around as if seeing the study anew and, abruptly, strode out of the room. His voice came from the landing: "Wait where you are."

I did as instructed, listening to his footsteps upon the stairs, and a minute later Holmes returned carrying two objects: a large, rather ragged cloth and a candle.

He handed the cloth to me and said, "Be a good fellow and wrap up that slide, would you?"

I stared at him. "For what reason? I had assumed that we had broken into this house to further our investigation rather than perform a burglary. If nothing else, I had supposed that it was of primary importance that we leave no trace of our presence here."

"It is a gamble, I admit," Holmes replied, "but certainly a calculated one. Now, will you do as I ask, or shall I do it myself?"

I began wrapping the large slide, reassuring myself that at least the ragged cloth, which I imagined might once have been used to polish silverware, would not be missed.

When I had finished, I watched my friend perform an even less explicable series of actions. He lit the candle with a match, then waited patiently for the wick to be exposed, blowing upon the flame occasionally to feed it oxygen. Then he bent to the level of the surface of the desk and tipped the candle to allow wax to drip freely from it and onto the wood.

"Ought I to understand any aspect of what you are doing?" I asked weakly.

"I am breaking a stalemate," Holmes said. "It is a more intrusive approach than I would like in usual circumstances, but now that I am in possession of all of the facts of the matter, and now that I have made an additional discovery that will afford us the upper hand over our opponent, I am eager to hasten this case to its end."

"And you are convinced that wax upon a table, and the theft of a personal keepsake, will achieve that?"

Holmes stood up and surveyed his work. He had created a large heap of wax on the desk where the glass plate had once lain, and around it a series of smaller lumps.

"Yes, I am convinced," he said.

"And yet you intend to say no more about the matter by way of explanation?"

Holmes only smiled.

"At times, Holmes," I said, "your behaviour seems motivated primarily to infuriate me."

My friend's smile did not waver, and seeing that no further answers would be forthcoming, I sighed and said with affected good humour, "Well, if nothing else, we appear to have confirmation of one earlier deduction: the fact that Israel Fay is our extortioner." I paused, then added, "Though I own that it now seems the lesser of our mysteries."

"Which do you consider the most considerable, then?" Holmes asked.

I glanced at the new pattern of paraffin wax on the desk, but decided not to pursue that frustrating line of questioning. "Given our circumstances, surely the primary puzzle relates to the whereabouts of Israel Fay." Then, before Holmes could respond, I added, "Or rather, I know that you will say that he is currently making his way to Kingston upon Thames, but the mystery concerns his vanishing act from this very building."

Holmes nodded vaguely, as though he had long since dispensed with this line of thought. "Yes, I suppose I ought to explain it," he said – but rather than return to the doorway, he approached the mantelpiece of the fireplace situated on the curved outer wall of the room. His long fingers traced its length, passing over the ornaments arranged upon it: a ceramic vase containing dried flowers, two brass busts of stern-looking men who might as well have been twins, a carriage clock and – the only incongruous items – a series of cylinders which, after momentary confusion, I recognised as large lenses taken from cameras. Holmes lifted each of these ornaments in turn, turned it over in his hands, then replaced it carefully in the precise location from which it had been taken.

Shortly, he turned and clapped his hands together. "Shall we go, then?" he said, for all the world if he had been waiting for me rather than the other way around.

He led me out of the room and down the staircase once again; I trod carefully to ensure the safety of the wrapped package I carried. As we descended, it occurred to me to say, "You went into the bedrooms earlier. Did you determine that there is truly only one occupant of the house?"

"Yes," Holmes replied simply.

At the foot of the stairs Holmes disappeared into the blackness, but then gaslight bloomed and I was forced to shield my eyes. Now I saw that the surfaces of the cabinets, the cameras and other photographic equipment arranged on high shelves close to the ceiling, and even the wooden panelling of the corridor walls were all coated in a thin layer of dust, and motes floated in the air before my eyes.

Holmes darted into one room and then another, and returned to me within less than a minute.

"It is as I suspected," he said with satisfaction. "There is no dark-room anywhere in the house."

I nodded, without understanding the importance of the pronouncement. "I thought you were going to demonstrate how Fay eluded us."

"Yes, yes," he replied testily. He spun on his heel, then paced along the flagstones that ran alongside the central staircase. I followed to see that the passage ended bluntly at a wall of white-painted panelling. Rather than abandon his search, Holmes pressed himself against first one panel and then another, his head cocked to one side as though he were listening to the very wood itself. Presently, accompanied by a triumphant clucking of his tongue, he stepped back as the rightmost panel depressed noticeably, then slid aside in its entirety, to be tucked away beneath the staircase.

To my surprise, what was revealed was an ordinary door. A heavy-looking padlock hung from the latch that had been added beneath its handle, but its shank was loose and the latch pulled back.

Holmes turned, then paced to the other end of the hallway. He bent to the window, which I calculated must be the one beside the portico at the front of the house, and pulled back the curtain very slightly. At first I assumed he would look out in the hope of catching sight of Israel Fay, but he seemed uninterested in the view. Instead, he took the matchbox from his pocket again, and lit a match but then immediately blew it out. Next he forced the end of the match between the window and its frame. Then, with utmost care, he released the corner of the curtain to rest upon the matchstick.

Without making any remark he strode back to the mysterious door under the stairs, pulled it open and gestured for me to join him as he peered inside. Stone steps led steeply downwards.

"I take it that this leads to more than simply a wine cellar," I remarked.

"Let us find out together," Holmes replied cheerfully.

Again, I insisted that he go first, though as I descended after him I felt that my rear seemed intolerably exposed, and I regretted that my secondary position meant that I had to rely upon Holmes's wielding of the pocket-lantern. The light was too meagre to be of much use to me, and I stumbled frequently, unable to put out my hands due to carrying the wrapped glass slide. I exhaled with relief when we reached horizontal ground once more.

We were in a rough passageway with a roof so low that I felt obliged to duck my head, even though the clearance was enough that I saw that I would not strike it. With a look of mild admonishment, Holmes took from me the fragile wrapped package. Undaunted by the lack of light to be seen anywhere ahead of us, Holmes took my arm and we walked together, pausing only when I tripped on a protruding stone or had any other cause to grumble.

After we had walked for what seemed an eternity, we reached an iron door. Without hesitation, Holmes pushed it open and passed through it. I hit my head on the beam, then tripped on the mossy steps that rose up immediately, and emerged cursing.

"Where in blazes are we?" I asked, turning in a slow circle. Dusk had fallen, and from the little that the pocket-lantern illuminated I could see that we were once again surrounded by trees, and furthermore that the forest was denser than the undergrowth directly around Snakeley Manse. When I turned to look at the door through which we had come, the combination of its low position, the mottled rust on its surface and the overhanging roots of the trees above made it all-but invisible.

Holmes craned his neck to see the stars. "I can only determine that we are north-east of our starting position, and I would estimate we have travelled a quarter-mile underground."

I peered into the dark woodland. "So Fay escaped this way. That is all very well, but where did he go after that point? I see nowhere that a cab, or even a horse, might wait."

Holmes made a tentative foray into the depths of the trees, then returned shortly. "You're quite right. It may be that some vehicle was waiting at one of the other exits."

"What other exits?"

Holmes subjected me to a haughty stare. "I know that it was hardly bright in that passageway, but sometimes, Watson, I fear that you go about your day with your eyes firmly closed. We passed numerous junctions on our journey to reach this point."

I frowned as I cast my mind back. In truth, I had noticed patches of darkness that seemed more profound than others, but as I had been content to allow Holmes to lead the way I had applied all of my faculties to surviving the expedition with my head and limbs uninjured.

"How many alternative points of egress do you suppose there may be?" I asked.

"I *suppose* nothing," Holmes replied in an affronted tone. "What do you imagine I have spent my time doing, while I have been examining maps of this area? By my reckoning, there are seven possible exits from the underground network. Few of them are marked on any map, but there are means of determining their locations. By way of example, the 'fogous', or 'fuggy-holes', of Cornwall, which supposedly stored valuables, or refugees from attacks, or were important to some Iron Age ritual, are visible from above as slight embankments due to the peculiarities of their construction."

I blinked in surprise. "Are you suggesting that these tunnels are thousands of years old?"

Holmes went to the metal door and struck it with his fist. "That period may be dubbed the Iron Age, and this door may well be iron, but I do not imagine that you are suggesting that people of the time were capable of forging such a thing."

I felt my cheeks flush. "No, of course not."

"These passages are precisely as old as the building itself, and the reason for their existence was similarly personal to the man who commissioned its construction. Some time ago you remarked that 'Snakeley Manse' is an unusual name, and the reason that it so poorly reflects the appearance of the house is that both its design and its name are fanciful confections. It was built only a little over sixty years ago, the folly of a rich man whose name was not even Snakeley but Fay – an American whose understanding of Scotch Christian traditions was evidently lacking, given his naming of the house as 'Manse'. Its dilapidated state is a consequence of Fay having owned several other, far more favoured, buildings. It seems that the fancy that gripped him when he created the specifications of Snakeley Manse left him equally quickly. Over the years, however, the other buildings were sold as the family's fortune dwindled, and Snakeley is all that is left – and yet it is now treated no less shabbily than when it was merely one jewel among many. Still, we need not concern ourselves with the Fay family's outlook on life. What is crucial is that these tunnels exist, and that they provide multiple ways of leaving Snakeley Manse."

"And I suppose now we will investigate the other six exits, in the hope of determining which one Fay has used?" I asked, unable to fully disguise my misery.

"Would you like to do so?"

"I confess that I would rather sprint all the way to Kingston to apprehend him there, even if it were to take me all night."

Holmes clapped a hand on my shoulder. "Then I will not subject you to either of those tortures. Given Lestrade's insistence that police support will not be forthcoming, I have made no attempt to waylay our extortioner, and neither would it be fruitful to attempt to guard the passages upon his return. We will return the way we came, and lock up the house like respectful burglars."

"Then—" I began, hope rising within me.

"Then we may return to London."

"To Kingston upon Thames?"

"No, Watson. To Baker Street, to home, to a good dinner and then to bed."

During our career together, the occasions upon which I have entertained the impulse to embrace my friend have been few, but this was certainly one of them.

CHAPTER TWENTY-THREE

Holmes hurried into his room the very moment we arrived at Baker Street, and before he shut the door I saw him yank the curtains of the windows closed. Though I was somewhat gratified to know that our adventure of that evening had tired my friend as much as I, when Mrs. Hudson brought to our rooms an improvised supper of cold boiled ham, fried eggs and thick slices of bread, I felt obliged to inform Holmes, for fear that he had actually fallen asleep.

The moment my hand rested on the door handle of his room, Holmes bellowed from within, "Do not enter!"

I froze. "I only wanted to tell you that food is on the table. Are you not asleep, then?"

The only response was an indecipherable muttering sound. I pressed my ear to the door, and was surprised to make out sounds that were entirely unexpected: the faint sloshing of water. Could it be that Holmes had installed a bathtub within his room? Absurd though the idea may have been, I found that it took no great stretch of the imagination to picture Holmes lecturing me about the virtues of rolling directly from bed into a cold bath of water, first thing every morning.

"What on earth are you doing in there, Holmes?" I called out.

"I am nearly finished," came the hasty reply. "I will show you the results presently. Do *not* open the door!"

I retreated to the table, and managed some small amount of ham and a mouthful of bread, though my eyes remained fixed on Holmes's door all the while.

Fifteen minutes later, it opened and Holmes emerged in his shirt sleeves, blinking in the lamplight. The room behind him at first appeared entirely dark, but then I saw that a gauze-covered bulb provided meagre illumination.

I rose and went to the doorway. Inside, I saw that Holmes's make-up table and the cupboards upon which he normally kept his boxing gloves were both littered with beakers and trays that appeared to contain liquid – these must have been the source of the sounds I had heard. Above these surfaces was strung a cord rather like a washing line, and this fanciful image was heightened by the fact that a number of items hung from the line, fixed with pegs. However, rather than clothes, the items were sheets of paper.

I moved into the room, squinting in an attempt to make out what was on the papers.

"You can bring one of them out here if you wish." Holmes's voice came from behind me. "Take the leftmost, which appears the most successful. The images are all identical, and it is only the quality of their development that differs. I had supposed that if I were in possession of all of the necessary chemicals, I would make short work of producing acceptable prints. I now see that there is some amount of skill to the endeavour."

I smiled despite myself, and told myself not to turn around to face Holmes, who would certainly react badly if he saw my satisfaction at proof of his fallibility. It was unusual for Holmes not to excel at an activity on his first attempt, and in the past I had found myself exasperated and not a little envious of his preternatural abilities. With exaggerated care, I took down the leftmost print and brought it to the light, and said in a deliberately placating tone, "Well, at least you managed it in the—"

I stopped speaking as I passed into the light and looked down at the picture I held. Its outer part was dark, and I at once recognised the circular frame of the window in the centre of Snakeley Manse. However, everything within that frame was a jumble of shapes and shades of grey.

Still staring, I murmured, "I'm sorry to tell you, Holmes, that something has gone terribly wrong. Perhaps you could not see the image well enough even after it was developed in the chemical bath. I'm afraid it is a nonsense."

Holmes took the paper from me and held it to the light. He inhaled thoughtfully.

"Perhaps I might assist you, if you make another attempt?" I said. "Or perhaps we could approach somebody more knowledgeable about such matters."

"There is no need. It is near perfect," Holmes replied.

I let out an involuntary bark of laughter, undermining my pledge to be kind. "How can you say so, Holmes? It's entirely indecipherable."

"Look again." Holmes took the print to the table, then piled the dishes together (to my great annoyance; Holmes might not have been hungry, but I had not yet had my fill of supper) to clear enough room to spread it out.

Grudgingly, I did as I had been instructed, positioning myself directly above the image with my hands resting on either side.

Somebody with a weaker constitution might have described the contents of the circular frame as nightmarish. Now that I looked more carefully I saw numerous heads bobbing at the upper parts, yet they were all overlapping as though they belonged to spirits capable of passing through one another. Similarly, the lower part of the image was a tangle of ghostly limbs.

"I see what has happened," I said confidently. "Holmes, you told me that the Frenchman's gun was capable of taking a dozen pictures in a short space of time. Inadvertently, you have reproduced all of them in a single picture!"

Holmes smiled. "That is precisely as it should be. Marey's device produces a single image, within which are superimposed all of the individual frames of a sequence. A modern moving-picture camera may be capable of the same feat translated onto a celluloid strip, but its accuracy – in terms of sighting through the lens as well as the film stock one would be compelled to use – is far lesser. What I require is to see the fine increments in the movements of the occupant of Snakeley Manse, and that is exactly what I have produced."

I looked in wonder at the picture once again. "Then you can make sense of this unsightly thing?"

"Naturally. Look, within a single second as the figure passed this window, the head bobs dramatically. That tells us much. Note also that the arm closest to the window swings conspicuously, whereas the other limb is all but invisible to us, suggesting that it is held more stiffly at the side, in line with the left leg. Most importantly of all, the legs move far from identically: the reach of the right is greater than the left. All of this contributes to an inevitable conclusion that the person pictured here has a marked limp."

Holmes's explanation had a powerful effect on the image, or rather, my perception of it. Now I saw that what he said was true: the bodies pictured could be individually discerned, and if I tracked the minor lateral movement from left to right, I could well imagine that I was looking not at a single, frozen moment in time, but was seeing several moments condensed and frozen. It struck me as rather like the effect of Muybridge's racehorses galloping on the spot when projected by his zoopraxiscope – yet here, instead of a sense of moving along at the very same speed as the subject, I felt rather that I was capable of moving *through* time, back and forth at will. I could not help but gasp at the trick.

"It's a marvel," I murmured. Then I registered what Holmes had concluded from his study of the picture. "Is the detail of the limp an important one?"

"It was the very detail I hoped to prove by this exercise."

"Ah. Well, that is good." Then, shyly, I added, "Ought I to understand *why* it is important?"

Holmes smiled amiably. "No, because it is your duty to ask questions about my methods, and it is mine to reveal them with a flourish."

I sighed. "That is true enough." I reached over to the pile of plates, retrieved a piece of bread and chewed it slowly. Then I went to my chair at the fireside. "Come, then. Sit, and perform your flourish."

"My apologies, Watson – there is no time for that at present. I must travel to Kingston to speak with Eadweard Muybridge after his lecture. The flourish will wait."

I baulked, having forgotten about Muybridge and the likely threat to his person that he would have received this evening. I reminded myself that we no longer believed that the threats were to be taken as real, but that they were simply reinforcements to encourage Muybridge to pay a ransom. Even so, he might well be in an anxious state at this moment.

"It is good of you to think of him," I said. "Perhaps I will bring my medical bag, in case of nerves."

Holmes stared at me with an uncomprehending expression upon his face. "I will not be visiting him simply to ask him about his health. It is vital that I consult with him immediately."

"Oh." I realised I had been a fool to imagine that Holmes might place mere human emotions above the importance of solving a puzzle. "Then—"

"You need not come. Finish your meal, Watson, and afterwards you will certainly require your sleep. A cab will be waiting outside at four o'clock tomorrow morning to take us to Israel Fay's house in Loudwater, at which point we will apprehend the culprit of these crimes. This time, you may bring your revolver."

CHAPTER TWENTY-FOUR

"I still do not understand why we cannot simply break into the house again, and catch Fay asleep," I whispered. I had no desire to spend another few hours cloistered in the undergrowth, which was at this time of the morning damp with dew.

Muybridge and Holmes were occupied in unpacking the equipment which I had discovered already in the carriage of the cab, along with our client, when I had climbed into the vehicle at the early hour of four o'clock. The case had taken up a full seat, with the unfortunate result that I had been pressed against the window for the entirety of the journey.

During this time, Muybridge had spoken little, responding only in perfunctory fashion to my questions about the events of yesterday. What I came to understand about the lecture at Kingston library has since been augmented to a great degree by what I learnt from the later newspaper reports (and I am conscious of cleaving close to what I understood that morning, in this retelling of events), but even from Muybridge's reluctantly divulged account it was clear that his extortioner had indeed struck again. Perhaps due to the impromptu nature of the event and the difficulties of preparation for the crime, the threat had not been delivered via one of the zoopraxiscope slides, but rather a static photographic print. After Muybridge had delivered his introduction in the upstairs study room of the library, with fifty people in attendance and more reporters who had failed to secure seats waiting outside the doors, he pulled down the rolled white cloth upon which his zoopraxiscope slides would be projected by the lanternist, George Fellows, whose services had evidently been retained since Liverpool, given that Muybridge knew well that he was innocent of any wrongdoing. In performing this simple action, though, Muybridge inadvertently revealed Fay's handiwork, and his audience responded immediately in shock and amazement. However, it must have been the case that at first few of these men could make out the details of the photograph in question, which was another print made from one of Muybridge's albumen stereographs captured in the Yosemite Valley. The photograph, a copy of which I found at a later date in one of his published albums, was titled 'Contemplation Rock, Glacier Point', and once again it depicted Muybridge himself, though only in silhouette. This time he was shown sitting upon the rock in question, which protruded from the very top of a mountain, the forest trees mere pinpricks beneath him, his legs dangling over the void – appearing for all the world as if his 'contemplation' was the thought of leaping to his death.

If any of the onlookers had been unable to make out all of these details or understand the significance of the choice of picture, they were certainly able to see the additions that Fay had made. The photograph was fixed centrally within the white screen, and was not at all large, but Fay had contrived to turn the already dizzying picture into a hallucinatory vision. Lightning flashes filled the air around the younger Muybridge, and beneath his dangling feet was a pit of spikes. The head of the tiny subject of the portrait was this time not vandalised, presumably because its status as a silhouette meant that Muybridge was already rendered faceless. Instead, the lightning bolts were all directed inwards as though they might strike him all at the same moment.

If the newspaper reports that I read later that day were to be believed, the crowd rose from their seats as one, edging forward to gaze at the awful spectacle, their gasps of horror merging to become audible from far along the hallway. Perhaps it was this physical interruption that caused Muybridge to realise that his lecture had been curtailed before it had truly begun. Before this aghast crowd, he tore down the white screen and stamped upon it, then bent to continue ripping it with his fingernails, bellowing in frustration and rage.

If I had known this entire story that morning, perhaps I might have spared Muybridge my questions – or perhaps I might instead have feared more for the additional erosion of Sherlock Holmes's reputation, given that when this awful scene occurred he was nowhere in attendance and, according to public opinion, must surely be accused of allowing this outrageous violation to be enacted. However, I digress, as little of this was clear to me at the time and therefore it did not contribute to my comprehension of the events of the morning. I will return to that narrative now, restoring myself to my ignorant state.

Holmes and Muybridge worked in silence, and despite the dimness before dawn, I saw that the machine they had unpacked was none other than Muybridge's famous zoopraxiscope.

In response to my unasked question, Holmes jutted his chin to indicate the house. "That building is riddled with hidden passages. Even had we searched for them all during our last visit, we would no doubt have missed at least one. Furthermore, I may have some small skill at lock-picking, but I cannot be sure of doing so in complete silence. To risk raising the alarm would be to risk losing all, as any of those internal passages may lead directly to the entrance to the underground warren, and there we have no means of effecting an ambush."

I glanced at the device, which was now almost fully constructed. "And… you intend to discourage Fay from escaping by distracting him with a moving-picture story?"

Holmes laughed, dismissing my question.

Since we had disembarked from the cab near to the Dolphin inn, he had carried a low stool. When I had noticed it I had been irked that he had not thought to bring a seat for me, then had reminded myself that Muybridge was far older than I, and no doubt exhausted by the early start to the day. However, now I saw that it was not intended to be sat upon at all. With an abundance of caution, Holmes made his way silently across the loose stone of the wide area before the house and placed the stool before the window to the left of the portico.

As Holmes retreated just as cautiously to our position, Muybridge remarked, "How does he move so stealthily? His movements are like those of a large cat. I only wish that I had my camera in order to make a record."

Holmes's feline powers seemed also to extend to his enhanced hearing. When he reached us he raised one foot and then the other, showing us their soles. "A large cat wearing rubber-soled tennis shoes, no less."

He held out his hands to receive the zoopraxiscope from Muybridge. "Is it ready for operation?"

Muybridge nodded. I saw that he had inserted one of his glass plates into the machine already; though I could not make it out fully now that it was in place, I noted that it was one of Muybridge's motion studies of the human form.

Holmes examined the device, too. When he was satisfied, he said, "Then for the moment I will simply place it where it must be located. I will light the lantern, but you will be responsible for lifting the shutter, and for any necessary adjustments to the focus."

Again, Holmes crept across the stones, holding the device aloft as though he were a royal servant conveying a crown on a pillow. With equal care, he placed the zoopraxiscope onto the stool and adjusted its protruding lens so that it was almost touching the windowpane before it. Only now did I remember Holmes's peculiar activity the previous day, when we had broken in to Snakeley Manse: this was the very window where he had inserted a matchstick to keep the smallest part of the corner of the curtains from falling into place. Evidently, the projection produced by the device was intended to appear *within* the house.

Holmes rejoined us, then turned to survey the arrangement. He clasped his hands together.

"Now gentlemen, we will adopt our positions. Watson, you are to guard the rear exit, and I will remain beside the front portico, ready to spring out the moment that the door is opened. Muybridge, your sole responsibility is to operate the zoopraxiscope, but mind that you do so without making yourself visible. Do you both understand your roles?"

We both nodded confirmation, though I could not help but add, "My role, yes, but not the overall plan."

Holmes regarded me blankly, as if this was a most foolish complaint.

"Do not trouble yourself with caution as you move into your places," he said. "So long as you are able to operate the device promptly, Muybridge, then some amount of noise is indeed desirable, in order to alert our prey – otherwise we will be bound to wait until he chooses to rise from bed. Now, good luck, and let us begin!"

Despite Holmes's assurances, I kept to grassy ground until I had no choice but to cross the loose stones to reach the rear porch. Revolver in hand, I adopted a crouching position beside one of its low walls. I heard the steady crunch of footsteps upon gravel, and when they stopped I visualised Muybridge bending to his contraption, lifting the shutter to reveal his moving picture.

For a long while nothing happened. Then, from the front of the house came the sounds of stamping feet. I panicked momentarily, and almost left my position in order to investigate, but then I told myself that it must be Holmes, making noise in order to rouse Israel Fay from sleep.

Sure enough, within seconds I heard sounds from within the building, at first upstairs and then the unmistakeable noise of somebody descending stairs in haste. The quality of the echo was odd, though, and I reminded myself of Holmes's claim of secret passages within the old folly. Fay might be much closer to my position than I had anticipated, coming from an unexpected direction along a staircase I had not yet seen.

Despite being primed for action, I made myself as inert as a statue, albeit a crouching one. I heard more sounds: a patter of feet on a hallway, and then a gasp of horror. I counted to three and no more noise came from within, but then I heard a gabbling, high-pitched voice. I tried to reconcile the sound with my expectations of Israel Fay's appearance. Was he not close in age to Muybridge, the men having worked together over many years?

I was not able to contemplate this puzzle for long. With a start I realised that the sounds of footsteps had resumed, and that they were proceeding in my direction. I placed my hands on the ground like a sprinter about to commence a race, and willed all of the muscles in my legs into readiness.

So it was that the very moment the rear door to Snakeley Manse burst open, I was upon Israel Fay, and I wrestled him to the ground without any need to threaten him with my revolver. Once he was subdued, I sat fully upon his shivering form and called out – entirely needlessly, of course – to Holmes. My friend appeared instantly at the corner of the building, closely followed by a terrified Muybridge. I stood and bent to roll over my captive to reveal—

The man was not Israel Fay.

I looked up wildly, into the house, babbling, "Holmes, he must still be inside!"

Holmes put his hand on my arm. "No, we have caught our man."

I stared at the man cowering beneath me. He was in his early middle years, and appeared a studious type, clean-shaven and wearing thin-rimmed spectacles, with a decidedly soft, doughy face. My initial assessment was that he was otherwise nondescript, but then a growing sense of recognition crept in at the back of my thoughts.

"I have seen you…" I said wonderingly. Then, slowly, "Was it not in Liverpool?"

As soon as I spoke the words, I knew that they were true. I could now visualise this same man, *sans* spectacles and wearing a sullen expression, standing and watching me balefully after having knocked me down outside the doors of the ballroom in Liverpool town hall. When I had asked him for assistance, he had simply stared at me and refused to cooperate. To my shame, I had taken him for an imbecile.

He did not reply. I saw now that he was shuddering all over, and that beads of sweat prickled upon his brow.

"You may stand, Mr. Bradwell," Holmes said.

I whirled around to stare at my friend, who made no comment as he fastened handcuffs around the wrists of our prisoner, who appeared to have abandoned all intention of fleeing.

"What? Then this is Israel Fay's secretary?" I cried.

Richard Bradwell continued to shudder. He stared at each of us in turn, his eyes wide as if we might be his saviours rather than his tormentors. Each time he stole a glance at the interior of the house, he shuddered anew.

"The very same," Holmes replied. He gestured to the open door. "Now, perhaps we ought to go inside where it is warmer. The police will arrive presently."

"I'm not going back in there," Bradwell retorted. "You can't make me."

Holmes smiled. "You are hardly in a position to dictate plans. But I assure you that you are safe. We have the means of exorcising the phantom."

"How can you—" Bradwell began, but he broke off, staring wildly.

Gently, Holmes directed him into the dim interior of Snakeley Manse, and Muybridge and I followed. I watched our captive with interest, noting his faltering walk as a result of his left leg moving more stiffly than the right.

Bradwell got as far as the hallway and then he halted, staring deeper into the house. I moved ahead to see what he was looking at.

Even though I knew of the trick of the zoopraxiscope, I was yet unprepared for the effect it had produced. Projected upon the white door leading to the underground caverns was the spectral vision of a man in motion, wearing a pale suit and with his arms outstretched before him as though he were expecting to embrace somebody. It was only now that I realised I had seen the images once before, in the study here in Snakeley Manse, from which Holmes had stolen the glass plate.

"Israel Fay," I said.

While Fay's posture might have seemed pleasant enough at the moment of its recording, in this gloomy context it appeared slow, looming and malign. The figure paced forward interminably, arms continually outstretched. At some point I understood that the sequence must repeat, but I could not determine when: it seemed only an endless advance.

Muybridge said, "This sequence has never appeared in my published work. It reveals little of the subject or the niceties of the manner of movement, partly due to being taken from directly in front, and partly because of Fay's insistence on remaining clothed. But he was adamant that he desired to act as model, even if only once. I obliged, and then gave the slide to Fay in Philadelphia, as a keepsake."

Bradwell remained aghast, but there was nevertheless a noticeable change in his demeanour. Slowly, he edged towards the locked front door of the house, watched closely by Holmes. As Bradwell passed the window where the zoopraxiscope was stationed, the ghost of Israel Fay blinked out of sight. Bradwell gave a long, low groan, and at the same moment he unconsciously stumbled back, and the ghost of Israel Fay reappeared.

CHAPTER TWENTY-FIVE

Soon we were all settled in Fay's study, which was certainly the most well-appointed room in Snakeley Manse. I had lit the fire already prepared in the grate, and Muybridge, who had arrived last after leaving the house briefly to rescue his precious zoopraxiscope, had made his way to the drinks cabinet and produced brandy for everybody, including Bradwell. To any observer we might appear a convivial group – that is, if one failed to notice that Bradwell was obliged to use both his hands at once to raise his glass, due to their being bound by metal cuffs.

I took Holmes to one side. "There is a great deal that I do not understand, but the most immediately concerning is whether it is only a ruse of yours to say that the police are coming. You have not called for them, and Lestrade made it abundantly clear that he would not offer his help speculatively."

Holmes patted my shoulder. "I assure you they are coming, and that they were summoned only after our arrest had been made."

"But how—"

"A letter was delivered to Scotland Yard at the appropriate moment by one of my irregulars. It makes clear, in the strongest possible terms, that the guilty party has been caught, and indeed it lists all of the crimes of which he is guilty, and an itinerary of recent events and their significance. I recommended that the local force in High Wycombe be alerted immediately."

No less confused, I said, "I still fail to see how you contacted your own messenger, though."

"The simplest of answers: I did not. The boy was given a precise time to deliver the message, and I trust that he did not fail. It is all a matter of confidence, Watson. I am confident of my messenger's reliability, and the system I devised was predicated by my confidence that at exactly seven o'clock this morning I would have successfully apprehended Richard Bradwell and collected sufficient proof of his crimes to make his arrest not only viable, but inevitable. My promise to Lestrade is intact."

I gazed at my friend in wonder at the bold gamble of summoning the police before they had cause to be involved. What would come next – perhaps solving a crime before it was committed?

"I think I might be horrified," I said eventually, "if it were not for the fact that Bradwell seems to accept the rightfulness of his arrest. He could not appear more guilty." I paused. "But Holmes... do you suppose that now may be the time for me to ask questions and for you to produce your explanation in a flourish, as you promised?"

Holmes smiled. "Yes, I believe it is."

"Then..." I turned to look at Muybridge, then retreated to one of the armchairs so that our conversation might include him. "For what crime, exactly, are we arresting Bradwell?"

Holmes put his glass of brandy on the mantelpiece, then moved to stand in the centre of the ring of seats, facing our prisoner. Since his shock at seeing the projected vision of Israel Fay, Bradwell was now impassive.

"Perhaps we will begin at the beginning," he said. Then he paused. "Or perhaps not *quite* the beginning. If we did so, we might go all the way back to Israel Fay's first encounter with Eadweard Muybridge in California in 1872."

Muybridge said nothing, but narrowed his eyes, as if trying to determine how closely his fate was to be intertwined with Richard Bradwell's. Upon entering the room he had gone directly to the central desks and lifted each of the glass slides in turn, perhaps wondering which of them might next have been intended to be vandalised and deployed as a threat against him.

Now addressing Muybridge himself, Holmes continued, "We might, indeed, note your own history – not only your work on the motion of animals and the human body, but also your injury in a stagecoach accident, and the death of Major Harry Larkyns at your hands."

Now Muybridge sat up straight, so violently that brandy spilled from his glass. "I remind you that I was acquitted on all counts, despite my refusal of the suggestion of any mental impairment. My actions were *just*, sir!"

Holmes bowed very slightly. "That is why I do not concern myself with it directly. I am only occupied with the *effect* of these events in your life, and how they were utilised by Israel Fay."

I offered, "Then you are speaking about Fay's desire to write Muybridge's biography?"

"Indeed. Fay understood not only that our client's unusual history could be shaped into a compelling account; he also realised that those events themselves had been foundational elements of his success in later life."

I saw Muybridge bristle again, but he did not speak.

"I restate that I make no judgement about the situation," Holmes went on, "only that it was so. Muybridge's work speaks for itself, but his celebrity has undoubtedly been in part informed by his personal affairs. Consequently, Israel Fay believed that a well-researched and well-written biography was only halfway along the route to his own success – success which he craved due to his mismanagement of his ventures. Fay determined that returning Eadweard Muybridge to celebrity—"

"Returning?" Muybridge thundered.

"Yes, returning," Holmes replied quickly. "You are intelligent enough to recognise that your prestige has waned in recent years, and you are intelligent enough to see that arguing otherwise would be in vain."

Chastened, Muybridge fell silent.

"We have already spoken about Fay's methods. He would revive the notoriety of Muybridge in the public eye, by recalling those past triumphs and controversies. His almost being run over by horses was intended to remind newspapermen, in the first instance, of Muybridge's work photographing those same proud beasts. The defaced images on the glass slides that amounted to threats against his person would restore to the public imagination the idea of Muybridge as embattled, and possibly himself as a dangerous man, embroiled in ugliness. But Israel Fay was not a young man, and he required assistance to carry out both of his endeavours – the writing of the biography and the threats against its subject. At this point in our story enters Richard Bradwell."

He gestured at our seated captive, and Bradwell nodded solemnly, then lifted his brandy glass in a mocking salute.

"Tell me," Holmes said, "upon your engagement, did Fay describe the full extent of your responsibilities?"

"He did not describe the torture we would put this man through," Bradwell replied, glancing at Muybridge sitting beside him with no trace of shame or even embarrassment, "but when viewed with hindsight, I own that he delivered clear enough hints that I would go further than simply transcribing his words. There was a great deal about moral attitudes, and about my own physical fitness."

Holmes nodded, appearing impressed at the secretary's forthrightness. "Before we dispense with it entirely, I am interested to know how far work on the biography has progressed."

Bradwell laughed and pointed to a sheaf of papers upon the twin desks in the centre of the study. "It is almost complete. As far as I am concerned, it is a simple account. Perhaps Muybridge's life is not as fascinating as everybody supposes. Fay was right: the book could only be made a success by making Muybridge's name potent once again."

The man's posture had changed dramatically while he had been speaking. All of his affected casualness had disappeared, and now he appeared angular, his shoulders held oddly as though there were a great weight pressing on his left side. I saw that both Holmes and Muybridge were watching him with great interest, too. It occurred to me that their respective fascinations might take very different forms: Holmes would derive meaning from the man's every movement, whereas in all likelihood Muybridge was interested in the posture and movement in its own right, watching Bradwell as an artist watches his subject.

"Then you admit that it was you who arranged for the horses to nearly collide with Eadweard Muybridge on the street," Holmes began, "and that you exchanged the glass slides for copies that you and Fay had vandalised?"

"Yes, I admit it," Bradwell replied without hesitation. "Each was a simple matter. Friend Muybridge here is hardly the most astute of targets. I was the driver of the carriages on both occasions, and at his lectures I could pass directly before his nose and he would barely look up."

Muybridge's cheeks reddened, and I was minded to reprimand Bradwell – but then I remembered that I, too, had seen Bradwell 'directly before my nose' and had suspected nothing. I had no desire to remind this cocksure hooligan of that fact.

"To sum up, then," Holmes said lightly, as if he were as yet unaware of the growing tension in the room, "all was proceeding well. The book was in preparation, Muybridge's notoriety seemed in the ascendant, in no small part due to the engagement of my own services to investigate the threats." He broke off. "Was that your idea, or your employer's?"

"It was mine," Bradwell said sourly.

Holmes beamed. "Then I congratulate you. It was a masterstroke. It was also your undoing, of course, but I applaud your ambition."

Ordinarily, I might have relished watching the confidence slip away from Bradwell's expression. However, another thought had edged into my mind and marred my enjoyment of the moment. Amid the excitement, I had forgotten that I had arrived at Snakeley Manse this morning expecting that we would arrest Israel Fay.

"Where is Fay?" I said, almost unconscious that the question had passed my lips.

"He is dead," Holmes replied bluntly.

I gaped at him, then at Bradwell, who was shaking his head.

Muybridge let out an agonised moan. "Tell me it is not true," he pleaded, addressing no one of us in particular.

"It is the truth," Holmes said, "and this man was responsible for his death."

Only now did Bradwell rise from his seat; while perhaps he intended it to be a leap to his feet, it was decidedly more awkward due to his bound hands and stiff left leg.

"I have nothing to do with Fay's disappearance," he insisted. "And I do not suppose that he is dead. All that I know is that he is not here, and has not been since I returned to Snakeley Manse. I had only intended to remonstrate with my former employer after my unfair dismissal, though I confess I also intended to remind him of the unorthodox nature of his instructions, hoping to use his misdemeanours as leverage. But there was no answer to my knocks or ringing of the bell, so I opened the door with the key that was still in my possession. I have been here ever since."

Holmes regarded him with a trace of amusement in his eyes. "And you admit that you have been continuing his scheme to threaten Eadweard Muybridge since your return?"

"I admit it freely. I am no innocent, Mr. Holmes. When the police come, I will tell them the same, and I will face the consequences."

Again, I sensed admiration in Holmes's response. "Quick calculations are in your very nature. To confess to one crime but to claim ignorance of a larger one is a wise tactic, in the circumstances in which you find yourself this morning."

"You maintain that Bradwell killed Fay, then?" I asked.

Holmes nodded.

I turned to look at the flames in the grate, drawing together associations in my mind, and cursing my slowness.

"I think I see it," I said slowly. "There is no dark-room here at Snakeley Manse."

When I turned back to the group, Holmes was watching me with an eyebrow raised.

"Go on," he urged.

"The housekeeper referred to deliveries of chemicals during the last months – the very same months during which Bradwell has been employed here. It is my understanding that these glass plates" – I gestured to the slides on the desk – "were appropriated during Fay's employment at the University of Pennsylvania, or otherwise taken from Muybridge as research for the biography; either way, they were already prepared and did not require being created here at Snakeley Manse. Furthermore, we have seen no suggestion of the use of chemicals in any of the threats against Muybridge. Therefore, I suggest that they were instead used to poison Israel Fay himself, causing his death."

Bradwell had affected a look of horror – I say 'affected' because I was convinced it was a charade. Conversely, Holmes beamed with obvious pride.

"Bravo, Watson!" he said.

"Then... I am correct?"

"No."

I exhaled loudly. "Oh. You understand that you rather raised my hopes."

"Ah, but you were halfway to the answer!" my friend said. "It is better than failing to leave the starting blocks, is it not?"

I shrugged my shoulders, all of the thrill of solving a riddle having left me. "Then what *did* occur?"

"Certainly, Bradwell poisoned Fay, over a period of two months or more. I suppose, Bradwell, that your intention was to incapacitate your employer over time, making yourself ever more vital to his affairs? It is certainly your name which appears on the documentation of your employer's recent investments in technology related to moving pictures. You are more far-sighted than Israel Fay ever was – indeed, one might argue that you were the very secretary that he had needed for many years, if not for your impulse to deceive everybody around you – and in time you may have made yourself a rich man."

Bradwell shook his head. "I have no earthly idea what you are talking about."

"Very well," Holmes replied, a trace of disappointment now entering his tone. "Then we will rely on informed conjecture at present. I maintain that you did make use of poisonous chemicals, probably daily, but that you never intended to kill Fay by this method, nor any other."

"But you said yourself that Fay was dead!" I protested.

Holmes looked sharply at me. Then he turned and, all of the intensity of his manner falling away abruptly, strolled to the fireplace. "Note my use of the word 'intended'. No, when Bradwell killed Fay, it was not premeditated."

"I deny killing him!" Bradwell bellowed.

"Of course you deny it," Holmes said amiably, "and I am sure that you were shocked at your own actions, the night that you killed him. You were incensed, were you not? I suppose you will not supply the information about what the source of your irritation was. Perhaps Fay was beginning to regret his ploy. Was he about to confess all to his old friend, Muybridge?"

Muybridge's face had turned beet red, as though he were being gradually deprived of air. He stared at Bradwell impotently.

Bradwell himself made no reply. His entire body was trembling, and he watched Holmes nervously as my friend paced up and down before the fire.

"Even so," Holmes went on, "I suspect that you retained some semblance of control, even then. For example, the shouting that the housekeeper heard that night – I imagine that was not the harbinger of your attack on Fay, but that you staged that apparent argument *after* Fay's death, as you developed a plan to cover your tracks?"

Again, Bradwell did not respond.

Holmes nodded as though this silence represented confirmation. "Then it is only a matter of determining the weapon."

He stopped before the left-hand side of the fireplace, took from it one of the pair of brass busts, and then moved to the right to retrieve its twin. He turned and held them up for display as if he were a surgeon lecturing to students in an anatomical theatre.

"This bust," he said, raising his right hand higher, "has been polished recently, with particular attention given to the square base. The other is coated in dust, like most objects in this building. I hardly need to say that if one were to grasp the bust at the readiest place – the head itself – its base would represent the striking weapon, and its sharp corners would prove particularly effective. Furthermore, a blow to the face would result in a distinctive wound that would be difficult to conceal or explain away. Did he die instantly, Mr. Bradwell?"

All our heads turned to the secretary, who nevertheless seemed aware only of Holmes.

"You have acknowledged yourself that this is conjecture," Bradwell said in a measured tone. "What you have described is fantasy. Clearly, you have no proof, and equally clearly, the police will not allow themselves to be persuaded by such a work of fiction."

Holmes replaced the busts upon the mantelpiece. "The traces of blood I have identified on the base of this statue support my accusation, but you are nevertheless correct. The policemen who will arrive here from High Wycombe will have little interest in my 'story', as you characterise it. However, the police at Bishop's Stortford are likely to feel entirely differently about the matter, as are the fellows at Scotland Yard."

If this pronouncement shocked Bradwell, he was clever enough to conceal it. I, on the other hand, gasped aloud, and Muybridge's gaze swung back and forth between Holmes and Bradwell as if the answer was to be found somewhere between them.

"When was it that you learnt about Fay's gift of the Mirror Lake photograph to Elias Griffin?" Holmes asked.

"I do not know what that is," Bradwell replied immediately.

"As you wish. Let us presume that it was a little over two months ago. Having come to know of its existence, and understanding that it was a greater, or at least a more immediate, prize than any potential success of Fay's biography, you determined that you would have it for yourself."

Still, Bradwell remained taciturn.

With a glint of mischief in his eye, Holmes added casually, "By the way, did you realise that the signature upon the picture was a forgery, by Fay's own hand?"

Finally, he had produced an effect on our prisoner. Bradwell's body sagged, and he slumped into his chair.

"I note that is not a full admission," Holmes said cheerfully, "but I take your response as encouragement that I am proceeding along the right lines. Yes, it is true. Your quest to recover the Yosemite photograph was predicated upon an error."

Muybridge voiced the objection that I had been about to make. "But he did not steal it! That photograph was burned in the fire – I read as much in the *Times!*"

"True," Holmes said. "It is another example of Bradwell's ability to recalculate quickly. Upon his initial visit to Chaloner House he located the picture in Elias Griffin's bedroom in the external annexe and made plans to steal it, but by the time of his return his intentions had changed entirely, with the dire outcome that has been well-reported."

"Good lord, Holmes!" I exclaimed as a new realisation came to me. "Are you suggesting that Richard Bradwell was the house-guest of the Griffins, and that he and Martin Chrisafis are one and the same person?"

Holmes bowed his head in confirmation.

"Then…" I began, rising from my seat and striding up and down along the hearth rug. "Then the body that was burned in the blaze… That was…"

"It was Israel Fay," Holmes concluded.

In a quavering, hoarse voice, Muybridge said, "But you maintain that Israel was killed by a strike from a mantelpiece ornament – and now you say instead that he burned. Which is it, man? Neither of these images will leave my mind in the coming days."

"Both are correct," Holmes said, and he was mindful enough to introduce a note of apology to his tone when speaking of Muybridge's ill-fated friend. "He was killed here at Snakeley Manse during an argument with Richard Bradwell, and then Bradwell contrived to dispose of the body in the fire at Chaloner House."

Still Bradwell did not respond to these allegations, but neither was his prideful manner intact. He no longer looked up at his accuser. Instead, he stared morosely at the fire as if he were entirely alone in the room.

"Bradwell posed as the fictitious son of Abraham Chrisafis in order to win Griffin's trust," Holmes said. "His aptitude for careful planning compelled him to regard his first overnight stay at Chaloner House as a reconnaissance, allowing him to identify all of the elements that would allow him to steal away the Yosemite photograph – and at the same time he intended to do away with many months of Elias Griffin's work on celluloid strips."

I had been following this explanation avidly, but now I held up my hand. "Why would Bradwell do so, if his instinct was to invest in moving-picture technology, which would include precisely such developments as Griffin was engaged upon?"

"Because Griffin's work belonged to him alone, and he was bullish about not making his work public until it was complete, and therefore no investment could be made. Furthermore, Bradwell, under the guise of his employer, had already made substantial gambles upon other companies which hoped to reach similar breakthroughs in retaining dye upon celluloid strips without discolouration. In short, Elias Griffin's success would have cost Richard Bradwell a great deal."

"Then the idea of doing away with it and at the same time robbing the man…" I trailed off and turned to look at the hunched Bradwell, regarding him almost with respect at his boldness.

"The dual opportunity proved too tantalising to pass up," Holmes concluded. "However, as I have said, Bradwell's accidental, impulsive killing of Israel Fay changed his plans entirely. The approach of slow poisoning to take control of Fay's investments was a sound one – repellent, naturally, but logically sound. After Fay's death, there could be little hope of maintaining full control of these affairs in the continued absence of the purported investor himself, and the publication of the biography of Muybridge could hardly be allowed to go ahead, if there was no Israel Fay to meet with the publishers. However, we have already established that Bradwell's mind is a remarkably quick one. He covered well for his mistake initially, staging a shouted argument in this very room, and then the next morning dismissing the entire household staff – and in addition, as far as any of them were concerned, dismissing himself. Once he was free of the immediate threat of discovery, he adapted his existing, and most ingenious, plan to his new ambition: ridding himself of the evidence that he had killed Israel Fay. If that could be effected, then there may have been some small chance that Bradwell might continue to arrange his employer's financial affairs for some limited amount of time, with the claim that Fay was away from home rather than dead. As we have seen, he would also use this time to change his approach to Eadweard Muybridge. If the publication of the biography could not be relied upon, the same plan that had been intended to increase Muybridge's notoriety could now be used for another ambition. It was a far blunter approach, but Bradwell was becoming desperate to gain whatever he might from the circumstances he had contrived. He decided he would simply demand money from Muybridge."

Abruptly, Muybridge leapt from his chair, throwing himself at Bradwell. I darted up to intercept him, yanking at his arms before he could strike.

"So I'm merely an afterthought, is that it?" Muybridge bellowed.

Bradwell gazed up at him, unperturbed. "Yes," he replied.

Muybridge's body became slack in my grip, in response to this bluntness. "And if I had paid the amount of one hundred pounds, would more demands have been made?"

"Of course."

Once again, I marvelled at Bradwell's calmness. It seemed that he had partitioned the accusations to which he would freely confess, and those that he would protest against vehemently. I had never known anything like it.

"I beg you, sit down," Holmes said to Muybridge. "I understand that you are irked, but we are straying from our narrative."

I guided Muybridge to his seat, and said, "Yes – you were speaking of Bradwell's new ambition of disposing of the body."

I attempted to visualise Bradwell arriving at Chaloner House in Bishop's Stortford. A detail occurred to me: I recalled that Edith Griffin's maid had heard the approach of a cab, and yet none had come close to the house itself. After paying the fare, Chrisafis might have taken from it a large packing case as well as his suitcase, then quickly deposited the former in the thickets nearby before presenting himself at the house. Then, he must have returned to retrieve from the packing case the hidden body of Israel Fay, late at night—

Without quite realising I was speaking aloud, I exclaimed, "The purple pyjamas!"

"Excellent, Watson," Holmes said. "They are certainly a key detail. What of them?"

"You discovered a purple thread in the bushes to the east of the grounds of Chaloner House. And the burned body – Fay's body, I mean – was wearing purple pyjamas, which indicates that the thread came loose when Chrisafis – I mean Bradwell – carried it from the woodland, where he had hidden the body, to the annexe."

"You are very close to the truth. But the unusual trail beside the annexe shows us that Bradwell carried a heavy case all the way to the door of the workshop. Of course, dragging the packing case would have taken markedly more effort than simply carrying the body as you have suggested, so why did he?"

I attempted to put myself in Bradwell's place that night, then gave an involuntary shiver. "Because hauling a cadaver over one's shoulder would be a horrific experience."

"Precisely. Not least if you had killed the man yourself, and were suffering an overwhelming sense of guilt. The less time spent in physical contact with such an unavoidable reminder of one's crimes, the better, wouldn't you agree, Bradwell?"

Of course, Bradwell agreed nothing of the sort, but Holmes hardly seemed irked at his reticence.

"It was for the same reason," he continued, "that Bradwell did not take the simplest approach to disguising the body. In order to pass Fay off as himself, he might simply have dressed the body in his own clothes. Instead, he went to the trouble of purchasing purple pyjamas of the very same design that Fay had been wearing when he was struck and killed here at Snakeley Manse."

I shuddered involuntarily, having momentarily forgotten that we were sitting in the very room where a man had been bludgeoned to death. I looked around me, half expecting to see a vision of Fay's tortured ghost, in the manner that had been projected downstairs earlier that morning.

"So," I began, speaking rapidly in an attempt to shake off the imagined spectre, "Bradwell made certain that Edith and Elias Griffin saw him wearing those purple pyjamas, knowing that it would secure the identity of the burned body upon its discovery. This same ruse meant that he was required to leave the house that night wearing the pyjamas and nothing more, and then when he dragged the heavy packing case from its woodland hiding place, they must have caught against a bramble and left the thread you discovered later."

"You have summarised the situation admirably. Of course, if not for his concern that some unforeseen thing might have necessitated the abandonment of his plan and a hurried return to his room, he might have had the good sense to change into the fresh clothes he undoubtedly left alongside the packing case in the woodland, before beginning his scheme that night. As it is, I suppose that he changed his attire only after the fire had been set. We would not expect him to wander the streets of Bishop's Stortford at night wearing only his purple pyjamas, would we?"

I found that I could not begrudge Holmes his obvious enjoyment at revealing the complexities of that night.

"I believe I can now anticipate much of this plan of Bradwell's," I said slowly, "though some of the smaller details continue to elude me."

Holmes laughed and we shared a look which often preceded his 'flourish'. It had occurred to me more than once in the past that at such times I behaved like a fairground barker, promoting Holmes as the main act.

"What questions have you, in particular?" he asked.

I considered this. "For one, how could Bradwell have dragged Israel Fay into a building that burned with such ferocity, and yet himself have escaped unharmed? And why would he have broken down a door that was patently unlocked?" I hesitated, then added, "And why was the fire as merciless as it was, given Griffin's natural tendency to keep his laboratory conditions safe?"

"These are all excellent questions," Holmes said. He checked his watch. "I imagine that we have time to work through them before the police arrive. Mr. Bradwell, would you like to supply the answers, or shall I continue?"

Bradwell did not even raise his head.

Unperturbed, Holmes again addressed his audience of two avid listeners, and a sullen third.

"I will proceed from the beginning of the events of that night," he said. "The first, and perhaps simplest, step was for Bradwell to secure the key to the workshop. Both of the doors to the annexe were locked from inside and Elias Griffin was asleep in his bed – but while Griffin was safety-minded, he was not as conscious of security as one might suppose. We know that the evening was warm, as had been those before it. Whereas Bradwell may have anticipated that much of his stay would be dedicated to acquiring a copy of the key, an easier answer presented itself."

I recalled my own experience watching Elias Griffin from outside the annexe, during his night-time excursion to the burned building. On instinct, he had begun to take off the jacket that he wore habitually, and then he had reached out his hand.

"The coatstand was directly before the window!" I said out loud.

"Indeed, and it was a warm night, and the window was certainly open," Holmes supplied. "Moreover, the keys were loose in the pocket of Griffin's jacket, so could be removed individually and without making undue noise." He glanced at Bradwell, who seemed to sink ever lower into his chair. "So we have dispensed with that particular problem. Now Bradwell was able to unlock and open the workshop door, and to deposit Israel Fay's lifeless body on the floor of the room. Mr. Bradwell may like to note that there is ample evidence of this activity, despite his attempts to avoid leaving traces. Watson, you will recall the peculiar trail on the sand track alongside the annexe? We have already established that it was produced by the dragging of the heavy packing case which contained Fay's corpse, evidenced by the depth of that trail, which was then hardened by the fire. But do you also recall its rise and fall? That was the first detail that suggested to me an irregular manner of walking. Bradwell was aware enough of his limp to keep to the grass when he approached the annexe, to avoid leaving footprints in the sand, but the characteristics of that trail, which veered to the left with each of his movements of that leg, were evidence enough of his presence. Muybridge, perhaps later I will show you the pictures I took using the chronophotographic gun which you kindly loaned to me, which can be used to accurately determine that Bradwell's gait matches exactly that which produced the marks in the sand path."

I noted that Muybridge had the good manners to appear impressed, though his eyes were glazed. I suspected that either he was fatigued and struggling to follow Holmes's story, or that perhaps he was preoccupied with the effects of Bradwell's plot on his own future.

"What is next?" Holmes mused. "Ah yes, the fire. In addition to the workshop key, Bradwell now had possession of the key to open the store-room in which the chemicals were very sensibly stored some distance from both the annexe and Chaloner House itself. It is a clever detail, to have used Griffin's own materials to cause the fire, but of course this introduced a risk of discovery of their usage. Astute as ever, after setting his trap, Bradwell avoided immediate discovery by refilling the partially emptied bottles of chemical solutions with water – a fact that proved simple to determine by smelling the contents. Watson, you will recall the puzzling detail that there were two water-jugs in the annexe, and yet none was present in the bedroom allocated to the guest then known as Martin Chrisafis – and that while Bradwell certainly brought the jug from his room to the annexe , that hardly indicates presence of mind, given that he did not also rouse the household as he left to investigate. That situation can be explained readily enough: in case of Griffin's water-jug being already empty of water that might be used to refill the bottles of chemicals, Bradwell brought down a full jug in preparation for the task. Is that not so, Bradwell?"

When the secretary did not respond to these claims, Holmes continued, "Your plan was to spread those flammable chemicals liberally around the workshop, then toss in a match. However, despite your ill intentions towards Griffin's work, you had no desire to add another death to your conscience. Evidently, your accidental killing of Israel Fay already weighed heavily upon you, as indicated by your attitude to his ghost, both this morning and in the days since his death."

"Did you say his *ghost*?" Muybridge asked.

Holmes had clearly anticipated the question. "As we have demonstrated, a ghost is whatever reminds one of the person who has passed on from this world. This morning it was a phantom projected by your zoopraxiscope. Bradwell's predisposition to react so strongly to its appearance was a central part of my ambitions to catch him to-day, and it was inspired by his own recent behaviour." Holmes turned to me. "I am speaking of the wax upon the glass slide depicting Israel Fay."

I shook my head to indicate that I was unable to make the connection.

Holmes put a hand on Bradwell's shoulder, a gesture that appeared almost paternal. "This fellow's mind is powerful, but it is also overworked, to the degree that he sees things that are not there. I have told you that his killing of Fay was a rare, impulsive error. Since that date, he has approached many aspects of his adapted plan calmly and coldly – but in relation to his former employer, he has tortured himself. The presence on the desk of a slide featuring Israel Fay was an aberration, as it was the only slide that Bradwell would certainly not employ as a threat – it would have represented an indication of the perpetrator that would be visible to witnesses as well as Muybridge himself. Moreover, the wax upon its surface indicated that it fulfilled a very different purpose: that of a shrine."

I gasped. "Then your theft of the slide was not only in order to use it as part of the zoopraxiscope illusion."

"Once I understood Bradwell's sentimental and superstitious nature, that plan came to me immediately – but you are correct to suggest that just as important was the *disappearance* of the slide." Again addressing Bradwell, he said, "When you returned from Kingston library last night, did you return to this room immediately?"

Bradwell continued to gaze at him balefully and in silence.

"I imagine that you did," Holmes said. "Your movements are as clear in my mind as if I were examining one of Muybridge's motion studies. You returned to this room to deposit the slides you had taken to Kingston with the intention of exchanging them for those you had vandalised – though in the event, the refusal of George Fellows to leave the zoopraxiscope unattended for any amount of time meant that you had been compelled to make your threat via the white screen itself. Once here, you could not help but notice that the plate featuring Fay was no longer where you had left it – perhaps you had taken to stopping before it each time you passed, your guilt overwhelming you and yet your superstitious nature preventing you from putting the slide away? Anyway, it was missing, and in its place you discovered heaps of wax, perhaps from the very same candle you had taken to burning upon the glass plate when you pleaded to a higher power, or to Fay himself, for relief from your conscience. My hope was that your imagination would conjure a supernatural scenario: that Fay himself had left the traces of wax in an attempt to torture you further. Therefore, the appearance of Israel Fay this morning, evocative of the pictures you had appealed to daily, but now shown at life-size and markedly more spectral, left you momentarily unhinged. Do not trouble yourself to confirm my account; I know that it is at least close to the truth, as this morning's outcome attests."

"That is all very well, Holmes," I said, "but those details are tangential to the explanation of Bradwell's behaviour at Chaloner House. That is to say, his desire to save Elias Griffin from becoming another death of an innocent to add to his conscience."

"You are a natural storyteller, Watson, and I thank you for keeping my account to the pertinent details. It is as I have said: for the reasons given, Bradwell contrived to remove Griffin from the building before setting alight to it."

I shook my head. "That cannot be so, Holmes. Elias Griffin was awoken from sleep and then rushed from the annexe *because* there was a fire."

Holmes laughed. "I maintain that there was not."

I gaped at him. "I have seen the burned timbers with my own eyes!"

The expression on Holmes's face was almost one of tenderness, as though I were a much-loved pet who had failed to perform a trick.

"Once again, Watson, you are conflating outcome with causation."

"What on earth do you mean by that?" I scoffed.

"I mean that Griffin perceived that his workshop was aflame, but what he saw was not the fire that would eventually destroy that part of the building. We spoke of this during our visit, Watson. What were Griffin's actions that night?"

I gazed at the far smaller fire in the grate. "He awoke, either due to sound or perhaps heat." At a glance from Holmes, I added, "Most likely a sound, as his bedroom was only partially burned even by the time the blaze was extinguished. Then he rose, no doubt quickly, and opened the internal door—"

"No," Holmes said, interrupting me. "He went to the door, certainly. Slow down your thoughts."

"He… he saw the fire through the window."

"Good. The glass of the window was very thick, was it not?"

"Yes. But still…" I found that I did not know how to complete my objection.

"In fact, it was Bradwell's own ingenuity that informed the trick we ourselves deployed this morning," Holmes said. He waited for Bradwell to acknowledge the compliment, but was disappointed.

I clapped a hand to my forehead. "He projected an *image* of flames onto the window!"

"Capital!" Holmes declared. "Even a short sequence might have been entirely convincing, seen through such thick and mottled glass. In addition, I suspect that Bradwell may have enhanced the effect – as you have stated, it was sound that awoke Griffin, and the sound of flames might easily be simulated by the crinkling of some stiff material, even the very celluloid sheets that would later be blamed for the conflagration." Again, he appealed to Bradwell, but the secretary's face remained turned towards the hearth. "So, Griffin saw and heard a fire. What then?"

"I still say that he would open the door. Foolish though it may have been, it would have been an understandable instinct."

"Quite so. He put his hand on the door knob – but then he withdrew it immediately. Did you not tell me yourself, Watson, that when you saw Griffin return to the burned room, he continually rubbed at his left hand?"

I nodded wonderingly.

"I determined from his daughter that he is left-handed. Therefore my assertion is that he grasped the knob with his left hand, suffered an immediate burn that made him reconsider his actions, and after that point he thought only of escape and the rescue of his workshop. If more evidence is required, I may add that the discolourations upon the door knob on the side of the workshop indicate that a small area of its surface was heated to a high temperature by some means – that is, even higher than the general temperature of the fire that would later break out – and of course that heat would have transferred through the cylinder to the opposite handle."

"Then Bradwell thought of simply everything!" I remarked.

Holmes chuckled. "Not everything. Griffin retreated to the main house, as planned, and then Bradwell set the fire. One notably gruesome detail is that he would necessarily have doused his former employer's face with the greater amount of the chemical solution, in order to ensure that he would not be identifiable as anybody other than Martin Chrisafis. Before he replaced the keys in Griffin's jacket, which remained upon the coat rack, he remembered to enhance the explanation that he desired others to reach, by breaking down the door of the workshop. As planned, the conclusion was later drawn that Martin Chrisafis had done so in order to access the building in the hope of saving Elias Griffin, but as we saw—"

"He forgot to lock the workshop door first," I concluded.

I looked at Bradwell, whose eyes were now closed. Given the precision of the great majority of his plans, I imagined that the revelations of these mistakes, tiny though they seemed to me, must have caused him great pain. I found that I revelled in the idea.

"Quite so," Holmes said.

He went to the window and drew back the curtain, and I saw that dawn had arrived. The light that now permeated Fay's cloister-like study had the effect of waking me, as if from a dream, just as the raising of the house lights in the Alhambra had done.

"Ah, here are the police," Holmes remarked as he gazed down to the driveway of Snakeley Manse. "Their timing is never less than impeccable – by which I mean that they reliably appear half an hour after any given event."

He returned to the hearth, gesturing for Bradwell to rise from his chair. The secretary did so without complaint, and walked ahead of Holmes and out of the room.

CHAPTER TWENTY-SIX

Neither Muybridge nor I stood up from our seats. For my part, I felt stunned, and Muybridge appeared entirely preoccupied with his thoughts. The only sign of life in him was as Holmes and Bradwell had passed: his eyes had darted, taking in each of them from head to foot.

I listened to their dual treads on the staircase, followed by the opening and closing of the front door.

Finally, Muybridge turned to me.

"One cannot deny that the young man had ambition," he said. "I find that I can almost admire the ability to think on one's feet, and to attempt to turn adversity into success."

A shudder passed throughout my body as I recognised the parallels between Muybridge and Bradwell. Muybridge, too, had killed in a fit of passion, and he, too, had avoided punishment, going on to achieve greater triumph.

"But the man is a monster," I replied in dismay, "and you were at great risk of being made another of his victims. Even once Fay was dead, taking with him the promise of the biography of your life, Bradwell then identified profit in extorting you. Even if he did not intend to dispatch you to Hell as he threatened, threaten you he did, and in full view of the public. Moreover, he has openly confessed that if you had paid the amount he specified initially, he would have demanded more, until you were ruined."

At this moment it occurred to me to wonder how the story might be relayed in the press – and here I will take an opportunity to deploy both the hindsight and foresight which are the privileges of the writer. As we know from our latter-day perspective, Muybridge's reputation was soon to be effectively reset to its former status, and an emphasis on his genius for photographic innovation has been at the expense of attention given to his former life and deeds in California, and indeed the wild threats against his person in England which have been our primary concern in this account. One may come across public records of the events of March 1896, but they are decidedly muddled. As for Holmes, it is possible to argue the case that the stain on his character remained – or rather, that he would do nothing to correct it. Though his triumph in capturing the perpetrator of the threats against Eadweard Muybridge was to be acknowledged fully in the newspaper accounts, over the years it has seemed to me that the initial sense of his failure to grapple with the niceties of the case has lingered. It is no consolation to me that Holmes cares little for his reputation, and it is my hope that this full account of what I intend to refer to as 'The Case of the Defaced Men' might serve to correct the public record.

Muybridge nodded absently, though he still appeared to harbour no ill feeling against the secretary who had entertained such malice against him. As if he had not been listening to a word I had said, Muybridge said thoughtfully, "I would indeed like to see that chronophotograph of the young man. Besides his obvious limp, there is much to observe in his manner of locomotion. Those strange, jerking movements might tell us much about a devious mind such as his – or perhaps it is the other way around, and the workings of the mind inform the behaviour of the limbs."

I considered this at length. At the Liverpool City Hall lecture I had joked to Holmes that one day crimes might be solved by means of examining figures in motion, captured and available for study. By this method time could be slowed down and, in the case of Marey's chronophotographs or Muybridge's zoopraxiscope images created by banks of cameras side by side, it could be arrested entirely. If the question of the hooves of the galloping horse all leaving the ground could be solved by a single glance at one of Muybridge's animations, what other mysteries might be unravelled as readily? The audience at the Alhambra had reached conclusions about the actions and motivations of a pickpocket shown to them on a screen, and when they desired to see the action replayed precisely as before, it was a wish easily granted. Truly, the arrival of moving pictures would make the world a less obscure place… and yet I found, conversely, that the idea of solving puzzles by this method left me more perplexed than ever. What place had the first-hand experience of reality in this new world?

Muybridge did not wait for my response. He continued in a pensive tone, "And your friend Mr. Holmes, too. I had assumed that my work would no longer involve practical photography, and only the curation of past efforts… but do you suppose that Holmes might consent to act as model for one of my studies? I recognised the oddity during our previous encounters, but now, following the triumph of his solution of this mystery, I have seen it again, far more pronounced…" His eyes shone. "His movements are… *most* unusual – they are fluid as a hawk in flight, or a wild cat upon the plains, yet they are at the same time constrained, efficient, controlled despite their sense of being *dangerous*. I have never seen anything like it."

Despite my earlier discomfiting thoughts, I could not help but smile. The world may have been changing, but some things – some *people* – would assuredly remain consistent. Though I knew that no consent would be given to having his motion studied in such a way, I nevertheless relished this new addition to my catalogue of fascinations related to my friend, the marvellous and unique Sherlock Holmes.

AUTHOR'S NOTE

In writing this novel I've drawn from a great deal of real-life events and artefacts. The examples of Eadweard Muybridge's photographs and zoopraxiscope slides are all descriptions of real slides (including the fascinating 'Head-spring, a Flying Pigeon Interfering'), apart from the images of Israel Fay, who is an invented character with no basis in reality. The references to Muybridge's work in Philadelphia and California, his appearance at the World's Columbian Exposition in Chicago, his association with Thomas Edison and Étienne-Jules Marey – and the killing of his wife's lover, Major Harry Larkyns – are also intended to be accurate, and any errors are my own. After moving back from the USA to Kingston upon Thames, Muybridge lived at various addresses; though he shared a house with his cousin, Catherine Smith, when he died in 1904, I can't say with confidence that he lived in that house in 1896. From around 1895 Muybridge was indeed engaged in compiling the book *Animals in Motion* (which was eventually published in 1899) and conducting a sporadic lecture tour, and he did give a lecture to the Liverpool Amateur Photographic Association at Liverpool City Hall on 19 March 1896. Of course, this period of his life panned out rather more smoothly than in this novel – I'm happy to say that no threats were made against him.

The timings of the early demonstrations of Auguste and Louis Lumière's Cinématographe and Robert Paul's Animatograph (also known as the Theatrograph) are as accurate as possible. Paul did demonstrate his device at London's Alhambra Music Hall on 25 March 1896, and his programme included films of cartoonist Tom Merry drawing caricatures of Otto von Bismarck and Kaiser Wilhelm II – you can watch the latter for free via the online BFI Player, which contains a wealth of early British film. 'Arrest of a Pickpocket' is another matter, though. In reality, this thirty-second sequence was only ever shown on peephole viewers, and the audience reaction in this novel is taken from the response to Robert Paul and Birt Acres' decidedly more static 'The Soldier's Courtship' in 1896; these two films vie for classification as the first ever British fiction film. Most other items on the Alhambra bill are drawn from real programmes, though not necessarily the same evening's entertainment.

ACKNOWLEDGEMENTS

Many of the details about Eadweard Muybridge's life are drawn from accounts in *Muybridge: Man in Motion* by Robert Bartlett Haas and *Eadweard Muybridge* by Marta Braun, plus Thom Anderson's 1975 documentary *Eadweard Muybridge, Zoopraxographer*. I'm also indebted to Stephen Herbert, whose online site 'The Compleat Eadweard Muybridge' was enormously useful, particularly its detailed chronology of Muybridge's life.

I've been interested in early British cinema for many years. Anybody keen to learn more about this fascinating period of cultural history would find the BFI/FutureLearn online course 'The Living Picture Craze: An Introduction to Victorian Film' valuable, and a rummage around in the free BFI Player will produce treasure after treasure.

I owe thanks to my editor, Cat Camacho, whose enthusiasm and engagement has always been hugely important, and to the Titan Books team at large.

Finally, thanks to my family, especially Rose.

ABOUT THE AUTHOR

Tim Major lives and writes continually in York. His books include the Sherlock Holmes novel *The Back to Front Murder*, weird science-fiction novels *Hope Island* and *Snakeskins*, short story collection *And the House Lights Dim* and a monograph about the 1915 silent crime film, *Les Vampires*. Tim's short fiction has been selected for Best of British Science Fiction, Best of British Fantasy and The Best Horror of the Year. He blogs at cosycatastrophes.com and tweets @timjmajor.